SING ME HOME

Lisa Ann Verge

Publishing History
First Print edition published by Kensington
Publishing as Wild Irish Rose
Copyright 1997, 2015 by Lisa Ann Verge
Formatted by Lisa Ann Verge
Cover design by Kim Killion

ABOUT SING ME HOME

"[Sing Me Home] is proof that people can change, one man can make a difference, and that romance novels can be funny, and lusty, and still cross into deeper territory."

—*Detroit Free Press*

"I love Ms. Verge's style. She scatters her puzzle pieces, then fits them into the most unlikely places. This one left me soaring."

—*Rendezvous*

"Lisa Ann Verge is one of the best medieval writers today."

—*Affaire de Coeur*

Ireland, 1307

Blessed with an angel's voice, Maura of Killeigh escapes from a convent determined to join a band of traveling players. They'll be her protection on the roads while she searches for the parents who abandoned her at birth. But once face-to-face with the seductive, sinfully handsome vagabond who rules the troupe, Maura wonders if she wouldn't be safer traveling alone.

*Don't miss Lisa Ann Verge's other sexy,
adventurous, historical romances!*

The Celtic Legends Series: Boxed Set
TWICE UPON A TIME: Book One
THE FAERY BRIDE: Book Two
WILD HIGHLAND MAGIC: Book Three
THE O'MADDEN: A Novella

Romantic Journeys Collection: Boxed Set
HEAVEN IN HIS ARMS
HER PIRATE HEART
SING ME HOME
THE CAPTIVE KNIGHT

The Cabin Fever Series
ALONE WITH YOU: Book One
LOST WITH YOU: Book Two
TAKEN WITH YOU: Book Three

Also available--the Novels of Lisa Verge Higgins

THE PROPER CARE AND MAINTENANCE OF
FRIENDSHIP
ONE GOOD FRIEND DESERVES ANOTHER
FRIENDSHIP MAKES THE HEART GROW
FONDER
RANDOM ACTS OF KINDNESS
SENSELESS ACTS OF BEAUTY

CHAPTER ONE

Killeigh, Kingdom of O'Carroll Ely, Ireland
The Year of Our Lord 1307

When Maura finally found the man she was looking for, he was stretched across a woman's lap, his fingers lost in her cleavage.

She stumbled to a full stop outside the campsite, still hidden in the trees, and tightened her grip on the basket slung across her shoulder. She felt as if she'd just come upon the sort of scene painted in the pages of the Abbess's Bible, full of wild-eyed demons and half-dressed women and long-tongued satyrs dancing around a woodland fire.

Stop.

Summoning her convent-training, she muttered a quick Hail Mary and then an Our Father. When she finished, she took a breath so deep that she felt her surcoat tighten across her breasts. Certainly the great wide world and all the people in it couldn't be as dangerous or wicked as the Abbess always insisted.

These people gathered around a fire were simply performers, she told herself, just traveling minstrels. The piper was playing the same reedy lilt that he'd played this morning. Another man was sucking on a bladder of ale, but in the village that same man had performed magic tricks that delighted the children. And the person she'd come looking for—the man now reclining on a woman's lap—she'd last seen him laughing as he wrestled with the baker's son while another minstrel took wagers.

She gave herself a good shake. It was too late to turn back, and she hadn't escaped the convent only to lose courage now.

She marched forward into the campsite. Swiping her skirt away from the flames, Maura rounded the campfire and stopped in front of the wrestler and his lover. As the man turned his head on its bed of fleshy breast, she tried not to notice that he looked like the very image of lustful sloth, sprawled out on the ground like that, his shirt untied so that the light gleamed on his chest.

He asked, "What have we here?"

The wrestler had a husky voice, as rough as she imagined his ill-shaven cheek would be. "My name is Maura," she said, startled by the odd thought. "I have some business with you tonight."

The piper's music squealed to a stop. The juggler's knives clattered to the ground. The wrestler stopped twiddling with his paramour's hair.

"Do I know you, lass?"

"Oh, I'm sure he *does* know you," someone interjected. "There isn't many an Irish flower our Colin hasn't plucked."

"Aye," another man shouted, "I'd say there isn't

a girl from here to Wexford that Colin hasn't deflowered. Tell us, lass, should we be worried about a father or a husband waiting in the woods?"

"I have neither father nor husband," she said, rattled by the sudden attention. "And I've never seen you all before you arrived today."

"Leave the girl be." The wrestler called Colin glowered at the gathering men. "Have you no eyes? This one's coif is as white as snow."

Maura's hand drifted to the ties of her linen coif, still tight under her chin, which she wore to tame, somewhat, the wild curls of her pale brown hair.

"Ignore the ravings of these jesters," Colin said, drawing her attention. "They make fools of good men for their living, and don't know better when to hold their tongues." He gazed at her through half-lidded eyes that held the flicker of flames. "Still, it must be a dangerous sort of business that would bring a young woman to our camp, alone, after dark."

"Not dangerous," she said. "I want to join your troupe."

Amid the minstrels' surprised muttering, the man called Colin raised his strong, black brows. Easing off his paramour's lap, he found his feet and unfurled to his full height. She arched her neck to look up at him, which was a rare thing, for she stood a half-head taller than most of the men in the village and all the brothers in the nearby monastery. But it was more than his height that made her suddenly catch her breath. He had piercing eyes. His pitch-black hair was tugged back by the ragged end of a bootlace. A single lock fell from his brow to brush his jaw. She had an odd, powerful urge to sweep it behind his ear.

Then the corners of his eyes sprouted little

crinkles, and she realized that he'd caught her admiring him.

The angel Lucifer was said to be beautiful, too.

Stop. She squeezed her eyes shut and said another silent Our Father. She promised to do two more Hail Marys before bed.

"So," he prompted, "you say you want to join our troupe?"

"I do." She hated the tremor in her voice.

"Do you have any experience, lass?"

The other minstrels tittered but she ignored them. "I've never been a traveling performer before, if that's what you're asking."

"Then how do you plan to earn your keep?"

"If you'll allow me," she said, "I'll show you."

His half-smile widened, showing a glint of teeth. He spread his hands in welcome as the minstrels crowded around.

Maura shifted her shoulder. The leather strap of a woven basket slid down to her elbow. She thrust her hand into the narrow opening and curled her fingers around the hunk of fur hiding within. She lifted her pet into the light. Nutmeg swiped his face with his little paws as he blinked his eyes open. She pressed her cheek against his soft gray fur, murmuring nonsense as she dragged a jingling length of bells out of her sack. She slipped the opening over his head. He chirred and blinked up at her.

"You have a performing squirrel." Colin rubbed his bristled jaw as if to hide a smile.

"His name is Nutmeg."

He'd been her pet for years now. The Lady Sabine, a laywoman at the convent, had bought the squirrel from a traveling performer, and then gifted the pet to Maura when Lady Sabine realized the squirrel was chewing away at the bedposts. The squirrel, oddly, only understood French.

Maura placed Nutmeg on the ground, and then, palming an acorn from a food sack hanging from her belt, she lifted it to get the squirrel's attention. When she gave the command, *debout!* he stretched up on his hind legs and tottered, upright, in a small circle. With another command, *danse,* he hopped from one back paw to the other in an awkward sort of jig. With a loop of the leash he began to chase his tail, faster and faster and faster until he was a blur of gray fur. With a final tug of the jingling leash, he crouched down, shook his head as if he were dizzy, and then rolled over to play dead.

She waited an awkward moment in silence for applause that didn't come. Then she tugged Nutmeg up so he would bob his head, as if he were bowing. She curtsied, as well. When she looked up, the troupe was still watching...waiting.

"He does more than dance," she said into the thickening silence. "He can roll a small barrel and ride on my head. And he has some other talents." She crouched down to remove Nutmeg's leash, and then she pointed at Colin. "Nutmeg, *Vas-y.*"

The squirrel raced towards Colin and clambered up the minstrel's hose. Colin's paramour squealed, then scuttled back as Nutmeg poked his head in the sack hanging from Colin's belt.

"This could be a very dangerous trick," Colin said, grinning at the bundle moving in the sack.

"Nutmeg, *Viens-ici.*"

The squirrel popped his head out of the pocket. In a flash he climbed down Colin's hose and scampered to Maura's side. The squirrel deposited a copper at Maura's feet and stared up at her with a twitching black nose.

Maura pinched up the coin. "Good pay for Nutmeg's performance," she said. "I thank you for it."

She popped the copper in her bag and eyed the man Colin in challenge, feeling a little tremor in her belly as the handsome wrestler eyed her back. As the moments passed and he said nothing, she wondered if her sleeve-laces were untied, if the night had frizzed her hair like it usually did, if the curls were at all contained beneath the white linen of her coif.

Then Colin's paramour sidled up beside him. The woman pressed her breast against his arm. Maura glanced at her, noting the brazen red hair, bright eyes, dark lips, and flushed cheeks. And suddenly, in her dull brown surcoat and common little coif, she felt as colorless and plain as the birds that pecked for crumbs outside the convent's kitchen doors.

"Enough of this foolishness," the woman said. "You've had your fun, Colin. Now tell this girl to go back to the convent where she belongs."

"Convent?!"

Staccato shouts of alarm stuttered through the campsite, like the minstrels had all been doused with holy water.

"She's likely to get you all hanged," the woman continued. "If she's found here, they'll say you abducted a nun."

"She hasn't taken vows," Colin mused. "Too much lovely hair spilling out over her shoulders."

"Looks to me like a fine, warm abbess," one of the men barked, eliciting a round of chuckles.

"She does have the look of an angel," Colin said, "descended among us to wash us free of sin."

"Huh," Maura barked, "and thus dirty the waters of the Shannon?"

She winced at her own words. She was supposed to be gracious and subservient. After all, she was here to ask a favor. But they stared at her like so many crows, and that made her nervous, and when she was nervous she got prickly, even when she knew better.

But the man called Colin only laughed, a sound that sent a not-completely-unpleasant tingle shooting down her spine.

"I recognize that laugh," a voice bellowed from a nearby tent. "Colin, what poor girl are you leading astray now?"

Maura turned to encounter the roundest man she'd ever seen. Waddling out of the tent, he pinched the bone of some roasted animal between his thumb and forefinger. His black-eyed gaze assessed her as he approached.

"Arnaud, we have a lady," Colin began, gesturing to her, "who would like to join the troupe."

"*Sacré*, if we were only blessed with as many patrons as performers, we'd be rich men." The oversized man twisted the bone in his hand as he assessed her. "Colin will give you a warm bed, but it's me who'll give you a place in the troupe, if you've got any talent."

Maura turned and narrowed her gaze on Colin. When she'd seen him fighting in the village this afternoon, so tall and brawny and full of chatter, she'd just assumed he was the leader of the troupe. He had such a straight-shouldered, confident look about him. Now she glared at him in accusation, but he just gave her a half-smile and a shrug.

"The lady," Colin said, gesturing to Nutmeg chewing an acorn at her feet, "has a dancing squirrel."

Arnaud shook his head. "We don't need any more rats in this troupe, even trained ones."

"I've earned many a coin on my own," she lied, her heart tripping, "playing Nutmeg for the children in the village."

"Children don't have English coin. Or meat or ale to barter." That black gaze, embedded in folds of flesh, made its way up and down her figure. "You're a pretty one. What other tricks do you know?"

She felt her face flame to the roots of her hair, and could only hope that the glow of the campfire masked it.

"No swiving then?" The big man sighed. "A pity. You've the hips for it."

The fat man turned around and headed back to his tent and she felt her hopes slipping away. This couldn't be happening. Nutmeg with his bell-dances and little blue shirts had been the joy of the convent and the center of attention whenever she'd visited cottages outside the walls. She had been convinced that these players would welcome her and Nutmeg's talents—and do it without question. And they were *minstrels,* not exactly the kind of people overly concerned about who they kept company with.

Yet she was being dismissed out of hand.

Maura's throat tightened. What was it about her that put so many people off? It must be like a smell, she thought, like the faint scent of onions, which always clung to her hands. Maybe she'd emitted this odor since birth, when her own mother had abandoned her.

"Can you dance, Maura?"

She turned to find Colin very close, his eyes upon her. Blue eyes, she realized, as blue as the summer sky.

"Dancing," she said, scooping Nutmeg back into his basket, "is the work of the devil."

"Can you tell stories?"

"Aye, of the saints' lives."

"We don't barter in those. Can you juggle? Tumble?"

A flush rose up her cheeks. She couldn't help but glance at an acrobat by the fire slinging her own ankle over her neck, all but exposing her privates.

He persisted, "Can you sing?"

"What matter if I could sing?" Of course she could sing. She sang every day at the offices, at the Mass. Only a common dotard couldn't sing. "You're not the man I have to convince," she said, jerking her chin toward the fat man tearing the last of the meat from a bone, hesitating at the flap of his tent. "*He* is."

"Arnaud's belly is empty, and when his belly is empty, he doesn't think clearly." Colin touched her chin to turn her face toward his. "If you've any hope of joining us, lass, you'd best lift that voice of yours in song."

She blinked up at him, feeling the fascination of this man shimmer over her like the wash of rainwater during a sudden storm.

This is a terrible, terrible mistake.

She pulled away from his blue, blue gaze, her heart and her thoughts racing. Maybe it wasn't too late. Maybe she could still sneak back into the convent. It was almost Compline, when all the sisters would kneel in the chapel. That was no guarantee that the novices wouldn't be twittering by the well, or whispering whilst they slipped through the gardens, or some other nosy creature would come out of the shadows to question her as to what she was doing, sneaking back into the convent after dark. She could still return to her home and escape this handsome man who looked at her as if he could see her naked.

But what would happen if she returned to the convent? She would take her place in the kitchens where she'd grown up, go back to making the meals for all the sisters and the laywomen in the community, be grateful as they always told her to be for having such a fine position. She could go back and continue to ignore the insistence that at her age she must choose between the veil or a marriage to someone like the butcher's son who kept finding excuses to wander to the kitchen door with slabs of meat she hadn't ordered, fine cuts that he'd put aside just for her.

Then Maura looked down upon the ring on her finger, twisting it, twisting it, twisting it, until it felt as tight as her resolve.

"Aye," she heard herself say. "Aye, I can sing."

She put Nutmeg's basket on the ground and ignored the minstrels who circled her in curiosity. She filled her lungs with the spring air as the first bit of drizzle began to fall from the sky. She closed her eyes and imagined herself in church with its echoing rafters. A song rose in her heart—*Angelus ad virginem*—The Angel's Address to the Virgin, one of her favorites. The music swelled in her head. She felt it pour through her body.

She opened her mouth and let it out.

CHAPTER TWO

"Arnaud," Colin said, chasing the leader of the troupe across the campsite, "you *cannot* let that woman go."

"If I took on every wayward girl you had an urge to prickle," the Gascon said, shifting a plug of pork to the other side of his cheek, "we'd leave a trail as long as Ireland itself."

"She's no whore." That had been clear enough. "You're a hard man, Arnaud."

"A hard man, you say? Haven't I enough charity here?" Arnaud waved toward Matilda Makejoy, the dancer of the troupe, sitting sideways upon a cushion by the fire, her belly swelling under the high-slung rope of her belt. "As it is we look less like minstrels and more like Mary and Joseph on the way to Bethlehem. Must we take in an abbess, as well?"

"Admit it," Colin said. "In all your travels, you've never heard a voice as fine as that."

Colin *still* heard her voice, even though she'd

stopped singing, even though she'd raced back into the woods as soon as Arnaud had dismissed her. He could hear it as if the sweet tones still vibrated in the trees. Her voice had pierced through him, pure and clear and tremulous, the kind of voice that brought wild men to stillness, that made lions lie down with lambs, that made sinners see the face of God.

"Yes, *oui*," Arnaud reluctantly confessed, "she has a fine voice—a singular voice—a voice worthy of the heavens. But is she to sing like that in an alehouse? She'll leave our patrons with no stomach for Maguire's riddles or the twins' tumbling."

"I'll teach her love songs."

"You'll teach her love, I've no doubt of that, but a woman can't sing with her quim."

"Stop for a moment and think." Colin stepped between the troupe's leader and the tent he was trying to slip into. "That lass has a voice fine enough to open the doors of kings."

"You'd have us singing at a royal court?" The Gascon paused in his chewing. "Us? Maguire with his dirty riddles? The twins with their legs in the air? Matilda dancing like a Saracen? You'd have the likes of us entertaining fine lords and ladies? Have you forgotten that we've been driven out of half the alehouses we've played in? That we had to leave the ripe fields of France because a certain someone swived the wrong man's wife? And we had to leave Wales because Padraig stole the wrong lord's gold?"

"France and Wales are worlds away. And English lords and ladies pay in gold, unlike the millers' wives and bakers' sons we entertain in these tiny villages. We'll make more and better coin than what we're taking in at rough alehouses and at crossroads."

"I won't do it, Colin."

"You won't do what?"

"I won't braid the rope you're going to hang yourself with."

Colin's jaw tightened but he held his own tongue fast. Arnaud knew nothing about why Colin had convinced him to bring the troupe to Ireland, but the old Gascon was clever and smart, and increasingly curious. The old man had sensed something was up that black night on the shores of Wales over a month ago, when Colin had stared across the phosphorescence of the Irish Sea, thinking, thinking, as his homeland called to him like the sirens of those Greek stories his teachers had forced him to learn.

Poor Arnaud looked at him now, waiting. He didn't know that the hangman's noose already weighed heavy around Colin's neck. It was simply a matter of time before it lay there in truth.

"Her voice is pure gold." Colin clapped a hand on Arnaud's shoulder. "And I'm going to fetch back the woman who'll put that gold in your pocket."

Colin turned on one heel and set off after the wench, ignoring Arnaud's shouts of warning. It didn't take long for him to see her crisp white coif bobbing in the woods by the light of the moon. He set his sights on that fine healthy curve of buttock and soon caught up beside her.

"A fine evening for a walk."

She tilted her head and laid a bright hazel gaze upon him, and it was as if the evening crackled with sparks and lightning, like the false fire he'd once seen exploding in the air at a Christmas feast in Paris.

Then she whacked him in the ribs with a stick.

Air whooshed out of him. He skittered back as

she gathered momentum for another swing, but not fast enough. She shoved the knotted end of the walking stick into his belly and sent him slamming against the trunk of a tree.

"Be off with you." She stepped back and swiped the stick through the air in warning. "What evil are you bent on, following me like this?"

"A fine greeting you give a man who follows you for your own good." He held up an arm to forestall another blow. "You're too pretty a lass to be traveling alone at night. Though you wield that stick well."

"I've wielded enough weapons against your like." She turned on a heel. "Now go back to your wretched troupe and leave me be."

"And where will you be going, Maura?" He gestured in the opposite direction from which she was travelling. "The convent is back there."

"I'm not going back to the convent." Her face tightened. "Not that it's any of your affair."

"You're heading for the north road then."

"Where else? There are few enough roads." She turned on a heel. "And those roads are long enough for two people to travel apart."

"And why would a convent-bred girl be traveling alone on the roads of Ireland?"

She swiped a curl off her shoulder. "So it's curiosity that's got you sniffing after me."

"You don't seem the kind for adventure."

"And what do you know about my 'kind?' Nay," she said, slashing a pale hand through the air, "don't answer that. We're not all like that redheaded woman of yours, you know." She shifted the weight of her pack and that odd little basket upon her back as she continued her angry stride. "If it's your curiosity that's got you nipping at my skirts, then I'll put an end to it and be rid of you. I'm off to St. Patrick's Purgatory."

Colin stopped in his tracks. She shot ahead of him, determined as ever, as if she hadn't just announced she was going on a pilgrimage to the most sacred shrine in all of Ireland, a shrine that lay on an island in Lough Derg, about three weeks' walk north.

He walked double-speed to catch up with her. "So you asked to join the troupe," he said, "to travel to a shrine."

She shrugged.

"Minstrels wander about, from village to castle to Irish homestead—rarely to a shrine. We go wherever luck and chance and a fair takes us."

"All the better for my purposes."

"And what purpose is that?"

"What matter is it to you?"

"People go on pilgrimages to purge their sins. I'd like to know what sin you committed that was so grave as to send you on the roads alone."

"It wasn't swiving, I'll tell you that."

"Oh, lass." A laugh rose up to his throat but he choked it down. "I'd take off my hat to any man who found his way through the thorns on you."

He knew there had been no man. It was written in the darkening of her cheeks, in the stiff carriage of her neck, in her way of walking that spoke of moral good sense. He avoided such women, but this lass was starting to feel like a challenge.

"You asked where I was going," she said, "and now I've told you. So go back to your troupe and leave me be."

"St. Patrick's Purgatory is three weeks' walk." He eyed her sack. "You've enough food for the journey?"

"Aye."

"You know how to work the miracle of the loaves and fishes, then."

"I'll make do better than you'll ever know."

"And lodgings?"

"You and your troupe camped in the woods without trouble."

"If you're thinking of sleeping in the woods, you'd best sleep with one eye open. Else you'll wake up to the breath of wolves, or the knives of ruffians."

"The only wolf I've seen so far walks on two feet, and insists on following me around asking questions, questions, questions."

"And how are you to pay to cross the Shannon? There are tolls at every ford, and few enough fords."

Her lashes fluttered. "I'm can swim."

"Others have tried that. The constable enjoys catching such toll-evaders on royal land. With you, he'll extract his toll in the way that will please him most, and you'll end up in the king's jail, less virtuous for your sin."

Her nostrils flared. "I'll trust in God."

"Spoken like a true novice, but then again," he said, daring to reach out and brush his fingers against the soft curls spilling out beneath the hem of the coif, "Brides of Christ are cloistered, and shorn to the scalp, and you most definitely are not."

Her pace quickened, but though she was tall and fast, he was taller, and faster, and more determined than she knew.

In frustration she said, "Is it the copper you're after? I'll give you back your coin if that's—"

"I won't take away a woman's fee, well earned. You could earn a great deal more."

"Sin pays well, I've heard. I've also heard that Saracens travel with carts full of concubines, but this is a Christian country."

"I don't dip my quill into my own inkwell, lass."

"And what could that possibly mean?"

"It means I don't swive the women in the troupe." Even in the moonlight Colin could tell she was blushing to the roots of her hair. "Also," he added, "I don't pay for my pleasure."

"Does your arrogance have no bounds?"

"There's no profit in lying. But your voice, Maura. For the troupe, there's much profit in that."

"Not says the man who pulls your leash."

"Arnaud thinks with his belly."

"A big enough thing—"

"—and empty as a cavern. We haven't greased our knives at a decent table since well before Lent. Which is why we are very much in need of you, though he'd eat his own shirt before he admitted it."

She turned upon him, pointing the stick whence they'd come. "Just moments ago your leader told me he had no use for a saint to bless the alehouses. He said that sin pays better than sanctity. He said my voice would be a bucket of ice water on the fire of profit. Then your minstrel brethren chased me away with their teasing and laughter."

"Don't blame the men for wielding the tools of their trade." He veered far enough away to avoid the spike of her stick. "A tongue is a blade that must be honed like any other, or it will soon grow dull."

"I won't be a whetstone for you and your men."

"Forgive them. They didn't know how to react. They've never heard anyone sing like that. You have the voice of an angel."

"Flattery now?" She stopped and turned on him. "I've seen men hop and jig like trussed roosters trying to get under a woman's tunic. Have you no pride?"

"We were felled by your song, every one of us."

"What kind of joke is this?"

"It's no joke. We need you. And you need us."

She crossed her arms and looked at him through narrowed eyes, still gripping the stick in one of her hands. It was a good sign that she wasn't swinging it.

"All our food and shelter comes only by the grace of those we entertain," he said. "The Irish are generous but poor. The English who rule them are rich, but think we are no better than spies. We entertain the first, but strive to entertain the latter. You," he continued, "could get us inside the great English halls all over Ireland…if you were to tune that lovely voice of yours to a different sort of song."

"A song about rutting no doubt. You'd like that."

He stared at her, from the tip of her cap, down over her full chest, to the tiny waist and the thrust of those ample hips, down to the toes of her slippers peeping beneath the mud-caked hem of her surcoat.

"I'd be a lying son of a cheat," he murmured, "if I told you I haven't thought of swiving you."

She didn't bat an eyelash. "There's the first bit of truth I've heard out of you all evening."

"Then admit this truth of your own—you need travelling companions, or you won't make it to St. Patrick's Purgatory."

Those dark eyes narrowed, the little nostrils flared, and Colin could tell he'd found her weakness, though he'd probably have to kiss her senseless to get her to admit it.

"I'd give a good portion of my dinner to know the name of the man who made you as prickly as a thistle, lass."

"Not name, minstrel, but *names.*" She uncrossed her arms. "In the kitchens of the convent, not a day goes by when some day-laborer or butcher or tinker tries to wheedle his way into my graces—"

"You worked in the kitchens?"

"I ran them, thank you very much. I've been doing so since I was sixteen. And so I know the true meaning of cupboard love."

A smile came over him. "I think we've just found a way to crack open Arnaud's hard little heart."

The next morning, Arnaud palmed the shallow bowl in one pudgy hand and lifted the rim to his mouth. Behind the shield of the bowl, he sucked down a gulp of the soup.

Maura stood before him, one foot tapping in the grass of the roadside campsite. She curled her hand tight around the handle of a long wooden spoon. Steam hissed out of the small cauldron hitched upon a makeshift tripod, and the last of the fire Colin had made for her now simmered to embers. Behind her came the slurping and scraping noises of minstrels setting to the last of their morning meal at the bottom of the cauldron—a cauldron they'd pounced on like wolves when she'd announced the food was done.

Arnaud lowered the bowl. Pinching a square of his mantle between two fingers, he patted his lips.

"Well?" Colin sat sprawled on the ground beside the leader, all long, loose limbs. "The wench can make a roast out of weeds, eh?"

She ignored him and instead eyed the mountain of the man. This wretched creature best show some appreciation for the labor and skill it took to stir up a soup of wild onions and herbs in less than an hour. She'd had to rise from her bed of leaves before everyone else to find herbs in the woods to add to the broth, dipping into her own meager stores of smoked bacon to flavor it. She'd been willing to make the sacrifice because the more Colin talked last night, the more the fiery edge of her impulsiveness receded. Three weeks' walk to St. Patrick's Purgatory! She hadn't even known there was that much road in all of Ireland, never mind this information about tolls to pass rivers and brigands with knives. Clearly she needed the protection of a crowd—even a wicked crowd—more than she'd even suspected.

At least, for all of the minstrel Colin's flirtation, he'd made no effort to force himself upon her when she made herself a pallet in the leaves last night—no force beyond the oozing glamour of the man.

Arnaud barked, "You learned to cook like this in a convent, girl?"

She stopped tapping and shifted her weight to the other leg. "I told you, I ran the kitchens."

"Convent fare is bland stuff."

"Not at Christmas," she argued. "Or at Easter. The convent at Killoughy is full of laywomen and noble girls. They're accustomed to fine fare."

"I'm a full-blooded Gascon," he muttered, "and I'm used to thicker stuff than this watery soup."

"Better meat will make a better stew."

"The soup wants salt."

"Aye, and it could do with a bit of cabbage and milk," she said, "but I didn't run across a cow wandering the forest, or conjured cabbage in full growth in the woods."

"Tell him what you can do with rabbit." Colin sprawled on one elbow like a libertine. "And fish—we often stumble upon fish flapping on the shores."

"I can poach fish in milk and thyme," she said. "Rabbit can be roasted with wild mustard rubbed into the skin." She hiked her hands on her hips. "I'll work with what the forest yields to us—but don't go and tell me how you find your meat or fish. I won't be a part of poaching or thievery."

"Admit it, Arnaud." Colin chewed lazily on a sliver of hazel bark. "She cooks better than Matilda."

Arnaud grunted. With two fingers, he scooped up the wild onions and sucked them into his mouth. He spoke through the last of them. "Colin tells me you're off to St. Patrick's Purgatory."

"Aye, that I am."

"Why?"

Maura straightened her spine. She found herself remembering the painful, gentle laughter of the Abbess when Maura first broached the thought of making this pilgrimage. Her parents had made it, she'd said, why shouldn't she? Then the Abbess had grown somber and rueful, regretting ever telling Maura about the group of pilgrims who'd passed by the convent around the time that Maura had been found, mewling, on the convent steps.

It's a foolish idea, Maura, no sense to it at all. You should be thinking about your future here.

Now Arnaud and Colin were looking at her, expecting an answer. "I'm making a pilgrimage," she insisted. "There's nothing more to say."

Arnaud clattered the bowl by his side, pinching

his mantle up again to clean his mouth. "You travel with us, we will know with whom we travel."

"I am Maura of Killeigh."

"Who is Maura of Killeigh?" he said, raising his meaty arms. "Adulterer? Witch? Will English knights come chasing after us, an irate father, or the men of the church?"

"I'm a free woman. I've made no vows, I'm bound to no one." She wished she didn't have the kind of skin that flushed whenever she felt ashamed. "I don't even have kin to chase after me."

"Every woman has kin."

"As a baby," she said, her throat growing tight, "I was abandoned on the convent steps."

"A foundling?" Arnaud grunted. "Did you come up with that story yourself, woman, to put off my inquiries? I've no stomach for nasty surprises."

"I would think a stomach such as yours must have room for many things." The troupe leader narrowed his eyes. Maura knew she should shut up, but this man was teasing her temper, and when she was mad she got prickly and couldn't hold her tongue. "Let us strike a compromise, shall we?" She swung around to gesture to the minstrels watching them. "I shall not ask why that dirty little man lacks an ear— for surely such was the result of an accident, not mutilation for the crime of trespassing. And the piper wears his hair over his brow like a monk just to show his piety, no doubt, not to mask a thief's brand upon his forehead. And I trust," she continued, gesturing to the twin women swathed in woolen cloaks, "that the acrobats wear their hair so close-shorn so as to keep it from getting in the way of their tumbling—not in payment for the crime of…selling passion."

"She's a hellion, Colin," Arnaud grumbled, as if she wasn't standing right there. "This one will scratch your eyes out rather than give you a soft word."

"She'll be all the finer for the taming."

The hairs on the back of her neck bristled. She shot arrows at him with her gaze but he only smiled as if they were flower petals falling from the trees.

"There are eight of us," Arnaud said, "and by the autumn we will be nine. You would have me take on this choir maiden who can do no more than cook."

"Arnaud, you are a man of great wisdom and business sense."

"I support a blind harpist and a pregnant sword-dancer. I am a man of *no* sense."

"But we need someone who is as lovely as our dear Matilda Makejoy." Colin gestured to one of the three women near the cart. Maura followed his gaze to a young woman whose long, black hair spilled over her swollen belly. "Our lovely Matilda will soon not be able to play the same sort of parts she did before."

"Playing parts?" Maura pointed the spoon at him, her suspicions rising. "Whatever you're set upon teaching me, it best be worthy."

"Do you hear her?" Arnaud raised the palms of his hands. "What could you possibly teach this abbess that would be worthy to take Matilda's place?"

Maura opened her mouth to say something, but Colin's sharp look stopped her. She bit her lower lip and thought about wolves, lusty toll keepers, and thieves in the woods, and tried not to feel as if she were about to sign her soul away in blood.

"Never fear, Arnaud," Colin said, smiling a slow, wicked smile. "We'll have enough time on the road to turn our foundling into a proper minstrel."

CHAPTER THREE

"So, you'll turn me into a 'proper' minstrel, will you?" Maura slung Nutmeg's basket over her shoulder as she caught up with Colin on the road. "Is there even such a thing?"

She was breathing hard as she kept pace with him, tired from packing all the cooking utensils back on the donkey, a job she set to with haste so she wouldn't have to think too hard about why Colin was grinning so much after Arnaud's agreement.

"Tell me, Maura." Colin turned that piercing blue gaze upon her. "Why do you despise us all so much?"

She blinked. "I don't despise you."

"Yet just the idea of training to become a minstrel puts a scowl on your pretty face."

She opened her mouth to speak but words of denial died in her throat. Was she really scowling? She supposed she should be acting more grateful, considering the circumstances, but scowling?

And did he really think she had a pretty face?

She shook away the vain thought, promised

another Hail Mary before bed, and then tried to control her muddled mind. She couldn't deny that she didn't embrace the idea of becoming a minstrel. The Abbess—the woman who had taken her in—had told such terrible stories about the sinfulness of traveling players. The senior sister had kept the nuns and novices shut inside the convent whenever a troupe passed through Killeigh. Maura had only managed to see them yesterday because it had been market day, and their stores of food were down to nothing, it being so soon after Lent. She suspected the Abbess had relented in the hope that Maura would go see the butcher's boy.

If Maura was honest, it was the *Abbess* who despised minstrels, and Maura believed whatever the Abbess believed. Why would Maura doubt a woman so well educated that she knew Latin and geography and all sorts of wondrous things? Certainly the Abbess came by her opinions fairly.

"There are three kinds of good people in the world," Maura said, using the Abbess's own arguments. "Those who pray, those who sow and reap, and those who protect the weak. Minstrels do none of the three."

"Ah, but we make all three of them laugh."

"Yes, by encouraging lechery with your acrobats," she said. "And by taking a poor man's hard-earned coin by encouraging him to wager on wrestling matches."

"We let them forget their troubles for a while—"

"—and their responsibilities."

"Of which they'll always have both. What harm is there in giving them a few hours' reprieve?"

She thought about this as she picked her way

around the puddles on the road. His words held truth, but she was having trouble focusing on it, too distracted by the scent that wafted off him, an exotic fragrance that made her imagine strange things—Turkish campfires, Saracen robes, the perfume of desert nights—things she'd only heard about listening to the convent girls' whispered, heated fantasies in the middle of dark nights.

Stop.

She closed her eyes and muttered three Hail Marys and then three Our Fathers, but knew that her sins were piling up. She needed to see a priest—and soon—for absolution.

Until then, she had to find a way to speak to this man without thinking about things she shouldn't.

"Your friends," she said, waving ahead to the rest of the troupe. "They seem very quiet today."

"Too much ale can leave a wad of wool in the mouth in the morning. They'll be themselves before evening."

"Tell me something about them."

That gaze again, the crinkles beside the eyes, that expression of knowing amusement.

"If I'm going to be traveling with them," she said, the back of her neck tightening, "I'd best get to know their names at least."

"Most certainly." He looked like he was trying to hide a smile as he gestured to his friends. "The man without the ear, the sooty-faced one who entertained all the children with his magic tricks yesterday. We call him Maguire Mudman."

"That's an odd name."

"Padraig Smallpipe is our piper." He gestured to the man dancing as he led the way. "And the lady in waiting is Matilda Makejoy."

Maura glanced at the pregnant, dark-haired woman swaying upon a donkey—no husband in sight, though Arnaud seemed attentive—and thought how very far she'd traveled from the convent where the worst of sins was to waste a bit of good beef.

"You know Arnaud," Colin continued. "He's a cranky Gascon who goes by the surname *Groshomme*."

"Fat man?"

"Ah, you speak French, and not just to your pet."

"Our Abbess is from Avignon, so she teaches the novices both French and Latin."

"But you're no novice."

"The Abbess made sure I received many of the same lessons as the novices and the laywomen there just for their education." She changed the subject by gesturing to the blind man walking with the acrobat twins. "Who's the harpist?"

"We call him Fingar Full."

She saw the harpist heft a handful of female backside. One twin playfully batted his hand away.

She said, "Fitting."

"And the twins," he added, "are Slaine and Sinead Shortskirts."

"Slaine and Sinead? Well, there are two names among you that have known baptismal water." She looked at Colin sidelong, ignoring the urge to tug that single, slender braid that trailed over his shoulder in the Irish way. "What is your nickname, then? Colin the Cuckolder?"

His teeth flashed bright. "I knew you had a tongue for this trade."

"You didn't answer my question."

He shrugged an impressive shoulder. "They call

me King Colin."

"Doesn't that fit like an old slipper."

"They fancy me a lost king," he mused, spreading his hand to the woods on either side of the road, "in search of my lost kingdom."

"King of an alehouse, I suppose?"

"Easy, Maura. You'll be getting a name, too, sooner rather than later, and it's likely I'll be the one to give it to you. 'Abbess' doesn't quite fit."

"Maura will do."

"I wonder if it will." He cocked his head at her. "On the road you have a chance to become someone you are not. Have you never wanted that?"

The question confused her. At the age of five she'd left her milk-mother and came to the convent to sweep floors, where she'd had the presence of half a dozen mothers always around. As she grew, she remembered seeing girls her own age working in the fields from dawn until dusk, but her duties were restricted to the small convent garden, and later, to the warmth of the kitchens. She'd thought herself well-placed, well-loved, for a girl without family, a babe left abandoned.

But then she'd been given the ring—the gold, crested ring that had been wrapped in her swaddling clothes—the ring now constricting her third finger. That's when she realized that her life was a false one, and there was someone else she was supposed to be.

"Your silence speaks for you," Colin murmured.

She shook her head. "I don't know what you mean."

"There isn't a soul on two feet who doesn't wish, now and again, to be someone else. I can teach you how, Maura." He squinted at the woods on either side of the road and then stopped walking. "This place will do as well as any. It's time for our first lesson."

Colin slid his fingers under the strap of Nutmeg's basket and then tugged it off her back. She reached for it but caught nothing but air.

"But the troupe," she said, glancing over her shoulder, "they'll be halfway to Athlone if we stop—"

"I know the way well enough."

She tightened her grip on her other pack as he curled his fingers around a strap. "If we delay I won't be able to cook a midday meal."

"Arnaud and the minstrels have lived a long time without your cooking skills. They'll make do while I teach you what you need to know." He gave her pack another tug. "Come, we have work to do."

With reluctance, she dropped her shoulder so the pack slid off her back. He placed it at the base of a tree with Nutmeg's basket. Startled by the sudden movement, Nutmeg jutted his head out and sniffed at Colin with a twitching black nose, before clambering atop the basket and darting into the woods.

She glanced over her shoulder to see the last of the minstrels—Fingar Full and the Shortskirt girls— disappear beyond a bend in the path.

Alone, then, on this sliver of a road surrounded by woods.

Alone, with Colin.

He came back to face her. "Late tomorrow," he said, "you'll be playing the part of a minstrel in Athlone. Athlone is the center of the king's cantreds, a city the English control, much to the chagrin of the surrounding O'Conors and McAuley's. The English like their entertainment almost as much as the Irish, even if they don't like the Irish as much."

"If they like hymns," she said, "then—"

"No hymns, Maura. You shall act in a play with me, taking Matilda's place."

"A play."

"For your first lesson, you shall pretend you are the young and lovely wife of a clerk. And I shall pretend, at first, to be your aged, miserly husband."

She planted her fists on her hips. "Play wife to your husband?"

"It's just a play, Maura. A *fabliaux*—"

"Give it a fancy French name, but I still know what it means."

He paused. "You've never seen a play, have you?"

She lowered her eyes. Maura was beginning to realize that there were many things in the world she knew nothing about.

"A *fabliaux*," he said, "is like a liturgical play at Easter or at Christmas. I've no doubt you've seen enough of them."

"Of course. I've even played in one."

"The Virgin Mary?"

"A lamb."

A strange look rippled over his face. He opened his mouth to speak but he stopped and then shook his head. "It's best if I do all the talking. Just do what I tell you to do, and this will work out fine."

He stepped closer to her. Though he didn't touch her, she felt the pressure of his presence magnify as if the wood itself were closing in on them. She wished he would tie his tunic properly. It was always gaping open from the unhooked edge and showing a stretch of tight, muscled chest. The man had the tall, brawny body of a legendary Fenian warrior, hair the black of the mythical Milesians, and eyes a laughing, vibrant blue.

She let her gaze drop to the hollow of his throat. It seemed the safest part of him to look at.

"The play begins," he said, "like this."

He raised his voice as if he were standing on a wooden platform rather than on a road pocked with cart-tracks and the imprint of horses' hooves. He began a rhyming recitation about a clerk 'full far in his age,' and the lovely wife 'he knew so well.' The words filled the place, as if they stood under the arched roof of some cathedral and not under the shade of trees whose boughs stretched above them. They were not touching, but his voice rumbled through her in a strange, intimate way.

He held out his hand as he finished the first stanza. "Walk to me, Maura. Listen to what I say and act as I bid."

"Foolishness," she muttered, but she slipped her hand into his nonetheless. His hand was warm, broad-knuckled, strong, and nicked liberally on the back—scars, no doubt, from wrestling for wagers. He urged her to walk in a circle around him, and she felt like Nutmeg being pulled on a leash.

> *"The woman he wived was no more than a girl,*
> *With skin as white as the sheen on a pearl,*
> *And eyes as green as the young summer grass,*
> *Full of innocence and vinegar and brass…"*

He tugged her a little closer with each circling loop, until she came so near she could feel the heat of him through her clothes.

His voice lowered in timbre.

*"Her hair swayed and rippled like wheat in the field,
with each movement of hip and leg and heel.
Broad buttocks she had, and breasts firm and high—"*

"That's quite enough of that." She turned her face away. "So this isn't about a saint's life, I see."

"It's a morality play nonetheless." The corner of his lips twitched in that maddening half-smile again.

She sighed. "Get on with it, will you?"

He tugged on her hand again, but this time he laid her palm flat on his chest. The touch was a shock—his body hard and warm, his chest rising and falling, and all her senses seemed to shift to her palm and the swellings and angles of the man beneath it. She locked her elbow to keep her distance.

He continued reciting while a wind rustled the woods all around them. He talked about how one day a minstrel came to the village. She could only raise her brows as he switched parts from husband to minstrel, leaning in as he looked down at her with a twinkle in his eye. He lifted her hand and pressed his lips upon her knuckles. The touch was wet and rough, and it made her heart skitter.

Colin kept talking, but the words became a dull murmuring in her addled mind. Between stanzas he whispered, *walk around me,* and she did as she was bid. *Stay still, keep your eyes lowered.* And so she did, as they continued to circle one another. *Turn your back on me, walk away from me.* And she did so, only to gasp as he seized her by the arm and jerked her against him so her back slammed against his chest.

The world went still. The birds stopped twittering in the trees around them, the wind stopped rustling through the leaves, and the clouds became fixed in place. Colin went silent. His breath ruffled the hair on her head. She felt his heart beating against her shoulder blade, steady and hard and fast. He shifted his grip to slide his hand across her abdomen. Maura felt something move deep inside her beneath the touch of that hand. A slow, sliding sensation that she didn't understand.

Splaying his fingers, he pressed her closer.

She waited, breathless, her pulse throbbing in her throat, waiting for him to recite the next line. All her senses focused on the rise and fall of his chest and the heat of him pressing against her.

He spoke just above her ear. "What would you do, Maura, if the man you loved held you like this?"

She remembered that soft, alluring voice. She'd heard it once before, back when he'd buried his hand in another woman's cleavage.

Then she slammed her heel into his foot. Spinning out of his grip, she turned only to find him grinning.

"That," he said, with a wince, "was not part of the *fabliaux.*"

"Well it *should* be."

"In this play, the lady grants the minstrel's love at last."

"The lady is a fool then."

She turned away, clucked her tongue for Nutmeg, and then caught the ball of fur bounding toward her. She lifted her pet against her cheek until Nutmeg squealed.

"Find me another part in your play, Colin the Cuckolder," she said, striding toward her packs. "I won't play the harlot for anyone."

CHAPTER FOUR

The minstrels danced into the royal city of Athlone. Padraig Smallpipe led the troupe, the ragged hem of his tunic twirling, his bare feet thudding upon the fresh spring grass, rat-tatting his tabor and piping a wheeling jig. Maguire Mudman, sporting a devil's mask, darted here and there among the crowd, acting the wild man. The twins, Slaine and Sinead Shortskirts, tumbled on either side of the donkeys, flashing bare thighs for the world to see. Colin sauntered behind, sporting only a loose, belted tunic and braies on this fine warm spring day, winking at pretty women as the sun gleamed off his hair.

Maura walked among them, mimicking their jaunty stride as best as she could. The pregnant minstrel, Matilda Makejoy, had rustled up a string of bells for her, so Maura would at least have the appearance of a minstrel as they made their noisy way into the city. Now the chimes jangled from her waist and banged her knees with each step. Despite the noise around her, despite the flash of swords Matilda hefted into the air, despite the scent of burning pitch emanating from Arnaud's torch, Maura's gaze fixed upon another sight, stranger than any she'd seen before: An enormous city.

This place bore no resemblance to the kind of village that clung to the walls of her old convent—that was just a cluster of houses, a baker and a butcher and a beekeeper, the sort of traders the sisters did business with. Sure, her home village swelled during the harvest time, when laborers drifted through to help bring in the hay for the cows' winter fodder. But what she was looking at now, from across the River Shannon, was no makeshift collection of hovels, but a sea of thatched-roofed houses.

The troupe crossed the stone bridge and danced into the thick of it. Scents assaulted her—the metallic taste of the air outside the blacksmith's shop, the stench of rotting carcasses around the tannery, the sweet scent of honey outside the waferer. In the narrow confines of the smoky convent kitchens, she'd long become used to the richness of conflicting fragrances. But here, the odors mixed and churned in the streets like a stew over-spiced, sickening to the smell. She tilted her head back to stare at the blue sky …and caught sight of a church spire.

She was long overdue for confession.

The street narrowed. Matilda, absorbed in her sword-dancing, paid her no mind. Arnaud's attention was fixed on the crowd. The others danced and piped and tumbled with no care for her. She wasn't expected to do anything now, anyway. Not until Arnaud scoured the alehouses frequented by the wealthy English of the place and found the one willing to give him the heftiest cut of the night's profits for their entertainment.

She saw an alley of opportunity and knew she wouldn't be missed at all.

In one swift movement, she took two steps sideways into the crowd. Pushing her way through the horde proved harder than she expected. Such a crowd, so many people! The Irish around the convent lived in scattered settlements, with huge tracts of pasture between them to graze their cows and plow under enough land to feed their families. She wondered how the meager fields she'd seen around this settlement produced enough food to feed all the beefy Englishmen she passed.

With the soaring spire as her guide, she wove her way through the streets as the piper's music dimmed and the push of the crowd eased. She slipped down a narrow alleyway and then turned into another. Finally, light streamed through an opening ahead, and she found herself in a courtyard facing a stone church.

She hiked her skirts, climbed the stairs, and pushed open the doors. The familiar coolness enveloped her. She paused to let her eyes adjust to the darkness. The scent of incense lingered in the air as if a Mass had just been said. She released a trembling breath, and something stiff and tight unwound within her. She'd been gone from the convent for only two days, yet standing here in the echoing presence of the church she felt safe for the first time.

Of course, this church was nothing like the small stone chapel that stood on the convent grounds and on the best of days could only fit a dozen sisters. Here, a rosette of colored light poured down from above the nave to pool on the rush-covered floor. She'd never seen such colored glass before. She'd never seen such a high-roofed church, so much space.

"You, girl, what do you want?"

The slap-slap of hard-bottomed shoes drew her attention to a young man in a long brown tunic making his way toward her.

"Good day, father," she began, bobbing in a curtsy. "I've come—"

"By God!" The cleric stopped short. "Are there minstrels in town *again*?"

Maura jerked in surprise. The cleric's hair hung to his shoulders, not shorn in a clergyman's tonsure, a sure sign that he'd not yet taken his vows of priesthood. Yet surely even a priest-in-training wasn't encouraged to use the Lord's name in vain.

"Oh, father," she said, "I'm not a minstrel."

"Are those sacramental bells, to be used at Mass?" he said, pointing at the chain of chimes looped over her hips. "And that stain on your face, is that the blood of the Virgin?"

She touched her face. She'd forgotten the waxy red spots Matilda had painted upon her cheeks. She'd forgotten that she hadn't worn her coif. Her hair hung loose. Suddenly she felt Nutmeg squirming to wakefulness in the basket slung across her shoulder.

"I've come," she said, with as much humility as she could muster, "to seek pardon for my sins."

"I've no doubt those sins are many and mortal."

She opened her mouth to speak, but a rush of mortification stilled her tongue. Of sinful thoughts, she had many. But a hundred times worse was the vivid, sinful dream she'd had last night. A dream where Colin was smiling and she a wayward woman far prettier than the girl-cook she was.

"I know why you've come," the cleric continued.

"You're here to confess your sins, listen to what good Father William says, mimic your penance—and then ridicule the whole sacrament later in the alehouses of Athlone."

She sputtered, "I'll do no such thing."

"Such vehemence. You play your part well."

It's not a part. She wasn't a minstrel. Not a real one, anyway. Yet she would not deny that she'd sought refuge among them. Nor would she speak ill of them, for they *had* taken her in when she would have foolishly set out on the road alone. Conflicted into silence, she cast her eyes down and twisted the ring on her finger and wished she'd scrubbed her face and worn her white coif and her plain wool tunic.

It just didn't seem right that she'd be judged by how she looked, rather than what was in her heart.

"Father William is at his table now, he won't see you." The cleric turn away and then relented, his mouth thinning. "If you must know, he takes confessions after Nones."

Maura's heart sank. By Nones, she'd be deep in an alehouse, working off the price of the minstrel's protection in a way yet to be determined.

"If you *are* truly repentant," the cleric said, taking her by the arm, "then you will return at the appointed time. Dressed more humbly, I trust."

Then suddenly she was standing in the blinding light of the square, the door of the church slammed shut behind her, listening to the scrape of the bolt into the sleeve. She turned and stared at the closed doors. A weakness spread through her as she realized she'd been denied the grace of the church.

Just then a crowd burst from one of the narrow streets. The horde exploded into the square to reveal the reeling progression of the minstrel troupe. Padraig Smallpipe and the Shortskirts twins twirled to one side, a whirl of flying yellow silk. Maguire Mudman donned his devil's mask and grasped his own crotch, as he raced amid the crowd, doffing a hat for tribute.

And there Colin stood. Too vibrant in the sunlight, all wicked blue eyes and crooked smile as he caught sight of her. The full-fleshed embodiment of the shadowy, ardent man who, in her dreams, had slipped his rough fingers in the valley between her breasts and then cupped one in his hand.

Her weakness tightened to fury.

"I told them I'd find you here." Colin held out his hand. "Come, little repentant. It's time for you to earn your keep."

She curled her hands into fists. "I won't do it."

No, she wouldn't play the harlot. She'd rather disguise herself on the roads as a boy—or an old woman—than get another greeting like the one she just had at the door to this church.

"Forsooth," he said softly. "You must."

"You can't force me."

"I'd never force a lady." He tucked a blue marsh-violet behind her ear so swiftly she didn't have a chance to jerk away. "But I promise to make it as painless as possible."

"Painless?"

"The first time is always painful…but pleasure soon follows."

Someone tittered nearby. Maura looked past him and caught sight of a gaggle of young women. With a spurt of anger, Maura wondered which one would have the privilege of feeling Colin's hand on her breast tonight.

She turned on him. "You're nothing but a common seducer, Colin."

"You wound me, lass." He clasped both hands over his heart.

"It's the truth that hurts."

"Faith, what have I done for you to think so badly of me?"

"You don't remember yesterday?"

"Ahh, yes." A gleam came into his eye. "I remember yesterday."

Another ripple of laughter through the crowd, a ripple that annoyed her. What game was Colin playing? He was talking too loud. He was making people think there was more to what she was saying than what she was saying.

She hiked her hands on her hips and addressed the gossips. "I'll have you all know that *nothing* happened yesterday."

"It's true." He cast a sad gaze their way. "Nothing happened, to my eternal regret."

"We were just practicing—"

"Yes, yes, practicing," Colin interrupted. "It takes some practice to get it right, doesn't it my friends?"

Amidst the laughter, she hissed, "Stop this. Stop it right now." The circle of observers had thickened and they were all ears. How could he do this in the shadow of a church spire, while the cleric's words still rang in her head? "You've had your fun. I'll have no more of this foolishness, and none of you."

He caught her before she could shoot past him, a grip of iron on her upper arm. "You had enough of me yesterday, then?"

"More than enough."

"It's true that there's enough of me to be had."

If a smile could dance off a face, Colin's would be bouncing a jig on the paving stones. The crowd around them was all but choking in hilarity. Her fury started to curdle. He was the reason she couldn't be absolved for her sins, and yet here he was, making fun of her before all of Athlone.

Well, she could play that game too, if she put her mind to it.

She yanked out of his grasp and turned toward the crowd. "Aren't men," she said, meeting the gazes of the women, "always so full of themselves?"

She was gifted with shouts of agreement.

"Be that as it may," Colin responded, "I'd rather be full in *you*, lass."

"Seems to me," she said, whirling to face him, "that you believe shepherds were looking upon you when you were born."

"I may not be God's gift to the world, lass, but many a woman would say I've got a worldly gift."

"A gift, you say? Truth be told, yesterday you came up a bit short."

Colin paused for a moment—a second's hesitation—watching her with a gleam in his eye. She took some pleasure in knowing that the laughter now rolling around them was finally at *his* expense.

"Lady." He bowed before her. "You surprise me."

"Has no lass found the heart to tell you this before?"

"None with so angelic a face."

"Then I'll be more blunt." She remembered something one of the milkmaids had laughed about after slipping behind a haystack with a day-laborer. Maura only had the vaguest idea of what it meant. "I can't help but notice that your beard—" she said, scraping a finger across his clean-shaven jaw, "—is little more than fuzz."

"Is it not a fine thing for a man to be free of thatch?"

"A lass can judge by the thickness of the hay whether the pitchfork is any good." The crowd laughed and she felt a trill of satisfaction.

"Remember," he countered, "grass does not grow thick on a well-beaten path."

"If the path is so well beaten, then perhaps your pitchfork is like a spindle—worn out by the using."

"Rather," he countered, "it grows smooth and hard and well-polished."

"And thin and short. And like all old spindles," she said, flinging her hand in the air, "it's best tossed out for a new one."

In the laughter that ensued, Maura turned her back to him, intending to escape, but his fingers curled around her arm again and he brought her up short. The next thing she knew, he'd swung her into his arms, thrust her hips against his, and forced her head back so she had no choice but to stare up at his face, inches from hers.

There, it was happening again—that strange sliding feeling deep in her belly, as if the world was slipping away beneath her. The laughter of the crowd faded to a rumbling in the distance. The sun shone bright on his head, sheening his black hair—more like a halo than the horns he deserved. And she couldn't help staring at that face, at those smiling lips with the sharp, white scar that cut across the lower edge, glowing white now with how wide he was grinning. She watched that grin while they breathed in the same air, and she once again smelled that exotic and unfamiliar fragrance—oranges, cardamom—the one that made the back of her knees soften.

He's going to kiss me.

She waited for it to happen, staring into those intense blue eyes, and for a moment she felt like she was a child at Christmastide, aching for the moment the feast wound down so the waferer would come out to disperse his honey-dipped sweets that melted in one's mouth. But when his lips finally descended, he didn't aim for her own swollen, waiting lips. His mouth fell upon her earlobe instead.

Once there, he sucked it in.

Had lightning flashed down from the sky, she doubted it could thrust more rippling exhilaration through her than the feel of his hot mouth upon her ear. She clawed her fingers into his tunic as his tongue rolled rough and he drew in more. Seized by spasms of sensation, she didn't realize that Nutmeg had clambered out of his basket until she felt the bite of his tiny paws on her shoulder.

"Nutmeg," she mumbled. "Nutmeg!"

Colin pulled back. The crowd barked in surprise. Nutmeg squealed at the noise. With a chirr and a flurry of whiskers, the squirrel ripped threads down her back as he lunged for the paving stones. Frozen by his hard landing, he twitched his whiskers, and then tore through the legs of the scattering onlookers to some distant, quieter place.

"By God's Nails, woman," Colin said in a booming voice, "what sort of rats have you been lying with?"

The laughter was deafening. But she couldn't speak—she could barely think—so she focused on

Nutmeg, her terrified pet heading off to places unknown. Tearing away from Colin, Maura scanned the square. She glimped a furry blur dart into an alleyway. She headed after Nutmeg while slapping her ear, trying to rub away the tingling sensation Colin caused in more hollows than her ear.

He was only play-acting, she told herself, as she raced mindlessly after Nutmeg. She was a fool to think his kiss meant anything more than that.

Far down the alleyway, she glimpsed a gray tail hanging from the thatch of a roof. "Nutmeg?"

The squirrel poked a black nose over the edge, chirring down at her.

"Come, Nutmeg." She riffled in her pocket where a few spring seeds remained from the squirrel's hurried breakfast. "You'll find few enough trees here, and most of them already occupied."

The squirrel sniffed the air, then shot away when a woman threw open shutters just beneath his perch. Maura saw him leap onto the next roof. She followed him, house to house, trying to entice her pet down.

"He'll come down sooner or later."

She turned to see Colin striding down an alleyway in pursuit, squinting up at the squirrel cowering in the thatch.

"You!" She couldn't look at those blue eyes, still ashamed at her body's reaction to the touch of his tongue. "You scared Nutmeg near to death with your antics."

"Even the most skittish creatures always come around." He had the audacity to grin at her.

"Everything you say has a double meaning—"

"Not everything. Sometimes I speak the truth."

"Stop," she said. "I went to church this morning,

Colin. I met a cleric. Do you know what he did?"

"He turned you away."

She flattened her hand on a wall, cut down at the knees by his knowledge.

Colin shrugged. "A church is the one place our kind isn't always greeted with open arms."

"I'm *not* a minstrel."

He raised a brow. "In that square, you played the part as if you were born to it."

"I played the part," she argued, "because I foolishly wanted to give back to you the teasing you forced upon me. Vengeance is a sin, too. Another I won't be able to confess until I find a pardoner willing to hear me." She crossed her arms. "It's sure you have no concern for the state of your soul."

"Ah, Maura." His laugh was gentle. "I lost my soul a long time ago."

She opened her mouth but no sound came out. She didn't know how to respond to blasphemy. Her entire existence had been focused on the protection of her immortal soul—filling her days with prayers, confession, absolution, grace, especially to avoid the kind of sin that had crept into her dreams last night.

"Here." Colin tugged the tippet of his hood over his shoulder and reached into its length. "I followed you to give you this."

He pulled out a battered leather pouch, crossed with patches. He uncurled her hand and settled the pouch in it. A few coins spilled out. English coins, stamped with the visage of King Edward I. They gleamed dirty in the midday sun.

"Your first earnings as a minstrel." Colin raised one strong brow. "Like it or not, you're one of us now."

CHAPTER FIVE

"Every last penny!" Arnaud gripped the donkey's bit and yanked the beast around the mud. "Gone, every last gleaming coin—flung to the breeze by our little Abbess. As if English farthings come so cheaply and so easily!"

I'll ignore him. I'll ignore him, Maura told herself, in rhythm with her walk. Since they'd left the town, and she'd announced what she'd done with her earnings, the heat of Arnaud's black gaze had bored a hole into her back. Well, she felt no shame in what she'd done with the money Colin had given her, though her stomach gurgled on nothing more than last night's sour ale—all the breakfast the troupe could afford.

She glanced at Colin to gauge his opinion, but that minstrel was concentrating on keeping the second donkey out of the mud.

"Stop tugging so hard, Arnaud." Colin gripped the frayed harness as he coaxed the second beast clear. "If you yank him, he'll buck or stop altogether."

"Let him buck—or stop—what does it matter?" Arnaud swung his free arm to the road stretched before them. "We'll earn as much playing to birds and the squirrels as we did playing to those tight-fisted Englishmen. No—" Arnaud interjected as Colin opened his mouth to speak "—you know the rules. We share *all* earnings equally. You had no authority to give those coins to her so she could piss them away."

She flinched. "I didn't piss them away."

"She gave it all to a pardoner, no less. Hear that, Colin? She gave our hard-earned pay to a *pardoner!*"

"That money," she said, "was better spent than any you ever earned."

Arnaud raised his face to the skies. "She thinks those coins actually went to the *church.*"

"That pardoner," she argued, "came from the hospital of Roncesvalles, in Spain—"

"A Spanish hospital, of course!" Arnaud's gaze searched the heavens. "Surely, a Spanish hospital would send a pardoner all the way to this godforsaken island to raise funds."

The comment struck hard but she ignored it. A holy man was a holy man. "He had the authority to forgive sins unconfessed—including yours."

Arnaud flushed an unhealthy shade of red. "Colin, do you hear what this wench is saying?"

Colin, struggling to ease the laden donkey out of the mud, lifted his head long enough for her to see the laughter he was trying to suppress.

Aye, he would laugh at her. She supposed he had expected her to spend that coin on trifles—ribbons and braid and the like—or on oatcakes and meat. The fact that she'd promptly dumped every last farthing in the hands of a traveling pardoner meant nothing to him. Colin had no care for coins, for wealth, certainly not for comfort—the ugly blue lump on his forehead and the cut across his chin from last night's fight proved that. But those coins meant pardon for the sinfulness of her straying thoughts. Better to have forgiveness for her soul than more meat in her belly.

"It wasn't all for me." Maura eyed Arnaud in rueful challenge. "With the way you all drank and sang and sinned in that town last night, you should be grateful that prayers are being said for your souls."

"*Oui,* such a generous pardoner, such a strong man, such authority!"

"Enough, Arnaud." Colin grunted as the donkey finally pulled a hoof out of the mud. "Leave her be."

"Are you defending her?"

Colin shrugged and then winced at the motion. Aye, he should wince, she thought. That cow-herder had thrown Colin over his shoulder as if the minstrel were nothing but a newborn calf. Still, Colin had fought with a ferocity that had shocked her. His teasing had laughter turned bitter when he stood across a village square eyeing a competitor. And he took each hammering blow of his opponent's fists with a bark of amusement, as if he welcomed the hand that would make mincemeat of his face.

She'd never seen a man welcome pain.

"Since it was my mistake, I'll give those coins back to you." Colin staggered away from the donkey, shook his arm, and caught the purse that fell from his sleeve. He launched it toward Arnaud. "Go ahead, divide it among the troupe."

Arnaud snatched the pouch from the air. "This is your wrestling money."

"That it is."

"You're missing the point," Arnaud insisted. "The Abbess shouldn't have given her own earnings away. She must follow the rules, or she can't be in the troupe at all. Wait." Arnaud eyeballed the pouch more closely. "This is the pouch you gave *her*."

"That it is."

Arnaud raised a brow. "You stole this back from the pardoner."

"The Abbess's pardoner has a weakness for gambling." Colin touched the lump on his forehead. "A weakness Maguire was happy to exploit."

Maura shuffled to a stop. Surely a pardoner wouldn't hang about a tavern, talking to the likes of the Mudman. Surely a pardoner wouldn't take the gift she'd given and gamble it away on a fight.

Her thoughts tripped over one another. The pardoner knew all the prayers in Latin. He had a pouch full of parchments with waxed seals, and a relic from St. Michael in a silk bag. How could it be that a man would proclaim himself a servant of God and then take that coin for his own sinful purposes?

"Hah!" Arnaud slapped the Mudman on the back. "That's my man, Maguire, taking back what's rightfully ours."

She turned away from the minstrels and strode headlong up the road, far ahead of the plodding donkey, trying to outrun her thoughts. The sisters had always warned her that the world was a sinful, dangerous place, but it kept revealing itself stranger and more treacherous than she'd ever imagined.

One thing was becoming glaringly clear. In the convent, she'd been raised a fool.

Colin slipped up behind her like a thief. She fixed her gaze on the mud sinking beneath her feet.

"Maura—"

"Don't." She couldn't bear to hear apologies, soft explanations, *pity*.

"All's well that ends well," he said. "You're still in the troupe."

"They're all going straight to Hell."

"Most likely."

He sounded so unconcerned. For her, the immortal state of her soul had been the center of her upbringing. Yet it bothered her how foolish she sounded for trusting everything she'd been taught.

"That troupe of yours," she sputtered, "is the very embodiment of the seven deadly sins."

"Are there only seven?"

"Matilda Makejoy looks in every craftsman's shop with eyes of the deepest green. She is envy."

"Envy?" Colin cocked his head. "By the way you blush each time you look at her belly, I would have thought you'd assign her a different sin."

"That boar you call your leader, he's gluttony if I ever saw it." The words rose up, pressing against her throat. "And that drunken harpist of yours makes double the sin."

"If enjoying meat and drink is sinful, Maura, I'll never be saved."

"Maguire is avarice," she continued, "and don't you tell me he lost that ear by accident, I know a poacher's mark when I see it."

"Clearly, there's no telling you much."

"The twins are vanity in the flesh. And that piper is sloth. I've seen cats that sleep less than he."

"In better beds, no doubt."

"And you," she said, reckless, "you are lust."

One dark brow arched and that smile slipped across his face. "Lady, you do me wrong."

"So were you searching for Heaven's Gate under that woman's skirts yesterday?"

He shrugged. "The two can often be mistaken."

"Only by a man who thinks with his beef."

She twisted away. Tears prickled at the back of her eyes. Why couldn't she control her own tongue? She hardly knew what she was saying, but she knew she sounded like a judgmental fool. She strode away from Colin, away from her shame, baffled at the strange ways of the world, furious at the sisters for raising her with blinders like a skittish horse.

"It's a blessing we took you on, Maura," he shouted. "We're missing one of the deadly sins."

"Anger," she conceded. Her breath felt hot as she blew it out. "I have good reason to be angry."

"Not anger," he corrected. "Pride."

After his accusation, Colin watched the anger leech out of her like ale out of a burst bladder. She refused to talk so he gave up trying. She didn't look at him for the rest of the journey, even as they camped, even as she chopped the wild onions and roadside herbs that she'd ripped from the verges of the road, brewing up a thin but flavorful soup as she brooded.

He felt as guilty as if he'd kicked her chattering little pet.

"Dinner's done." She knocked the spoon on the edge of the pot. "It's hot, so mind your tongues."

The minstrels made their way to the fire, dug their spoons out, and fell upon the stew. She marched over to where she'd deposited her pack and Nutmeg's traveling basket, a bit away from the campsite, under the shelter of a tree.

He watched as she made a fuss brushing the mud off the hem of her skirts. The bright yellow ribbon that hemmed her kirtle had already faded under the rain and dirt. Her sleeves sagged, showing off the gleam of her pale shoulders.

Damn it all to Hell.

"And what do you want?" she asked, without venom, before he had even reached her side.

She was sitting with her knees up, stroking the white belly of her pet, who sprawled across her lap.

"We've been invited to the castle of the O'Dunns," he said, pausing a few feet away. "These are Irishmen, Irish lords, not English, and we have to come up with a way to entertain them."

"Irish lords, English guildsmen," she muttered. "Matilda says they all piss in the same sort of pot."

He raised his brows. He'd seen her walking beside Matilda's donkey today, but he hadn't realized they'd been talking.

When he'd accused her of pride, he'd plunged the arrow deep.

"They do," he conceded, "but an Irish chieftain expects a higher level of play-acting, and Arnaud has promised them a fine young songstress."

"I heard as much when Arnaud came upon the O'Dunn's man on the road." She scratched the squirrel under the little tuft of his ear while the squirrel's black eyes fluttered closed. "I suppose you won't let me sing *Angelus ad virginem.*"

"Arnaud would prefer some song of love to please the ladies."

She took a deep breath, those white shoulders rising and falling in a way that pulled on him, and not solely in his braies. Innocence, he thought grimly. He'd forgotten what it looked like. He'd forgotten, too, what it was like to be that young, constantly surprised by the strange ways of the world.

"Will you teach me a song, Colin?"

She tilted her face. Her cheeks and forehead were beaded with steam and flushed from the heat of the cooking fire. Her lower lip trembled. He wanted to touch that lip, prove to her that the world could be a sweet place. He wanted to feel that lip give under his own mouth when sharp words weren't rolling past it.

Damn, he had an itch for her.

"Walk with me," he said, gesturing toward the deeper woods. "I'll teach you a song but we'd best do it away from the mockery of these minstrels."

Rising, she deposited the sleepy ball of fur back into the woven basket she'd hung on a branch, and then fell into step beside him.

"I suppose 'Holy Trinity Save Me' wouldn't be considered a love song?" she asked, as they wove through the trees.

"It's not hymns that we're singing, lass."

"If it were, I'd prefer 'Sin Threatens Our Ruin.'"

"Aye, I could see how you would." He cast her a smile as he remembered their earlier conversation. "My favorite hymn is 'My Body Is My Soul's Foe.'"

He caught her surprised look.

"Well, then, if it were hymns we were choosing," she added in a small voice, "I think I'd best learn 'Answer Not Insult.'"

He heard the oblique apology in her words, but she did not meet his gaze. They walked in silence for a few minutes, long enough for him to notice the flecks of dirt that speckled her skin, making her look freckled and mussed and earthily appealing.

"Teach me what love song you will," she finally said, in a rushed little voice, "but please *not* the 'As I

Roved Out Into The World' song I heard Maguire singing yesterday. There were endless rounds of that, and I believe my ears are still blistered."

"We can find you something better than that." He pulled his attention away from the way her hips filled out her kirtle. He riffled through his memory, going back to his student days at the school for bards at Emain Macha, the royal seat of Ulster, when he spent hours sitting around the peat fire listening to a wizened bard chant old poems.

He asked, "Do you know the story of Deirdre and the three sons of Usnach?"

"Aye. Sister Agnes used to tell us that one, and stories of the Fenian warriors, too."

"I know a song about Deirdre's farewell to Naoise, when he insists on returning to Ireland—"

"—despite Deirdre's dream that he will be betrayed as soon as he steps foot on his homeland."

He paused. "You know the song."

"Only the story. I had an education of sorts, living amid the nuns. Though it hasn't served me well outside those walls."

She filled her lungs with air, and he watched the rise and fall of her full bosom, the nipples well delineated against the wool kirtle.

His cock took notice, too.

"Teach me that song," she said, "before I have second thoughts."

Colin paused by a thick oak and ran through the song in his head as he traced his hand over the furrowed bark. "Matilda's voice is better than mine, but I suppose I can muddle my way through it."

He began. "*Farewell, dearest love, the tide doth rise…*"

He spoke-sang the words, transported back to

the springtime woods of his student days, composing verse to be chanted to the strum of a harp. He remembered the feel of the strings beneath his fingers, the coaxing of the music from his mind, the thrill of simple composition.

"'A hundred thousand times farewell, yet stay awhile...'"

Those days felt like a hundred thousand years ago. It must be the woods that brought back such memories. In a vague way he remembered this place, the roll of the land and the slant of the starlight through the trees. He could have passed through these woods ten years ago and not remarked upon it. They were not far from Connemara now, not so far from the salt spray of Galway Bay.

He imagined he could smell brine on the wind as he sang the last verse, *'No—I shall cry no more. No, I shall cry no more.'*

Maura stood in silence for a few moments after he was done. "Is that the whole song then?"

"Aye."

"It's a simple love song. If I'd sung something like that yesterday instead of you and I playing that farce in front of the church, I can't imagine I would have gathered half such a bag full of farthings."

"You were good in front of the church yesterday, but this will bring in coin from the ladies instead." He stepped away from the oak and approached. "You need to memorize the words, Abbess."

Once again he spoke the words, line by line, making her repeat them until she could recite them alone. He watched her lips as she mimicked the melody. The hollow of her throat quivered. Her voice had a strange quality to it, stranger all the more for how she could turn it, in her fury, to a screech harsh enough to shave a man's beard.

"Do you think you know it now?" he asked, when she'd repeated the words twice.

"It's simple enough."

"Then I'll hear it again, with feeling, lass."

She launched into the song just as the moon peeped out behind a cloud. Her voice was ephemeral—weightless, yet as powerful and invasive as sunlight through water. He'd heard many a voice in all his years of traveling. A fine Italian songstress he'd known had once brought the whole court of Toulouse to tears. Maura's voice had such a quality to it—an undefinable thing, elusive and infinitely engaging. This was no ball-and-cup trick—she had real magic in her throat. But now he noticed that her voice carried only a shadow of that magic.

In the silence after her rendition, he clucked his tongue in disapproval. "Where's my songbird of *Angelus ad virginem?* You won't be pleasing the O'Dunns using your little girl voice."

She hiked her hands onto those magnificent hips. "Are you complaining, Colin?"

"You have an Irish harp of a voice, Maura, but just now you plucked it like an untrained boy."

"That gravel you call a voice is better?"

"I never claimed to be a singer. But I know what you are capable of."

"'*Angelus*' is a song worthy of the effort."

"And this isn't?"

"It's just a simple love song."

"Love, my lass, is never simple."

"No doubt you've taught many a poor woman that lesson."

A shadow crossed her face and she took a step

away from him, but it felt like she'd stepped back a hundred leagues. Indeed, he couldn't deny it. He'd had his fill of women, too many faces in too many places. For the past ten years he'd drowned his sorrows in what pleasure there could be had. Strange that standing before this innocent, he couldn't remember the look of a single one of them.

Then he remembered that, raised as cloistered as she was, Maura had likely never had a kiss.

"You know nothing of love." He heard her breath catch. "Don't deny it."

"What difference does that make?"

"When you sing '*Angelus*,' you're singing about a devotion you understand."

"I must know love to sing about it?"

"It helps."

"You've years of wantonness on me, Colin. I may as well stop trying right now——"

"Are you quitting on me, lass?"

Those hazel eyes narrowed, her little nostrils flared, and Colin could tell by the tightening of her jaw that he'd found a weakness.

"I sang your love song," she said. "What more do you expect from me?"

"Passion."

Her sharp intake of breath left her mouth open. He felt the familiar slide of weight into his loins. He rasped his palm over her cheek, across her ear, to rake his fingers deep into her hair. The curls sprung soft against his fingers. He heard a slight tear of her coif as he plunged his fingers too deep. He lowered his head before she could think, speak, or stop him from doing what he'd wanted to do since she'd marched so boldly into the campsite outside of Killeigh.

He pressed his mouth against those soft, soft lips. They pillowed beneath his. She tasted of salt and fresh herbs. He sensed the shock that arced through her, and in its wake, a weakening of spine, a suppleness of body. Fragments of poetry sifted through his mind like so many broken promises.

He nudged her lips apart, wanting to be the bellows to prod this spark of passion into a fire, wanting to feel her shudder against him in the pleasure he knew he could give her. But what he tasted as she made a sound in the base of her throat was something he'd not tasted in so many years so as to forget the flavor. What he tasted, as her fingers worked their way up his chest, was a surprise so sudden, so sweet, so fresh that it weakened his knees.

Innocent passion.

By God's blood, he wanted this one in his bed. He wanted to lay her down on the ground and feel her tremble as he dragged his hands up her thighs. He wanted to burrow his head between her legs and taste her until she arched up in pleasure. He wanted to slip his aching cock deep into her cleft and move inside her until she cried out for more.

He pulled away to see her dazed gaze full of bewildered curiosity, and then the man he once was— the better man, the honorable idiot he'd thought he'd drowned in ale and pleasure—stirred within him.

He stepped away from her.

It took every ounce of his will.

Then he chucked her under the chin, pretending he didn't carry a stick the size of a tree trunk in his braies.

"That's passion, Maura," he said. "Best we leave it at a taste."

CHAPTER SIX

The mead hall was alive with revelry. Serving girls hipped their way through the crowd. Ale splashed from horns raised in toasts. Two fires crackled and spewed up a stinging haze to the smoke-holes gaping amid the thatch on either end of the hall. The air smelled of venison roasted in honey, the bones of which littered the trestle table amid the soft white flesh of boiled wild onions.

Maura stood in the shadows, her back against the wood of a roof-tree, her gaze traveling over the seated Irish warriors with their flowing mustaches and glowing faces. The O'Dunn had ordered the trestle table pushed to one side of the mead hall to leave a space open for the troupe to entertain. Now, the twins wrapped themselves in knots on the rushes, their white thighs jiggling like pork fat as their tunics rode up their legs. Their bodies stretched in ways Maura never thought possible. The room rang with the bawdy comments of the Irishmen while Maura tried to swallow the dry lump growing in her throat.

She was to perform next.

She plucked at a splinter on the post, wishing it was just the usual nerves that had her twitchy. She'd always been a little edgy singing at feast days, standing before all the black robes and crisp white veils and sharp, expectant eyes—but working herself up only made things worse. It was Colin's kiss that tormented her now, as it had since Colin had marched her back to the road to rejoin the troupe last night. The feelings that kiss had unleashed had grown in intensity, and now she stood here, breathing hard, fingering the thinness of her silken kirtle, wishing he hadn't touched her even as she wondered when he'd kiss her again.

"If you pull at your dress anymore," a female voice whispered in her ear, "you'll pull it apart."

Matilda's musky perfume wafted over her, the same scent that clung so faintly to the fibers of the bright yellow tunic Maura was wearing. She turned to find Matilda's dark eyes alive with mischief.

"It'll be easier than you think," Matilda said.

Maura let go of the roof-tree. The pregnant minstrel had taken a particular interest in her tonight, helping her choose this costume. This dusky-haired woman concealed a sharp mind and an even sharper eye. Maura was grateful that—for the moment at least—Matilda had misinterpreted the reason for Maura's anxiety.

"I can't imagine they'll want to listen to a dull convent girl," Maura murmured, "after watching those twins."

"You're here for the ladies," Matilda said. "No mistress of any castle would ever allow us to enter the halls if the only entertainment we offered were shaking breasts and flashing white thighs."

Maura blushed. She'd gotten to know Matilda better during the long walks between towns, but she hadn't yet become accustomed to her frankness.

Matilda mused, "When I first started dancing in front of crowds, I used to pretend they were animals."

"Animals?"

"Look at The O'Dunn." Matilda nodded toward the redheaded chieftain seated in the center of the bench. The metal beads on her costume jingled with the motion. "He's a pig," she said. "Definitely a pig."

Maura sucked in a breath as she noticed a wicked resemblance to a pig in the chieftain's flushed cheeks and upturned nose.

"That woman next to him, his wife." Matilda said, tapping her chin with the drinking horn. "The one who looks like she swallowed cow dung. Yes, that little mouth." Matilda mimicked the woman's pursed lips. "That white cap tight on her head. The little black eyes looking here and there, all about. I'd say she's a weasel."

Maura would laugh if she weren't feeling as tense as Nutmeg when she commanded him to walk a slender rope held taut between her hands.

"The rest," Matilda said, dismissing them with a wave of her beringed fingers, "they're all chipmunks, squirrels, and skittering little vermin—"

"Are you scaring the lass to death, Matilda?"

Colin swaggered over to them, hazel-mead sloshing out of his cup, and instantly Maura became aware of how very low this kirtle was cut across her breasts, how gossamer the bright, shiny fabric. She felt half-naked under his perusal, as devoid of modesty as she always found herself in her dreams.

"I'm giving her a little advice, no more." Matilda tapped him on the chest. "I haven't warned her about you—not yet."

Then Matilda sashayed away, leaving the two of them alone behind the screen.

She searched his gaze now as she'd searched it every time they looked at each other since their kiss, and found in that gaze a guarded, quiet amusement. How could he appear so calm, she thought, when inside, she was a storm of feeling?

"This won't do, Maura," he murmured. "This won't do at all."

Colin reached for the ties of her coif and pulled them free.

"No," she gasped, grabbing for her coif as he swiped it off her head, catching nothing but air.

"Hold still. You're as skittish as a mouse under a hawk's shadow. You have straw in your hair from the stables, it needs to come out."

She flattened against the roof-tree as he thrust his fingers in her hair. His fingers caught on a tangle he worked loose. Her heart kicked up a beat. Around them the servants fretted, delivering ale and mead. Beyond the screen, couples groped in the darkened corners, cups fell to the floor, feet shuffled, the door squealed opened as someone left in search of a privy.

She stood there pressed against the post letting Colin run his fingers through her hair, her voice lost, her mind gone fuzzy. Long, languid strokes. The stroking brought to mind those evenings when the laywoman Sabine would try to comb her hair into submissiveness before the darkness winked away the day. But this wasn't the silent cloister, and this wasn't

Sabine's ivory comb raking its way down Maura's shoulders. Rather than making her sleepy, every stroke of Colin's fingers generated a crackling heat.

He said, "You shouldn't keep this riot of hair so bound up. That wasn't God's intent."

"What…what…do you know of God's intent?"

"Hair like this is meant to tempt a man."

She meant to push him away, she really did, and that's why she flattened her hands on his chest. It had worked before, this kind of push, it had sent many a day-laborer skidding through the turnip peels, or tripping into the washing trough, but slapping Colin's chest was like banging a rock wall, and suddenly she found herself leaning into him and flexing her palm to better feel the throbbing of his heart.

Then thick fingers curled around her arm, and they weren't Colin's.

"Bed her after," Arnaud said, his brow gleaming with sweat. "Right now she must earn her keep."

Maura found herself tugged into a golden circle of firelight, into the haze and noise, the twins passing her as they scampered off with a flash of blue silk. Padraig Smallpipe scuttled away from the trestle table to give way to Fingar, coming to the center with his harp in hand. Arnaud left her standing there alone in the light with the trestle table before her, with the men and women of the clan laughing and drinking mead from their horns. A man gestured toward her and said something she couldn't hear amid the noise.

Little by little, the talk faded. Pair by pair, all those eyes fixed upon her. She glanced in panic at Fingar. The harpist lifted his blind eyes to the light pouring through the smoke-hole. A smile shimmered across his face as he stroked the first strings. Maura breathed in, let her eyes flutter close. She opened her mouth. The music of the harp strings shimmered in the air. Fingar stood, poised, waiting for her to begin.

A log snapped in one of the hearth fires. A cup dropped, clattered on the floor and then skidded across the reeds. Clothing rustled. Fingar strummed the opening to the song anew and the harp's strings vibrated to stillness again. Maura heard Arnaud wheeze somewhere in the darkness behind her.

She blinked her eyes open. The O'Dunn turned into a boar before her eyes, all tusks and drool. The weasel grew teeth and all but slithered across the table. The rats pressed in upon her. Arnaud's gaze pierced the bones of her spine. She'd felt the lash of Arnaud's tongue enough to know this was her last chance to redeem herself, to stay on with the troupe.

Maura flattened her palms on her thighs, felt the silk slip smooth beneath her hands, then turned back to the darkness, seeking out something, not knowing what it was until she laid eyes upon Colin. There he was, leaning by the roof-tree, wiping mead off his chin, that maddening half-smile upon his face. There he stood, one shoulder abutting the pole, one ankle crossed. He swiped another horn of mead off a tray and raised it toward her in a toast, then pressed his other hand over his heart.

You know nothing of love.

She narrowed her eyes, thinking of the feel of his lips upon her mouth, thinking of the dream she'd had last night, the one where she'd let him slip his rough, scar-nicked hand between her open thighs.

And then she turned back to O'Dunn-pig and his wife-weasel. The music swelled in her throat until she could no longer hold it back. She dropped her head back to open her throat and sang the song until it vibrated in the smoke-filled rafters.

Colin lagged behind the troupe on the road to Tuam, watching the way the sunlight reflected off a certain linen coif. Since Maura's triumph at the O'Dunns'—a triumph that had filled their pockets with groats—his little innocent had become the minstrel's pet. Maguire Mudman kept offering ale. Padraig piped away, making up words to a song about a lovely young songstress. The twins, twittering like larks in their guttural tongue, wove a garland of wildflowers to drape around her neck. Even Arnaud had stopped muttering and complaining.

He watched this from a distance and told himself that he was content. His innocent little songstress had learned her lessons well. She was a minstrel now, and Arnaud and the others would take care of her long after Colin was captured and hanged.

So when they passed a certain huge oak stump by the side of the road, Colin hung back. This stump was all that was left of the tree that had been struck by lightning years ago. Beyond it, there lay a shallow stream that led to a pond that he knew too well.

When the troupe rounded a bend, he stepped into the woods. He strode through the familiar hills until he reached the pond between two hillocks. There he paused, listening to the calls of morning birds and the breath of a breeze while in his head came the roar and clash of memories.

Greenery now feathered the branches, screening the scars of lances and swords that had once slashed these trunks. Saplings sprang from the dark earth where blood had once pooled. Wandering around the banks, he wondered how long after the battle it took for the blood to dry. He wondered where his men were buried. He stopped now and again, wincing as some combination of light and shadow, some knotted limb or tangle of branches loosed a dark memory.

He'd done a fine job trying to forget. The castles of Gascony, the hamlets of Normandy, the narrow winding streets of Paris, the well-beaten roads of England—good places for a man to lose himself, as good as a bladder of ale, a horn of wine, dancing and music and laughter, or the soft white arms of a willing woman. He'd thought he'd found what he'd been looking for: That life was happiest when it consisted of intervals of joy, strung one after another, like a rope of luminescent pearls wound in a woman's hair.

Now he crouched at the edge of the pond, splashed water over his face and slicked his fingers through his hair. A man's path was blazed by so many decisions, one after another. The last time he'd gazed into this pond, he'd been a youth with a bloody sword. Now what lay before him, reflected in the surface, was a mangled distortion of his own father's face. Same dark hair, same eyes. Yet so different in temperament, it was as if they were not kin at all.

Ten years of exile. Had he become man enough to fulfill the vow he'd made to his dead father?

He jolted up. The toe of his boot disturbed the water, shattering his reflection. This was nothing but a pond. The sound of sword-stroke had long faded, the last drop of blood had long sunk into the earth.

I can still turn away.

He girded his belt and turned his back to the pond, thinking how easy it was to believe his own lies.

CHAPTER SEVEN

Colin lifted a square of blue silk and waved it at the crowd around him. Men and women spilled out the back door of the alehouse to watch. A baker, his black hair flecked with flour. A butcher, his leather apron marked by blood. A candlestick maker, his hands swollen by bee stings. Clean-shaven faces, close-cropped hair. No multicolored cloaks here. No flowing mustaches, no braided *culans* hanging over the men's shoulders. Beyond the flax of the alehouse thatch, he glimpsed the stone cylinder of the castle—the forbidding spike the English had planted in Irish ground to claim it as their own.

When he was last here, Tuam had been only a summer ring fort, a small mound of earth used by the O'Manns for hunting in the nearby woods. Now it was full of Englishmen—Englishmen and at least one treacherous Irishman by the name of O'Kelly who'd passed the troupe on the road, riding proud on his palfrey, heading straight to that English castle.

Tonight, Colin thought grimly, he would remind O'Kelly of his treachery.

And so it all would begin.

Colin snapped the scarf by a corner, then balled his hand and tucked the end in the tunnel formed by his fist. His gaze gravitated to a woman whose eyes began to glitter with knowing amusement.

"Good day to you, my lady." He mimicked a courtly bow. "Would you be so kind as to assist me?"

She agreed with a lazy smile. He shoved the scarf into his fisted grip and asked her to poke it in tighter. She did, with a sturdy finger, taking her time with the ins and outs of the task, while bawdy comments flew around them.

"Faith," he said, addressing the crowd, "I'm usually the one doing the poking."

The words fell from his lips by rote, though he knew by the laughter that the joke had worked easily. He'd made the same joke a thousand times before, in French, English, and Langue d'Oc. He'd performed the same tricks and rolled with the same sort of woman in patches of spring clover all across Europe.

He leaned into the woman as she finished. "Did that satisfy you as much as it did me?"

She pursed her lips, still deciding. He raised his clenched hand and muttered a few words of Latin—*veni vidi vici*—then held his fist out to the wench again.

"Time to yank it out, my lady."

The woman pinched the tip of the scarf between her thumb and forefinger and then tugged at it with languorous slowness. He released a grunt of relief as the knotted end popped out.

"Lady," he muttered, "don't stop now."

She continued to pull, and out of his fist came another scarf, knotted to the first, a gossamer thing the shade of peaches in summer. The crowd gasped, and even the lady stopped seducing him with her eyes to raise a brow as a succession of bright silk scarfs slipped out of his fist. Colin let his grin widen and made comments about the length of it, all the while wondering in the back of his mind why the sight of such a pretty, willing woman left his cock limp.

When the last scarf fell out of his fist, the crowd applauded and Maguire, on cue, popped into Colin's place. The little man gathered farthings into his hat even as he started a tale about an itinerant priest and the peddler's daughter. Colin backed out of the clearing, avoiding the woman's seeking eye, and ducked into the alehouse. He came out of the other side into the brightness of day.

One sweep of the streets and he glimpsed the unexpected—a white coif, pure and clean. Maura, standing in the shade of the blacksmith's shop.

Colin's gut tightened. Maura should be safe at the camp, not wandering around this English town alone. She wore her kitchen-servant garments, not the bells and rouge and silks of a minstrel's trade. As he watched, three burly apprentices pressed close around her. He shot across the cobbles and without a pardon muscled himself between the men.

"There you are, Abbess." Colin draped an arm across her shoulders as he eyed the apprentices. "Angling to get me in a fight with a blacksmith?"

She blinked up at him in surprise. By God's Nails, the wench didn't even know that three men were closing in around her, three Englishmen who wouldn't give a moment's thought for her welfare. If he hadn't shown up, she could have ended up on her back on the smithy's floor, servicing the lot of them.

"This good apprentice," she began, trying to wiggle the weight of his arm off her shoulders, "has been kind enough to explain how metal is molded."

"That's not all he'll mold, if he gets a chance."

She tilted her head and gave him a scolding eye.

"My lady," one of the apprentices said, as he shifted a bellows off his shoulder to set its point in the dirt. "Is this your husband?"

"No…no," she said, "He's just—"

"Then be off, minstrel." The apprentice eyed Colin's cape and the jagged hem of his tunic. "She won't be meddling with the likes of you."

Colin's nostrils flared. The apprentice was young and burly, with swelling, work-reddened forearms. As a rule, Colin avoided tangling with blacksmiths wherever he traveled. They were strong enough to pull teeth out of a man's jaw. But after seeing the traitor O'Kelly riding the roads so freely this morning, Colin was in the mood to flex his muscles. He felt a familiar rush to his head, a warmth of anticipation in his blood, as he curled his hands into fists.

Maura seized his arm but he shrugged it off.

The smith lunged first, tossing the bellows aside before barreling into him. Air whooshed from his lungs. He and the blacksmith, locked in a hold, plunged onto the road, bumping into passersby until they tripped to the ground. Pebbles needled Colin's back as they skidded to a stop against the alehouse wall. Then Colin seized the blacksmith by the scruff of his leather jerkin and tossed him off, leaping up just as the apprentice rolled to his feet. The blacksmith charged again, but another man emerged from the shadow of the shop and darted between them, holding out one meaty hand to stop the apprentice from attacking.

"Do your fighting on your own time, William.

You're mine until vespers." The sweaty-faced master blacksmith fixed his glare on Colin, assessing him up and down. "A piece of sterling says my William will beat the guts out of this one."

Then Maguire Mudman twisted out of the crowd like a whirlwind. "Is it going to be a fight, then?" With a toothless grin, he flipped a silver coin in the air. "A piece of silver, then, for the minstrel."

"A ha'penny on the magician!"

"A groat on the blacksmith—"

"Double that for me—"

Maguire pulled out his wax tablet and began scratching wagers. Colin took measure of the blacksmith as he wiped the blood from the corner of his lip. Aye, the apprentice was strong and quick, and the blow to the belly had been a surprise, but Colin had several inches and a good five stone on him. Staring at this puffed-up young man, Colin didn't give a damn about the bids. No matter how the wagers fell, he intended to beat the stuffing out of this boy.

Then there she was, standing before him, anger radiating from her like heat from a kiln stone.

"What are you thinking," she whispered, "haggling over me like some market day harlot?"

"What are *you* thinking," he retorted, "wandering around this town alone?"

Her gaze faltered, but only for a moment. "I'm in a public place, amid a crowd—and not far from where you and Maguire were working." She crossed her arms. "I've been traveling on these roads long enough to be aware of some of the dangers, Colin."

He grunted. She shouldn't wear that coif, Colin thought. Hair like that shouldn't be hidden under a bit of linen. "You're dressed well for your wanderings."

"Don't change the subject."

"Where's Nutmeg? Your bells, your silks?"

"I don't always play the minstrel."

"I like you better as the minstrel."

"Whether I'm minstrel or maiden, you keep your distance, I've noticed."

She regretted the words the moment she said them, he could tell by the way her skin bloomed pink. He knew what she was talking about. He'd made a point of not being caught alone with her lest he be tempted into teaching her more lessons about love. She was too innocent to understand that he was staying away from her for her own damn good.

So he jerked his chin toward the apprentice, now swaggering back to his anvil. "Your blacksmith won't keep his distance, I'll wager you that."

"Don't be talking nonsense." She fingered the ring upon her hand. "William was telling me how such a ring could be made."

"William, is it?"

"It's a fine Christian name."

"I'm sure he yearns to hear you whisper it." He frowned. "What's this about your ring?"

"Never mind about that."

She turned with a flip of her tunic and marched into the shadow of an alleyway, escaping so fast that Colin knew he'd touched a nerve. He brushed the dust off him, saw that Maguire was busy taking bets, and then eyed the apprentice who had taken a stance near the front of his shop to pound a crescent of reddened metal with an iron mallet. With a challenging grin, Colin made sure the boy saw him set off after those twitching hips.

He caught up with her just as she stepped out of

the alleyway into the open space that spread before the city gate. He grasped her by the waist, ignored her cry of surprise, and pulled her into the shade under the thatch overhang of one of the shops.

A rider galloped past, harness and bells jangling.

"Watch yourself, Abbess." Her hair smelled warm. "You'll be crushed under hooves."

"I'm in more danger now, I think."

"You have to take care." He felt his throat tighten. "The troupe needs you now."

"Stop with your flattery. The troupe doesn't need me, and I'm only here until St. Patrick's Purgatory. Which," she said, pushing out of his grip, "I've recently been told is *north*, while all this time we've been walking *west*."

"I warned you back in Killeigh that a minstrel troupe follows the fairs." He seized her hand before she could slip away. "Now tell me what's special about this ring that you risk flirting with blacksmiths."

Her lips went tight and she tried to tug her hand free. He ignored her efforts and eyed the ring. Its face was scratched and worn, but the metal was heavy and untarnished, a sign of true gold.

He said, "This is no tinker's work."

"Of course it isn't."

"I know you didn't steal it. Was it a gift?"

"This is mine. It has always been mine." Her mouth moved but she seemed to be having some trouble forming words. "I found out, not long before I left the convent, that this ring had been discovered in my swaddling clothes."

He met those guarded eyes and remembered how she'd told him she was a foundling. A woman without a family. A woman without obligations, without the weight of unfulfilled promises.

Envy pierced him to the bone.

"You go to strangers to ask questions about a ring," he said, tightening his grip on her hand, "but you didn't think of asking me."

"What would you know about such a thing? You and Padraig are the only true Irish in the troupe, and you're all wanderers to a man. I need to see some similar insignia. I need to speak to villagers, local people on the road to the shrine. Or," she added with a lift of a brow, "a blacksmith who might know something of the forging."

"That blacksmith of yours knows ironwork, not the working of silver and gold."

"He knows more than I know."

"This troupe has been to France, Gascony, England. We know more than you can imagine."

She went mute, her jaw tight as she stood with her back against the wall. He eyed the crest upon the ring, worn to flatness, nothing visible but a scratch of even lines that looked something like the rays of the sun. The pattern looked familiar. He struggled to remember where he might have seen such a thing…but it became difficult to focus on the ring. The scent of heather seeped out between the wattles of the candle maker's hut and clouded around them. It roused memories of fresh grass and how it smelled crushed under a woman's back. His thoughts wandered to the softness of Maura's breasts, his gaze to the poke of her nipples under her tunic. He found himself thinking of things better meant for a man with a sturdy, profitable trade and a secure future.

"Well?" She leaned toward him. "Do you know something about it, or are you just using this as an excuse to play finger games with my hand?"

Such stormy hazel eyes, such sun-struck curls poking out from beneath that white coif. A whiskey-brown fleck of a beauty mark lay just above the arch of her left brow. Her skin looked so soft it seemed that a breeze would bruise it.

He didn't think the world could hold such innocence.

"What do you want to know about this ring, Maura?"

Her lashes swooped down to cast shadows on her cheeks. "You'll make me say it," she said, "and then you'll mock my foolishness."

"I will not."

A breeze siphoned in from over the walls of the city and whirled in the cleared space, raucous with peddlers' cries, soldiers' demands, the clatter of wheels over pebbles, the laughter of children. She pulled her lower lip between her teeth.

"Let me guess then," he said. "You joined us hoping to find the owner of this ring."

"No, I didn't have hopes as high as that."

"But you'd hoped to learn something."

She shrugged. "It was a better plan than sitting in a convent, forever wondering from whence it came."

"So this pilgrimage to St. Patrick's Purgatory is nothing but a story."

"Not exactly." She kept taking the pink flesh of her lower lip between her little white teeth. "Around the time I was found on the convent steps, a large group of pilgrims came through Killeigh, stopping for a while to rest in the fields. They were on their way back from St. Patrick's Purgatory."

"You assume your mother was among them."

She shrank into herself a bit, the hollows of her shoulders deepening.

"So you decided to walk the same pilgrim's road." He rubbed a thumb across her knuckles. "To search for the insignia. On a silversmith's shop, or hanging from the post of an inn. To ask questions of strangers in the hopes they'd remember a detail from over twenty years ago."

She tilted her chin, but her voice came out small. "I didn't realize that the world would be so…big."

Colin thought of the roads of Gascony, the vineyards of Bordeaux, the woods outside Paris, the cobbled lanes of London, the bustle of Dublin and Wexford, and swallowed the laugh that rose in his throat because ignorance was not a sin, and should never be mocked.

"I wouldn't take the veil," she said suddenly. "So the lady Abbess kept insisting I should marry the butcher's boy. He'd been courting me at the kitchen door for months, with no encouragement by me."

Colin felt a kick of jealousy at the thought of some dirty grunt ogling Maura in a back courtyard.

"Oh, he's a fine enough man," she continued, "and he has a good trade, but I was given this ring, you see. Once this had been given to me, how could I just go on with my life, pretending the ring didn't mean anything?" She sought answers in his face. "How could I *not* set out to find the truth?"

He let go of her hand and found himself cradling her face in his hands so that she couldn't look away from him anymore.

Soft, confused hazel eyes.

"The world is big, but it's not so strange, Maura." He eased her deeper under the thatch overhang.

"Babes are left on convent steps more often than you think. That's the desperation of unwed mothers bearing their lover's children, or families who cannot feed another mouth. Only in stories do you hear of midwives spiriting away children born of noble patrons, tucking a token in their swaddling clothes."

She flinched. "I don't fancy myself noble blood."

"I would."

Such soft skin. Her brows arched like wings. Freckles like tiny constellations on the swell of her cheekbone. Hazel eyes bright with questions. A face like a carved stone angel, except living, pliable, warm.

She whispered, "You think I'm a fool."

"No." Her lashes glinted amber. "I think you're the last bit of innocence on the face of the earth."

"Ignorance, you mean."

"No. It was courage that sent you out of that convent." He ran a thumb across the tear that fell from her eye. "But happy endings are rare, Maura. As much as I would give one to you, if I could." He pressed a thumb on the indentation in the middle of her lower lip. "Abandoned babes never find their true parents, and minstrels never turn out to be kings."

Dismay, desperation, and shame rippled across her features. Guilt needled him. He hadn't wanted to hurt her. He wanted to tell her it could be a great gift to be unburdened of family expectations, never to carry the encumbrance of some long-set destiny. He wished he could teach her to embrace her freedom, and give herself over to what life was meant for.

Capturing moments of joy.

His gaze fell to her lips and a feeling he couldn't identify rushed through him, so strong and fierce that he wanted to kiss her with the same intensity that he craved a bite of the first red apple in September.

Instead he closed his eyes and pressed his forehead against hers, feeling the heat of her skin, the slight hiss as she drew in a long, deep breath. He wondered what the hell he was doing, rolling his thumb down the curve of her breast, only to lift his hand and bury it in the curls lying against her neck?

It was all muddled in his mind. Everything had been muddled since he'd visited the site by that pond where his father had died, since he'd seen that damn traitor O'Kelly riding high on his horse. It was this English town, this Irish countryside, the knowledge that he was hurtling toward an inevitability he'd avoided for ten long years just when he had a reason to slow it down, to stop it—if just for a moment.

If just for this moment.

A passerby bumped him from behind. Colin tore his face away, long enough to see that her hazel eyes, usually so sharp, were now as mellow as honey mead.

He thought, *one kiss.*

One simple kiss.

Her lips quivered under his mouth. Sweet and eager, guileless and innocent, she was like a flower raising its face toward the sun. He tilted her chin with one finger so he could slant his mouth against hers— kiss her more deeply—and then, moments later, he gripped that chin to pull her away before he, too, became lost in this dizzy rush of desire.

He had to leave her.

Inches from his face, she whispered, "Colin."

His heart thumped at the sound.

As he turned on his heel, he wondered if anyone in the whole of his life had ever said his name with such sweetness.

CHAPTER EIGHT

In the English castle that evening, Arnaud—gleeful that the troupe had been invited to perform for such noble company—pulled her aside to tell her that the baron had demanded to hear 'the foundling songstress.'

"Your fame has grown," Arnaud told her, with avarice in his eye. "Sing well."

So Maura took her place when her time came. English and Irish nobility sat hip to hip on the other side of the trestle table, the air taut with expectation. She wasn't nervous, not about performing. She was too preoccupied thinking about that singular moment in the heather-scented shade of the candle maker's shop, when Colin had touched her face, murmured sweet things against her hair, and—once again—left her alone and aching.

Now, in the dim firelight, by the strumming of Fingar's harp, Maura let the music flow through her. She didn't want to repeat the song she sang at the O'Dunns'. So she sang an old Irish song that Fingar had taught her that very afternoon, when Colin had abandoned her under the overhang amid peddlers and washerwomen and visitors through the gates.

My love is like the sun
That in the firmament does run,
and always is constant and true,
But his is like the moon,
That wanders up and down,
and every month it is new.

She wanted to believe that Colin was just keeping to his promise to steer clear of the women in his own troupe. But a small voice inside her wondered if it were something more. Maybe she repelled him. Maybe he sensed that scent she emanated, some phantom odor that put people off.

She knew too well how it felt not to be wanted.

The sound of applause brought her senses back to the great hall. She curtsied and melted back into the shadowy chaos of the dark side of the room, where the troupe members jostled awaiting their turn. She headed toward the servant's door intending to go into the courtyard and check on Nutmeg, to make sure the cats that swarmed the keep hadn't found a way to knock her pet's basket from where she'd hung it on a peg in the stables.

Then Colin burst through that door.

She didn't know he was Colin, not at first. He was masked. He brushed by her unseeing, his cloak flapping against her as he passed. Only when she caught the scent of cinnamon and cardamom in his wake did her heart do a little skip-beat of recognition. He wore clothes she'd never seen before. Beneath his plaid cloak, run through with many colors, lay a knee-length saffron-colored tunic, edged with embroidery at the neck and hem.

She took a swift, shocked breath. She had seen such clothing before. The O'Mores of Leix, who held their Irish stronghold not far south of the convent of Killoughy, had a man among them—a *filidh,* a court poet who kept the clan's history, and wrote great epics about their battles, their leaders, and sang them at festive occasions to the strumming of a harp. She'd seen that *filidh* once, traveling on a fine horse toward the monastery up the road. He and his like were allowed to wear a traditional robe of six colors, only one color less than the robes of Irish kings.

She covered her mouth, wondering what Colin was thinking. Clothing separated noble from common laborer, and there were enough Irish chieftains amidst this crowd to know the difference. At least he wore a mask, and not just to hide the bruises blooming from the afternoon's fight with the blacksmith's apprentice.

"Listen, my lords," Colin said, as his voice sent sleeping birds fluttering amid the donjon rafters, "to a tale I will tell, of a king of wretched fate, and the kind of man we all know too well."

The room went still as the restless birds took perches among the rafters. Golden light brushed the forearms of men who had leaned forward to get a better look at Colin, as if they, too, were surprised to come upon an Irish bard.

Colin paced around the fire as he started the tale. His voice rose and fell as he wove the story to life. No one called for ale. The bones of the meat lay untouched upon the table. Through the stillness of her shock, Maura leaned forward to hear him better.

A cold chill scurried up her spine and birthed gooseflesh all over her body. The nuns had warned her that the minstrels dabbled in a sort of sorcery. No Italian player could play the part of a *filidh* better than Colin was playing him, right now.

But this couldn't possibly be. For a *filidh* must study for twelve years in one of the bardic schools—a place reserved for the younger sons of only the most noble of Irish families. A *filidh* must spend hours— weeks—composing in the darkness of a sod hut, and memorizing the compositions of others.

Colin spoke of battles and bravery, of defiance and determination. He spoke of a time when the Irish tribes fought constantly. The guests didn't seem to care that he told an Irish tale to a crowd more English than Irish. She was as caught up as they in the passions of Fergus MacEgan, the brash warrior, battling to keep something that had always been his.

Fingar's harp strummed in rhythm with the story. As Colin spoke of hordes of men galloping across the fields, their shields gleaming in the sun, Fingar worked the pads of his fingertips over the high strings. It was as if everyone in the room could hear the distant drumming of hooves over the hill. *They are coming nearer,* Colin would say, and the plucking would become more distinct, the hoof beats louder—then— *they are here!* The music became harsher, harder as Fingar plucked the strings between fingertip and curved fingernail—Clash! Clash! Like the strike of sword against shield, like the clatter of armor and the crack of hoof, and then, suddenly, all was silence.

"Then it was over," Colin said, his voice dropping, "and Fergus knew he'd been betrayed."

Something shifted in the room as Colin

continued. Maura heard Arnaud's swift hiss in the dimness behind her. There was a rustling at the trestle table, the sound of a bench scraping through the rushes, the slap of a hand on an arm, hard murmured words. Behind her came the skitter of many feet. The noise annoyed her, for Colin was still telling the tale, and she was angry about how Fergus had been betrayed by a distant kinsmen, a fellow warrior, a man that Fergus had called a friend.

"Come," Arnaud whispered in her ear as he curled his fingers around her arm. "We must leave."

"I'm not leaving." She tugged her arm free. "He's just getting to the best of it."

Caught up in the story, she waited for the inevitable. She felt a tingle of fear when Colin faced the trestle table and breathed a curse vile enough to make the hairs stand up on the nape of her neck.

"Evil death and short life to O'Kelly.
May spears of battle slay O'Kelly.
The rejected of the land and the earth is O'Kelly.
Beneath the mountains and the rocks be O'Kelly."

"Come, woman." Arnaud yanked her into the shadows.

She followed Arnaud out the servant's door, just as she heard the sound of a sword scraping out of a scabbard.

Colin was gone.

Maura and the troupe fled south, where the sparse woodlands ceded to a stretch of rolling, rocky earth. White limestone houses spotted the landscape, their thatch hanging so low as to brush the ground on two sides. Rock-pile fences curled over the soft hills and snaked across the fields, separating patches of earth sprouting as rich as emerald, and others glowing as golden as winter wheat, and all of it gently scoured by a wind smelling more and more of the sea. She searched that landscape daily, hourly, by the minute, hoping to see some glimpse of Colin riding toward them.

Days passed with no word.

Maura trailed after the troupe, blocking out the sound of Maguire's voice as he belted out yet another verse of 'The Bastard King of England,' with Padraig piping the drinking tune lustily behind him, and the twins giggling at the end of each bawdy verse. Maura strode, head-down, angry at their indifference, for they acted now as if they'd never had a certain Irish wrestler among their troupe.

She wondered if she'd ever lay eyes upon Colin again. She wondered, too, why her heart ached so much at the thought.

She winced as something sharp dug into her heel. Flopping down upon a stone fence, she hiked up her foot, thrust her finger into the hole in the heel, and rolled it around until she found the offending stone. Pinching it out, she hurled it skipping across the rocky path. A cow in a nearby field lifted its head and snorted into the misty air. Maura planted her elbows upon her knees and sank her face into her hands.

Maguire's rag-clad legs came into her vision.

"What have we here? A calf lost from its herd, mooning and moping about as if its mother had just been sent to slaughter." Maguire's breath blasted Maura's face. "I've got another riddle for you,

Abbess."

She straightened up to get away from the ale fumes. Maguire had buzzed after her all the way from Tuam. He'd hung around her like a gnat when they'd stopped to play in another stinking alehouse in Athenry, and spent his days filling her ears with the filth of his repertoire.

She had a strange feeling that the little man thought this attention was a kindness, that he was distracting her from worry.

"Another riddle then?" she said. "I'd think I would have heard them all by now."

Maguire barked a laugh, and then thrust his chin in the air like a rooster about to crow.

"Stiff standing on the bed,
First it's white and then it's red.
There's not a lady in the land
That would not take it in her hand."

Maura sighed, stood up, and set her foot back upon the path. "Another heartwarming riddle from the dung heap of your mind."

"Know you the answer, Abbess? Speak!"

"It's stiff on the bed, you say?"

"As hard as iron, Abbess, straight and tall."

"First it's white, and then it's red."

"When well-tended by a fine woman, it does grow and become so."

"Any lady would take it in her hand?"

"Personally," Maguire said, "I prefer it in the lady's mouth."

Maura narrowed her eyes at him. "Cracked between her teeth, I think."

Maguire winced, crossing his knees and mock stumbling.

"And chewed thoroughly, I'd say."

"By God's Nails—"

"Or boiled in a pot with turnips and a bit of meat."

"Cruel wench you."

"So cruel? To treat a *carrot* so?" She kicked a spray of pebbles into the grass. "A carrot stiff in the garden-bed, ripening from white to red when well-tended. Maguire, your japes are becoming as stale as the ale you drink."

The little man frowned, scratching a nit out of his beard. "Your wit has grown these weeks. I have another."

"You have a hole above your knee
and pricked it was and pricked shall be
and yet it is not sore
and yet it shall be pricked more."

She sighed and scraped her knife out of its sheath. "It wouldn't be this sheath you're talking about, would it?"

Maguire smiled and clapped his hands and skittered away. She wanted to scream, *do you care? Do any of you care?* She wished they would all stop their laughter and prancing. Not a word about Colin's fate had come back to them. Arnaud had shrugged and brushed off her questions, telling her never to ask a man a question he doesn't wish to answer, telling her to keep her mind on performing, that's what would put food in their bellies. A fine friend he was for abandoning Colin to a chieftain's blade, she'd told him, or a hangman's noose without a never-you-mind.

She didn't even know if Colin lived or died.

Now they walked hell-bent for Kilcolgan, in the exact opposite direction of St. Patrick's Purgatory, passing plenty of villages, Colin's name and his fate carefully left out of every conversation. How long and weary the roads seemed without him sparring with the troupe, honing the blade of his wit upon her, flirting sometimes.

Kissing her, now and again.

Maguire whirled on her again and she glared. "Have you no better thing to do than play the fool?"

"'Tis my profession, lady." Maguire danced a ring around her. "Think on this: If I stop playing the fool, am I still a fool? And if so, who's to say if I'm playing or not?"

"Is that wretch bothering you still, Maura?"

Matilda waddled her way toward them. Her girdle lay right beneath her breasts now, to make room for the belly distending her tunic. Her boots lay tied together across her shoulders, and she'd pulled her hair away from a face pale of rouge. Without her silks, Matilda looked like the dairymaid of the Tuscan countryside that she'd told Maura she had been before Arnaud had lured her into the troupe.

Maura linked her arm with Matilda's, to give the woman someone to lean upon, though Maura dodged Matilda's brown eyes full of sympathy.

"Save your riddles for the fair of Kilcolgan," Matilda said, setting her eye on Maguire. "Not all of us need show off our wares between towns."

"You're jealous, Makejoy, that I can work my wits and still earn a penny by it." Maguire darted over and gave her belly a pat. "What man wants to climb a mountain for the mounting—and find the cave well filled?"

"A man with a spade hard enough to dig, Mudman, and not a limp tatter of a spoon like yours."

They started as the sound of a horse's hooves came up the road. Around the bend rode a man on a large palfrey, his dark cloak flapping behind him. Maura and the other minstrels skittered to the edge of the road to make way for him, but he rode past and then stopped, barring the way.

Maura wondered if he were a toll-collector, a common sight wherever the English had settled, until Matilda draw in a sudden breath and gripped her forearm.

The man shouted a question to Arnaud. Maura heard the name Colin, and her blood went cold.

"A bard you say?" Arnaud stepped up and pinched the flesh beneath his chin like he was thinking hard. "You're looking for an Irish poet?"

"He was masked," the man said, "and disguised among a group of minstrels much like yourselves."

Her blood rushed. Colin had escaped!

"He was last seen in Tuam." The rider spoke a usurper's English. "Have you been to Tuam?"

Maura eyed the rider. He rode bareback, like the Irish, though he spoke English. His hood was pulled low, covering most of his face against the spatter of rain. There was no doubting the authority in the set of his shoulders, or the richness of the studding on the horse's harness, or the sure grip of his hands on the reins. But a man such as this, traveling alone, made her think he wasn't English law.

Perhaps O'Kelly had put a reward on Colin's head. She wondered how many other lone riders searched for Colin in the woods of Ireland.

"Ah," Arnaud said, "I know of whom you speak. He was in our troupe not too long ago."

Maura sucked in a breath. Did Arnaud have no sense of honor at all? Did these minstrels betray their own so easily?

"*Oui*, I know him," Arnaud repeated, planting his fists on his hips. "He has caused us all more trouble than he's worth, I'll tell you. He's a stubborn, reckless *bête* without a bit of sense in his head. He has dragged us into his battles but tells us nothing, and then leaves us scurrying out of castles like rats."

The rider asked, "Where is he now?"

"I don't know and I don't care. If you find the bastard, string him up too high for even the ravens to find."

Rich laughter rumbled out from beneath the hood. The rider dismounted with a snap of his cloak, then shoved the hood back upon his shoulders.

Colin's grin lit up the world.

Maura stood, dumbfounded as the troupe rushed him. The minstrels' laughter filled the air. Colin embraced a snarling Arnaud in a bearish hug. Padraig slapped him on the back. Matilda fixed his face in her hands and kissed him flat on the lips. The twins tumbled and hopped like children begging for wafers.

Maura covered her mouth with both hands, staring. She'd imagined him hanging by the neck from a tree on the side of the road, denied a good Christian burial. But his black hair gleamed on his shoulders, his eyes crinkled in laughter, and his face was marred with no more bruises and cuts than usual.

He told his story in pieces. How he'd dodged The O'Kelly's blade, then called on the Baron of

Tuam to protect the guests in his home. How the baron shouted for the fighting to stop. The baron had reminded O'Kelly that there was a hefty fine for killing a bard, one hundred and twenty good milk cows, and then ordered the angry Irishman to stop reading insults into a simple story. Colin bowed out, stole O'Kelly's horse, and took a direction opposite of the minstrels to confuse the men O'Kelly then sent to kill him. Releasing the horse, Colin had shadowed his own assassins until a messenger summoned them back. Colin suspected that O'Kelly had finally realized he was only adding credence to Colin's words by chasing him down, and then decided his pride wasn't worth one hundred and twenty good milk cows.

Colin slapped the horse and sent the fine palfrey down the road, borrowed, so he said, from a toll-collector who had fallen asleep over his ale. He smiled at this, too, the swaggering thief. Then Colin lifted his gaze above the heads of the troupe and locked gazes with her. He shouldered his way through the circle, all pride and foolish courage.

"Well, Maura?" His breath smelled of green hazel-shoots as he leaned close to her. "Shall I not get a proper greeting from you?"

The shock of her fist against his cheekbone jolted her to the shoulder. He stumbled back from the surprise, tripped over the rock-pile fence and sprawled to the grass—sending Nutmeg, who had perched himself upon that fence with a cracked nut in his paws, reeling into the field. She stomped over to Colin, clambered over the fence, and braced her feet on either side of his hips. She glared down at him as he wiped his mouth and looked bemused at the blood upon his fingers.

"Did your mother drop you on your head when you were born?" Her anger bubbled like a stew left too long over the fire. "What were you thinking, playing a *filidh* and taunting an Irish nobleman with a bard's curse? You could have got yourself hanged."

The bloodied grin widened. "Would you mourn for me, Maura?"

"I don't mourn for fools."

He seized her by the hips. Her knees gave way, her boots skidded in the damp grass, and she fell atop him, bouncing against his hips.

"I missed you," he murmured, "all those nights in the wet heather alone."

She slapped her hands on his chest. "I was well rid of *you*."

But the words came out shaking, for the anger receded under the onslaught of another sensation, something deeper and fuller and far more troubling. His cloak smelled of damp earth and wood fires. His hands tightened on her hips. All those secret dreams rushed to her mind, when she was in just such a position but as naked as the day she was born.

He rumbled that maddening laugh, that maddening, all-knowing laugh.

"You promised to bring me to St. Patrick's Purgatory." She paused on a breath, trying to control her anger. "Fulfill your promise before you get yourself hanged."

Then she leaned down and kissed him, tasting the blood in his mouth and the slickness of the mist on his bristled skin. She kissed him until he kissed her back, his fingers curling into her hair.

"Aye, *a stóirín*." He pulled a fraction away. "That's the kind of greeting worth a hanging."

CHAPTER NINE

"*Alors,*" Arnaud interrupted, "there will be enough time for this later, when we're in Kilcolgan and safe from the English, eh?"

Maura sat up with a start. Then, realizing exactly what she was sitting on, she scrambled to her feet. Colin took his time rising, smiling at her with a look that made her blood roar in her ears. Knowing laughter came from behind them, where the troupe watched.

She should know better by now. A man like Colin would eat her up in one swallow and then be looking for another course by the break of day, but as she turned back to the road she couldn't lie. She did not regret kissing him like that.

"I can't believe you're here, living and breathing, after what you did." She brushed the dirt off her tunic as she stepped onto the road, avoiding Matilda's amused eye. "What were you thinking, wearing a bard's robes and putting a curse on an Irishman who was sitting in the room?"

"That Irishman and I have an old grievance."

"A grievance? Did he cheat you out of your wagers in a fight? Steal the heart of a woman you had your mind set on?"

His smile flickered. "Jealousy becomes you, though there be no reason for it, *a stóirín*."

My treasure. The word shot through her. She'd never been anyone's only treasure.

"Some time ago," he said, "O'Kelly chose the English over the Irish for his own profit. He needed to be reminded that some people haven't forgotten what he's done."

Maura knew little of the fighting between the Irish and the English except that it seemed to be going on all the time. "O'Kelly isn't the only Irishman who's in league with the English."

"He's the one that mattered to my family."

"So now you tell me you have a family who holds grievances with Irish chieftains."

"Having a family," he said, "comes with obligations. Something you might measure against the weight of that little ring of yours."

She dropped her gaze to her ring, then hid it in the folds of her tunic. Back in Tuam, he'd spoken to her gently about her foolish hunt for her mother, more gently than the Abbess ever did, more honestly than the Abbess, too. Still, she didn't like to be reminded of her ignorance.

So she changed the subject. "Do you realize how you had everyone worried? I'd thought for sure that the chieftain O'Kelly had run you through with his sword and left you bleeding to death in the rushes."

"The only injury I suffered," he said, patting his mouth with the back of his hand, "was a bruised lip."

"I think you enjoy fighting." She remembered his bloody grin and the light in his eye whenever an opponent approached. "Sometimes I think you've got your mind set on getting yourself killed."

"Would you miss me, if I did?"

Yes.

During the few days he was away she'd missed him sorely. He confused her with his kisses and then his coldness, his whispered words and then the way he set her aside. Had any man come to the kitchen doors of the convent acting like this, she would have had nothing to do with him. She'd have forgotten him the minute his shadow slipped away from the door.

But she was changing in ways she didn't understand. She felt it in the marrow of her bones. She used to mark the roll of her days by the clang of church bells, and now she hadn't been to Mass in weeks. Back in the convent, she'd rarely walked farther than the hundred yards to the village and back, and now she measured her days by how many miles they'd put behind them. She'd been so afraid of all the uncertainties of the world when she first considered this path. She thought she'd miss the sound of stew bubbling in the pot over the hearth fire, or the scent of gravy simmering. She'd thought she'd always be cold on the roads without the warmth radiating from the stones, or she'd be hungry so far from a well-stocked larder. The truth was the exercise brought her to the pot with an edge to her appetite that made any plain roadside soup taste like a meal fit for kings. Every road brought new anticipation of what grand sight might appear around the bend.

But the changes in her went far, far deeper. On Sundays, she used to collect a list of her sins to be ready for confession—sins like anger at Sister Siobhan for forgetting to water the garden, vanity and covetousness for yearning for Lady Sabine's comb, lapses in ritual like forgetting evening prayers after a long day cooking for Easter. How petty those immoralities seemed now that she'd abandoned the sisters, only to sing in thin silks in an alehouse and willingly sit spread-eagle atop a minstrel man for the sake of a desperate, wonderful, delicious kiss.

And yet, none of this felt like depravity. Deep in her heart she knew that something wonderful could happen if she gave herself to Colin. Something the nuns would call sinful, dangerous to her body and her soul. All her life she'd spent within smoke-tinged walls, safe from the rain and cold, taught the ways of the world from the pages of a Bible, only to realize that those ways were more wondrous and more complicated than she'd ever imagined

Perhaps the real sin was to hide in ignorance, comfort, and safety rather than dare to live.

The thought stayed in her mind as Padraig piped them all toward Kilcolgan. The town itself was no more than a cluster of thatch-roofed houses lorded over by a stone castle. They traveled past it, following the river beyond a small chapel until they reached a makeshift alehouse close to the inlet shore. The people inside rose and shouted and clapped their hands at the sight of their approach. While Arnaud talked terms with the owner of the alehouse, she sat on a bench with the wind flapping the tarpaulin above her, putting Nutmeg through his paces for the children who'd gathered at the sight of him. The reddened rays of the sun cast the thatch overhang into shades of amber and gold as the sun sank like the wink of a great eye. Soon peat fires flared and darkness cast its blue-black hand upon the alehouse.

They sat to a dinner of flaky cod and a plate of something buttery and salty from the depths of the sea, all washed down with honest ale that lit her belly with a glow. That queer warmth intensified as the dinner ended and Padraig set to his pipe, playing the sort of music that made a woman's toes tap upon the ground and her fingers rap against her knees and her heart beat a little faster.

Maura urged a nervous Nutmeg back into his basket, and then searched for a sturdy peg on which to hang the basket for the night. Around her, the fishermen clapped, waiting for their turn to whirl with Matilda and the twins, their feet stomping upon the packed-earth floor, the wind snapping the tarpaulin above them to the beat of the tabor, and farther beyond, the tide rushing up the inlet to wash the muddy shore. Padraig's pipe wailed through her. Maguire punctuated the music with his hoots and howls, the fishermen with the sounds of shouted Irish, and everyone pounded the beat with their feet.

Her gaze found Colin's as if drawn by a force beyond her own will. He wove through the dancers to face her, his hair wild, his eyes gleaming with all the promises of the world. He showered her with a bouquet of primroses and cowslips, while around them the fishermen's leathery faces crinkled into knowing folds.

He held out his hand.

The devil will tempt you, Maura remembered the Abbess saying. *Out in the world, the devil will tempt you with music and mead and mirth, he'll tempt you into a dance, and that's the first step toward sin.*

Maura put her hand in Colin's. In her mind she saw those fires that lit the countryside during harvest time, when the day-laborers pitched camp just outside the convent fields during that month of hard labor. In her mind she heard their music, too. Somehow, at the end of the day, they always found the energy to dance with the girls of the kitchen—the girls the Abbess hired to help during those busy months, those girls who spun every morning into the kitchens red-cheeked with excitement, their feet tapping to the music still, their voices and their eyes full of secrets.

Colin drew her into the dance and she stopped making excuses for what every bone in her body ached to do. They danced in circles, changing partners and twirling in giddy abandon with hooked arms and flying feet. Wasn't it strange to have strangers touch her and not want to slap their hands away, for surely the laughter seemed honest enough.

It was always Colin she came back to. With the tug of his fingers, she moved with him, she moved against him, she moved to his command. This was nothing like the prancing she'd sometimes dared to do around the trestle table of the kitchen as she cleared up the remnants of the night's dinner and made partners of the spoons and the tongs, of the knives and the ham bones.

As the excitement flowed through her, she began to understand what drew the women into the fields in the moonlight. Her limbs grew supple, she felt as buoyant as if she skipped upon water. She smiled back the smiles in the shining faces around her. What a motley group of fishermen and alehouse wives and black-handed tanners. All men and women, no more, no less, caught in the bright joy of the moment.

Ah, there he was again, on the next change of partner—reaching out for her—and then she felt the brush of his palm against her waist, and the rough rasp of his hand as he closed it over hers. His face was only a breath away from her own, she could smell the hazel-mead he'd been drinking. The room whirled around them as he drew her about—so strong, so sure—as if her feet never brushed the ground. Her breath came fast through her lips and the heat of the fire singed her back as she passed close. Above the sky twirled, the heavens winking down upon them. Laughter bubbled up inside her and muddled her head. She couldn't stop—she wouldn't stop—Heaven help her, she never wanted to stop dancing.

Time escaped her, or perhaps they danced in the crease of it. It was like Beltane, when the old stories said the season of darkness came to an end and the season of light began. But in the deep night, there was said to be a crack in time, a moment when this world and the other merged and the creatures of the Otherworld slipped between the veils and danced on earthly soil. Gazing around at these minstrels with their painted faces and bright silks, with their laughter and their music, it was not too far a stretch to think she'd been captured. Maybe in the morning she'd wake up alone on a knoll by the side of the road with only the throb of strange liquors in her head and wondrous fading memories of music too beautiful to bear remembering.

So when Colin tugged her hand, she followed him without resistance out of the circle of revelers. They closed ranks behind them without a break in the rhythm. With her tunic gripped in her free hand, she followed him down to the river's edge where the stronger music was the wash of the tide rising.

He tugged her toward a cluster of overturned boats. Then he cradled her, and there was his face, that handsome bristled face hovering above hers. There was that smiling mouth, descending upon hers.

She welcomed his kiss without hesitation.

His mouth was firm, expert, urging her to part her lips. She felt the brush of his tongue against her own. The shock took her by surprise and she pulled back so she could catch her breath. But he kissed her again, tilting her head with gentle hands, teaching her how to strengthen that frisson of pleasure skittering up her spine as his kisses deepened.

She was vaguely aware that they were still moving against each other, as if they still danced around the fire, and suddenly she felt the lip of a cart behind her, digging into her backside. He pressed her onto the bed of the cart. Through half-closed eyes, beyond the sweep of his dark hair, she saw the streak of the stars across the sky as the world tilted and she lay flat. He climbed in beside her, shuffling her farther in until she felt the full length of his body pressing, ever more urgently, against her.

She kissed him as the moonlight bathed their shoulders. The night wind brushed her face. She played with his tongue as Padraig's pipe wailed in the alehouse beyond, as Matilda's voice rose in song. They kissed as the buckle of his belt snagged on her leather girdle, tangling them close.

Short, eager kisses. He pulled away and she couldn't help herself. She pressed her forehead against his. Something changed inside her—like the sudden rising of dough slapped into grease, burning and expanding at the same time. Her heart raced, but no longer from the breathless whirl of the dance.

She thought, *don't speak. Don't speak.*

His hand slipped under the hollow of her back. His lips captured the lobe of her ear, his tongue traced a trail down her jaw, and the wind cooled the place where his lips had been. He urged her closer so her breasts flattened against his chest. Liquid sensation flowed through her body and seemed to pool between her legs.

He slipped his hand over her buttock and she jerked in surprise as his fingers trailed in the cleft between. He kept going until he gripped her thigh and nudged it to spread her legs apart. Only when she felt the rasp of his woolen hose against the tender inside of her thighs did she realize that he'd pulled up her tunic. She spread her knees wider for him, wanting him to touch her. She didn't like the hollow feeling growing inside her and she sensed he could fill it.

She was not ignorant of what lay between a man's legs. Watching the day-laborers wander to a tree to pass water, she knew a man had a part different from a woman, a long part like a thick rope, so Sabine had once told her, whispering answers to her curious questions. She knew from the talk of the kitchen girls that the man's part grew long and hard, and men liked to press that part inside a woman.

Now Colin yanked and tugged and she moved her bottom until the tunic was wadded somewhere around her hips. She felt the breath of the night air on her bare thighs and even higher, where the wind had never touched. He rolled over onto her and she felt *him,* the man part of him, hard and hot and long just like the girls had confessed. She pressed against it, a reflex she hadn't expected.

It felt good to feel him there.

It felt *right*.

She blinked open her eyes to meet his gaze and saw a man she didn't recognize. This was not the laughing Colin she knew, not this stone-faced man with the flicker of a muscle in his cheek—surely, this was not the same man who had laughed and danced with her only moments before. This wide-shouldered creature whose muscles flexed beneath her hands stared down at her with a look in his eyes she could not fathom.

Maybe she didn't look like the woman he knew, either. She felt like a stranger in her own tingling skin. Her cheeks felt red-hot, her lips swollen from kisses, her breasts tightening almost to the point of pain, made tighter as he suddenly passed his fingers across them, then focused on one nub, rubbing it through the wool.

"Maura," he said, his voice a rasp in his throat. "You could kill a man with wanting."

She grasped his head. "Don't fill the night with words."

She curled her fingers into that hair soft enough to strike envy in any girl's heart. She moved her own hips against his body in a way she thought would put the twin's acrobatics to shame. With a low groan, he tugged her skirts until they slipped out from under her. The wooden slats of the cart felt rough upon her backside—at least until he slipped his fingers into the cleft between her legs.

She made a noise in her throat she didn't recognize. Her own body bore down upon that invading hand. She threw her head back at the sensation of his touch. One of his fingers slipped inside her and she started to shake. He probed and she felt a stretch, a pressure.

He went still.

She blinked out of her blindness and whispered, "Colin."

His face was unreadable in the shadows, the stars bright beyond the silhouette of his body. He moved his fingers again, probing in that magic way, and he muttered something, words she could not hear, because suddenly she couldn't think anymore.

She *wanted.*

She slipped her hands beneath his tunic, searching for the ties that held up his hose. Her fingers quivered against his flat abdomen, but she couldn't seem to find those ties. She felt his finger slip out of her and she whispered, "no no no," until he started stroking her, short little strokes at the top of her cleft. Something inside her tightened to unbearable tautness, then tighter, with each stroke of his wet fingers—*where are those ties*—and then she gave up with the ties and grasped his shoulders because with his stroking she was about to fall somehow, coming closer with each slick stroke, and then she sank her fingernails into him as a sensation swelled, rising, rising, rising—

Oh.

OH.

CHAPTER TEN

Colin held Maura until she stopped trembling, though his own body ached for release. He took a measure of satisfaction for having given her pleasure without saddling her with potential consequences. Of course, a better man would never have tempted such an innocent, no matter how strongly Maura had asked for this with her eyes.

But he'd had ten years to accept that he was not a better man.

Now he distracted himself from the softness of her by noting the summer constellations spread like milk in the sky above—the bull, the twins, the crab— listing them by rote until his head ached, a dull throb to match his still-aching cock. He breathed the scent that clung to her hair and tried not to imagine what it would be like to sleep next to this woman every night, to live a normal man's life.

He slipped his arm from under her and inched away. She didn't move as he laid his mantle over her. He shuffled down to the edge of the cart and slid off. His feet sank into the mud as he followed the gleam of moonlight to the edge of the shore. The black expanse of the river shone with strange light, winking here and there on the ripples of current.

Maybe it had something to do with the scent of the sea, the softness of the air, or the blue-white quality of the starlight, but standing on this familiar shore all the old poems rushed to his mind as surely as if he were a young man reciting them for his father's approval: *To Fergus, nephew of Tadhg, son of Uilliam, nephew of Fionna...* He could recite his genealogy back to the King of Ulster, still farther to the nephew of the King of Connacht, every name shrouded in the martyrdom of the battlefield. It was a story of jealous Irish tribes competing for a slippery high kingship, defeating themselves with their own divisiveness, fighting for pride rather than uniting against a powerful mutual enemy.

He glared over his shoulder at the town of Kilcolgan. The stone donjon loomed, a black shadow against the stars. The English knew how to conquer and subdue. They came as one army and seized land and built a castle to guard every port, to take tolls upon every road, to watch the land from on high. In the years since he'd been gone, Ireland lay like a pincushion under their dominion, making the Irish kingship nothing but legend. The poems he had spent his youth memorizing no longer mattered, yet here he was, drawn back to this bloody ground like a vengeful ghost, no wiser than his own ancestors.

He wandered back to the cart and the woman sprawled upon it. He hung his hands over the creaking side and pressed his chin against the salt-stained wood. Her hair fanned like a halo around her head. He had nothing to give this innocent but an evening's fleeting pleasure. Even masked, he'd taken a reckless chance at Tuam by satirizing O'Kelly. How long it would take before someone figured out his identity and hunted for the price upon his head?

His father wouldn't wait to be caught. He'd attack now and preserve the element of surprise.

But he was not his father.

Then he reached out to bury his fingers in Maura's hair, wondering how much longer he could pretend this was his life.

Maura emerged from the shadow of the church into the bustle of the fair of Kilcolgan. An onion-seller hawked her wares nearby. A stray dog yipped, then darted out of the path of a broomstick. People milled about the stalls in the square. Coins clinked, trades were bartered, bickered and shouted, English farthings changed hands for pasties and pies. She leaned against a carved stone column, staring at Colin.

He stood as still as a roof-tree as he stared at the looming donjon that lorded over the town. A devil's mask hung from the ties at his neck, upside-down and askew on his back. He sported a tunic of horsehair on his lanky frame. Apparently he'd taken Maguire's place this morning, playing the wild man among the crowd, to draw the fairgoers into the alehouse. But he played no wild man now, standing as still as stone.

She approached, her heart in her throat. "It's a fine day to be sightseeing."

He flinched. She took some satisfaction in that. For he'd left her to wake up to the cool light of morning alone, dazed, her whole body aching and strangely tender-sore.

"So it's you, lass."

So it's you, lass, as if they hadn't spent the night entwined on a fisherman's cart doing things she'd spent the morning confessing to a local priest, sinning twice over because she wasn't sure she was repentant.

"In my grandfather's father's time," he said, "that castle wasn't there. It was a hunting lodge, winter lodgings for the O'Maddens, so they would have fresh fish for the forty days of Lent."

She mumbled, "A hunting lodge."

"The MacEgans stayed there often, as well. The clans were close, cousins."

"Is this the way you usually put off your women," she stuttered, "chattering nonsense the morning after you have had your way with them?"

Heat rose to her face. As she squinted up at the castle she thought that starlight was far kinder than daylight. A woman could hide in the night what secret parts of her the glare of morning exposed.

Colin's gaze flickered to the church behind her. "You're straight from the confession box. Newly anointed and ruing last night's passion?"

"You'll tease me now?"

He had the grace to look chastised.

"I told the priest," she continued, "that I wouldn't put off my pilgrimage any longer, that I'd be setting off in a day or two, for penance," she said. "And truly, I'm *trying* to go to St. Patrick's Purgatory, but it seems that you keep making us change directions. Are you such a vagabond that you can't even stay in a woman's bed till the morning?"

"If I'd stayed any longer," he said, "you'd have lost that lovely innocence, and ended up like Matilda."

Flushing anew, she cast her gaze away from the glamour of him. She'd suspected he hadn't finished the act, but she didn't dare ask. If what Colin said was true, then last night she had skirted along the edge of sin—tasted the icing upon the honey cake—but did not actually take a bite. She hadn't known that a woman could feel pleasure and not pay the price.

The knowledge tingled a new awareness in her.

And then she looked back at him, and he was smiling at her, a soft strange smile, and her heart stumbled. She could smell him—clean and cold as if he'd bathed in the sea. Water dripped from his *culans,* and water stained the front of the horsehair shirt.

He tugged one of her curls. "Tell me, Maura. What would a fine lass like you want with a penniless vagabond like me?"

Now there was a question she couldn't answer. Truth be told, she hadn't thought it all through. Her mind and heart had turned to Colin, with as much impulsiveness as when she'd set out of Killeigh with the idea of finding her long-lost mother, with no more guidance than a scratched old ring. But while she searched those eyes of blue, she knew what she wanted. She felt it clear through to her bones. She wanted to dance with Colin. She wanted to taste his kiss. She wanted to journey to the land they'd visited last night, and go farther, without guilt and regret.

He raised his eyebrows. "Is it marriage that you're after, then?"

The back of her throat dried up, and a new ache was born in her chest. Why should she be surprised he'd know such a thing, when she'd hardly grasped it herself? It wasn't as if she'd fought in his embrace last night. Like every other maiden, she found herself looking upon his battered nose and his strong shoulders and dreaming of things she had no business dreaming of, wanting things she had no right to want.

"I want what any woman wants," she whispered, wishing the fair would swell and swallow her up. "I want to be an honest woman."

"You want a name," he said. "A name for a nameless foundling."

"No."

He raised his brows at her.

"I wasn't dropped from the sky onto the convent steps." Her throat was impossibly tight. These past weeks she'd done nothing but put farthings into thieves' hands and got lies in return, and grew ever more ashamed of her former foolishness. "I have a name," she persisted, "I just haven't found it yet."

He upped her chin in the palm of his hand. "And yet you stand before me willing to take a name you don't even know."

She knew that Colin wasn't all that he seemed, that there lay some hurt within him, a powerful guilt that made him put himself in the way of blacksmiths' fists, that made him hungry for quick pleasures that never satisfied and thus must always be fed, a shame that made him mock high ranking men while hiding behind a mask and pushing the troupe hither and yon for reasons he did not disclose.

She still wanted his kiss.

Here I go again, she thought. *Here I go, playing the wayward woman in the shadow of the church, succumbing to glamour.* But the thought passed like a breeze. Nothing mattered under the power of Colin's touch, now that she understood the joy that could come of it.

"It's the man I want," she said. "Not a name."

Colin's expression shifted, like he couldn't pretend to be amused anymore. Suddenly, he said,

"Leave with me, Maura."

She startled. "Leave?"

"Right now," he said. "Right this moment."

"But Arnaud—"

"—has run this troupe for decades, he can do well enough without us."

He eased her back against the limestone of the cloth maker's hut and then caught her mouth with his own. Water dripped from his hair and trailed between her breasts. A sharp, sweet ache speared through her. His kiss was never enough, never, never enough.

Then, suddenly, they raced through the crowd, through alleys where the sun beamed light between thatched roofs. They danced across the center gutter, rounded a peddler's stubborn donkey, and dodged a stray dog tearing at a captured hen near the poulterer's shop. Her heart slammed against her ribs as he tugged her in his wake. The devil's mask banged against his back, smiling at her. She swept up her tunic to free her feet from their tangle, but she stumbled and Colin caught her.

He laughed as he caught her—a strange, wild laugh that should have given her pause, because it brought to her mind a memory of him grinning through bloodied teeth as he faced a fighter—and maybe she would have paused, if he hadn't at that moment twisted her into the shadows to make her senseless with more kisses.

She didn't know how long they'd been kissing when a voice cut through the bustle of the fair.

"Colin?"

Colin ignored the deep, questioning voice, not even pausing to raise his face from where he ran his teeth against her throat.

The voice again. "Brother?"

At that word, Maura opened her eyes. Beyond Colin, a beggar stepping out of the crowd. He wore a patched tunic and gripped a walking stick. A silvery scar trailed across his cheek, then disappeared under rags covering one eye. The beggar stood with his mouth agape, an alms bowl hanging from his neck.

"Brother," the man repeated, raising a hand against the sun. "Brother, turn and look at me."

Colin raised his head from her throat, fixing his unseeing gaze on the limestone wall behind her.

"Murtough." Colin's jaw went tight. "It was you that I saw begging at the church steps."

"Ten years." The beggar ventured a trembling smile beneath the rags—a madman's twitching grin. "It's a long time to make us all wait."

Colin's attention shifted to her face, his bright blue gaze becoming as brittle as the colored glass she'd seen in the cathedral at Athlone.

The beggar said, "You're the only one left of us, Colin."

"I know."

A hush fell upon the street. The bustle she and Colin had raced through had stilled, and the place had gone so quiet that she could hear the wind rustling in the thatch above her head. Though most of the English couldn't possibly understand the Irish language, many stopped at the sight of the beggar holding out a trembling hand to the minstrel playing the wild man, as if what was happening before them was nothing but a play.

"You've finally come," the beggar said, making the sign of the cross so his alms rattled. "Finally, you'll take your place as the true MacEgan."

CHAPTER ELEVEN

"Should I lower my head in obeisance when I see you now, King Colin?"

Colin stiffened at the sound of her voice, strained from the swift climb up the hillside just outside of Kilcolgan. He'd retreated to this high point not just to get away from her questions, but also to eyeball the stretch of countryside below, particularly the ribbon of road that led to the town of Shrule where his brother Murtough insisted they all travel—into the very land for which he would soon be spilling blood.

"So you want to pay obeisance?" he asked, forcing his voice light. "I admit, it'd be a fine sight to see you on your knees before me."

He saw a spark in those eyes, but she didn't bite back. Her clothing rustled as she settled on the ground, an arm's length away from where he sat, close enough that he knew she intended to stay awhile. He wished she would sit farther away. He wished he could prevent her from witnessing what was to come.

"So this is your lost kingdom then," she said,

waving a hand over the scene. "All these little English towns?"

He supposed she deserved an explanation. She'd been patient enough in the square, after he'd embraced his brother and then gathered the minstrels to bustle them out of town. They couldn't stay and risk the chance that someone had heard Murtough, in his reckless excitement, shout the MacEgan name.

"These were MacEgan lands once." He gestured to the north. "Three days from here, between Lough Corrib and Lough Mask, lies Fahy, once the castle keep of the MacEgans."

"Colin, the English have settled here so thickly even the wind has forgotten the sound of the Irish."

He agreed, in part. In the genealogy it was said that the MacEgans had controlled all the lands bordered by Lough Mask and Lough Corrib to the west, to the rounded Slieve Aughty Mountains to the south, to the river Suck to the east, to the wild tribes of Clan Morris and the O'Conors to the north—more land than he could now see, though the June air shone with clarity. But in his grandfather's father's time, the English had built the cluster of towns that now controlled the lands. For three generations the MacEgans lived peacefully as subtenants of the English baron, a mockery of vassalage since they rarely paid tribute or gave homage. For generations, the MacEgans had lived side by side with the English and didn't care a wit. To the Irish of the land, the MacEgans were still the chieftains.

But that was a big bite of a tale to swallow, even for this cloistered young woman who believed in the stuff of impossible dreams.

"All this time," she said, grasping her knees,

"you've been calling yourself King Colin, making a big jape of it all, and now I'm to believe that you've been mocking me with the truth all along?"

"Murtough told you the whole tale, I'm sure." At the base of the slope a fire flickered as daylight began to dim. From the height, Colin could see his brother's walking stick gleaming as Murtough gesticulated with it, a bladder of ale swinging in his other hand.

"Your brother told a tale, but he may as well be reciting stories of Cú Chulainn or the Fenian men."

"The old tales are the only riches any of the MacEgans have left."

"So I'm to believe that the man I've seen juggling the breasts of sinful women—the man I've seen brawling with blacksmiths—is the mighty MacEgan?"

He flinched. Even Maura could see into his craven heart and know it wasn't made of legend.

"Your brother did tell me one thing that struck true," she said, fixing him with that sharp hazel gaze. "He told me about a boy, a sixth son, who was sent off to a monastery at Emain Macha to learn to be the clan's poet. A boy who came back in his fifteenth year with a bard's skill."

It had been Christmastide, he remembered it well. He'd had a head swirling with legends, eager to show off his skill on the harp, eager to show his father how fine a *filidh* he would be for the clan.

"Strange thing about this boy," Maura continued. "He told a tale that year, a tale so moving that no MacEgan present has ever forgotten it."

Colon picked up the bow he'd left beside him, testing the tautness of the string. He'd worked for weeks on the composition of that poem, keeping pure to the ancient language of the poets—keeping it in perfect rhyme. The content had been just as rigid, just as ancient. It was a proud poem of bloodlines that stretched past to the kingship of all Connacht, a poem about the bright victories of the MacEgan ancestors, of the continuing honor of the clan's birthright, of the clan's God-given destiny. Because he knew, above all things, that a *filidh* must stroke a patron's feathers by vaunting their bloodlines.

"Colin."

"Aye, that damn poem." He laid the bow on his knees. "I was showing off for my father, no more."

"Murtough said it had an effect."

"The English baron had just died," he said, "leaving only daughters as heirs. So the question of who would control the lands that had once been MacEgan's hung in the air. A change in power is always a dangerous time. And there I was, launching into that poem in a room full of young warriors—"

"You couldn't have known what would happen."

"Aye, I did know. It doesn't take much to set MacEgan blood stirring." He cocked a brow at her. "You know that well enough."

She jerked to her feet, turning her face away from him. "That story you told at Tuam, the one that got you in so much trouble with O'Kelly." She paced, her leather shoes scraping across the rough surface of stone. "That was your father's story, wasn't it?"

"Yes."

"If Murtough speaks true," she said, "then the war your clan fought is over and lost."

Aye, lost. Lost, lost, lost. According to Murtough, what was left of the MacEgans clung to a precarious existence in the Partry Mountains, west of Shrule, forced to live as best as they could under the leadership of his ailing—if not already dead—cousin, Brendan. There, if Murtough spoke true, they warmed themselves by the fires of old stories and whispered Colin's name, waiting for his return.

Maura said, "You've got four brothers dead, another blinded in one eye, and the MacEgans pushed to the edge of the world. Did you think, by coming here, you could set that all to rights?"

Colin's smile dimmed. A bird swept low over them, screeching in warning. This woman could turn that tongue against a man and slice him clear to the bone.

He said, "I am the only son who isn't dead or maimed—"

"And thus smart enough to know better than to fight lost causes."

"How rich it is that you talk of lost causes, with that ring of yours, and your wild hopes of finding your family."

"I don't have to spill blood for what I seek." She clutched the hand that bore the ring. "But who do you plan to kill? Your brother spat on the names of a long list of men. Are you to kill the O'Shaughnessy's and the O'Heynes? Or are you going straight to the English baron who controls these lands—Lord William Caddell?"

William Caddell.

Colin's nostrils flared. He remembered the wash of Galway Bay upon the shore. He remembered the sight of the tattered army around him, the remnants of his defeated clan. He remembered standing there, barely twenty years of age, thinking of the three brothers who had died in the wars, the father hastily buried by the side of that pond, the fourth brother lying upon a makeshift litter in the purple of twilight upon the coast of Connemara, his face soon to be a death mask—thinking of all the waste, all the battle, all the grief. He remembered, too, the sound of horses coming from the woods behind him, the sound of swords scraping unsheathed as his warriors prepared to die. But the horsemen who crashed upon their hiding place were his own men, carrying Murtough—blinded in one eye by the sword of William Caddell—blinded yet spitting a hundred thousand curses upon William the Black, just as Colin's father had done as he died beside that lake.

And all the men had turned to *him* with vengeance in their eyes, as if a twenty-year-old poet could be the warrior MacEgan.

"Colin," she whispered, drawing him back to the height of the hill, the June breeze that didn't smell of blood. "If everything Murtough is babbling is true, then there must be a price on your head."

"Wasn't it you who said the devil would stretch the rope to the ground, if I ever found myself hanging?"

"Don't use my words against me." Her eyes were wide, too wet. "What are you going to do if you get yourself caught?"

"Die. It's how the legends usually end anyway. And the wars."

She gripped his sleeve. She shifted so she was on her knees before him. "You can't do this, Colin. Not you," she whispered, tugging at the wool of his tunic, "not the man with the enchanted heart."

Something moved inside him as he looked down at her lovely, fair face with its winged brows and the freckles on her temples—a strange sliding of heart and mind, a dangerous sense of doubt and reckless hope. He wondered, in the days to come, whether he would ever see such gentleness in anyone's eyes again.

"You wanted to escape before Murtough found you," she whispered, in that husky songstress's voice. "There's a whole world out there, free of the past, free of what cannot be changed. Let's run away, like we planned."

He traced her jaw with his thumb and let himself imagine another man's life. He imagined traveling with her through rolling green hills, sleeping among the cows and waking with them lowing on the warm hillside. He imagined the bubble of a kettle over a fire, while they slept upon a pallet of fresh hay. He imagined picking the straw from her hair every night after kissing her cheeks pink. He imagined waking up to the first rays of the sun with her curled in his arms, with nothing but their bodies and a thin blanket holding back the chill. He imagined swimming in a hundred different rivers, building a new home every night by the side of the road. He imagined shedding his name, disappearing into the world, drowning in this woman's arms.

In some ways, he'd lived that life already—at least a darker, meaner shadow of it. But for all that he pretended he enjoyed the oblivion found in ale and willing women's arms, his obligations had eaten away at him. He could not ignore the family that called to him anymore, and still call himself a man.

He caught the edge of her lip with his thumb. "Go back to the camp, Maura."

"Colin—"

"I must do what I promised my father. I intend to put an arrow through William Caddell's heart."

CHAPTER TWELVE

Maura watched as Maguire crouched in the dust of the road and squinted at the donkey's raised hoof. The Mudman grimaced and then stood up with a sigh.

"A rock was there and gone," he announced. "But it left a fine deep rut, that's what's causing the beast to limp. It needs to be washed and bound, and the donkey rested for at least a day."

Arnaud threw up his arms. "Bad luck dogs us like a rat after an apple cart. We'll have to camp here and put off Shrule for another day."

Maura nodded. The twins bobbed their heads. Fingar slipped his harp off his back as if in resignation, and Matilda pressed the flat of her hand against her swelling belly. Then Maura sidled a secret glance toward Colin, standing with his arms crossed.

Colin pushed away from the tree and sauntered toward the donkey. "A rock, Maguire?"

"Aye, a rock." The Mudman frowned. "Are you doubting my word, then?"

"I'm admiring the way you taught the beast to limp," Colin said. "Will he do it on command, like Nutmeg?"

Maguire chewed a piece of grass to the other side of his mouth. "I won't push this donkey harder. We'll lame him for good if he doesn't get a day's rest."

"Strange that all this bad luck happened as soon as Murtough climbed on that farmer's cart and left me behind with all of you."

Matilda made another low groan and clutched her abdomen. Maura stepped quickly to her side, as did the twins.

"Come, Matilda," Colin said. "You'd be more believable if you hadn't been singing like a maiden on May Day all morning."

"What would you know of it?" Matilda took Maura's arm as the twins lowered her to the grass. "You know nothing of childbearing except how to make one."

"It's a wonder you all haven't starved to death with how badly you play your parts." Colin eyeballed the troupe. "Don't you understand? Once Murtough reaches the MacEgans, they'll send someone out to fetch me. All you are doing is putting off the inevitable—"

Foolishness.

She'd spoken aloud. She knew because suddenly he looked at her with those angry eyes as if he knew that she had orchestrated all of this. Turning around, she set her foot into the lush grass off the side of the road. She swung up Nutmeg's basket and hiked it over her shoulder and then trudged into the shadow of the woods without real direction, knowing only that he'd probably follow.

She had to stop Colin from reaching Shrule in any way possible.

"Don't be long," Colin shouted, "or I'll come after you."

"Now there's a promise," she shouted back. "I'll take my time, then."

She plunged into the shadows. She took a grim pleasure in the snap of twigs under her feet. She kept her mind on the blind need to save the man from a folly she still could not comprehend.

Colin the Minstrel—an Irish chieftain.

The MacEgan.

She reached a river and kicked a stone over the surface. It skipped twice across the water before sinking into the current. She swept Nutmeg's basket off her back, hooked it on a broken branch of an oak tree, and then sank down on her haunches. She dropped her chin into her hands and looked for answers in the shimmer of sunlight on the water.

Through a break in the trees, in the distance, she could just see little streams of smoke that marked the English town of Shrule. She wished she could obliterate the whole town with a single thought. She wished she could erase the past three days. Things weren't right anymore. She was still a kitchen maid out on a foolish quest, but he was no longer Colin the lecher. He was a stranger walking in Colin's skin.

"I know you're not as deaf as Padraig."

Colin came through the trees, his shirt billowing open, showing a glimpse of uncompromising chest.

She said, "You didn't have to follow me."

"But you knew I would. Don't deny it," he said as she opened her mouth. "We're all playing our parts here, Maura, but you're smart enough to know this won't change anything."

She jerked to her feet, startling Nutmeg where he rustled in the grass. "So you'll play the part of the fool?"

"Don't."

A bird chattered in the boughs of the oak. A pebble tumbled into the shallow water. The scream of the insects soared. Colin gave her a long look and then turned to walk away.

"You made a promise to me, Colin," she said, raising her voice. "You promised to bring me to St. Patrick's Purgatory."

It seemed like a hundred thousand years ago. What a fool she'd been, thinking she could find her parents by simply setting out on the roads of Ireland. The world was bigger than she'd ever imagined. And she was just beginning to realize that better things could be found upon the road than what she'd originally set out to find.

"The shrine will not disappear," he said, in an odd, gravelly voice. "And Arnaud is a better escort than ever I could be."

"You're breaking your promise."

"Yes."

"Not even a twinge of conscience."

He showed her a face without humor. "Don't try to save me, lass."

"How about you saving *us*, then? If you've got killing on your mind, it's likely we'll all be hanged."

"They won't know I'm one of you."

"Is that another of your promises?"

His face darkened. He wheeled around and headed back through the trees, away from her, out of her life. For reasons she still struggled to fathom, she had to make sure that didn't happen—at any cost.

"I suppose this has been nothing but a bit of business between you and me." She stomped down to the river's edge and nudged one slipper off with the toe of her foot. "I sing for my supper, and you kiss me until I want to make feet for children's stockings."

He stopped in his tracks. She felt a trill of success. She kept him near for one moment longer.

Now that he was watching, she tugged at the ties of her tunic. "Oh, I've been listening to Maguire," she said. "What else does he call swiving? Being in a woman's beef? Playing in cock's alley? Aye, I'd have quite a vocabulary to bring back to the convent with me, if they will have me back at all."

"What are you doing?"

She dragged the length of her tunic over her head. "I'm hot and dusty, and the river looks cool." She flung the tunic away, then hiked up the skirt of her linen under-tunic to pluck free the garter that held up her stockings. "And I'd best get used to stripping off my clothes in front of strange men, since you're so determined to leave me unprotected."

She felt his gaze on her pale thigh like the touch of a feather. She yanked off one stocking and tossed the black wool in the growing pile of her clothing. She flashed leg in the bright sun as she undid the second. Then, deliberately, she tugged at the ties of her coif and pulled the linen cap off her head until her hair tumbled over her shoulders.

In all her life, she had barely undressed in front of any of the sisters or even the kitchen girls. They took baths in their own shifts, which provided some measure of modesty. But here she was standing in her thin under-tunic on the banks of a river, letting a man she hardly knew stare at her body.

It was a strangely powerful feeling, to be able to hold the attention of the rover she'd vowed not to succumb to, the kind of man the sisters made a point of warning her against, to be able to force him to stay in one place, all because of her body, thinly veiled, outlined through the thin linen by the light.

"Is this all that men do, then?" She circled her bare toe in the water. "You stand about and stare at a woman? Faith, Matilda led me to believe there was a lot more sweat and grunting in it."

"A wise woman," he said, his voice husky, "would put her clothes back on."

"There's a fair in Dunmore." She tugged her under-tunic a hand's span above her knee, feeling the cool breeze whirl under the linen. "That band of masons we passed told Arnaud about it, I heard them myself. Dunmore is northeast of here, in the direction of St. Patrick's Purgatory. I suppose it's as good a place as any for me to start earning real wages."

"You earn real wages singing—"

"—and what will become of me after you're gone, and we have no real reason to wheedle our way into the halls of kings?" She squinted away from him, over the river, thinking up all of Maguire's nasty phrases. "Arnaud won't suffer my singing and Nutmeg's dancing. All the world will be calling me a barber's chair, since every man in every parish will have a turn in me—oh!"

Suddenly he was behind her, dragging her back against his body with a shock of contact. She smelled him—leather and rain and something else, something musky and private and exciting. He breathed hard against her head as the wind pressed her under-tunic flat against her legs.

She wanted this man. She wanted him now, by the cool waters of this river, upon the sweet clover with the warm June sun pounding down upon them.

This didn't feel at all like sin.

She lifted her hand and wove her fingers into his hair. He stood as tense as a harp's string. His arm tightened. He twisted her and she saw the bright blue sky blazing beyond his dark head. Then, suddenly, the pebbles of the river bit into her knees, the cool water splashed beneath her body as he laid her down in the shallow waters. The river chilled her shoulder blades—a thumb's depth of it, no more, but enough to lick at her buttocks and send her hair fanning out, pulled gently with the current.

An expression flittered across his face that she could not read. His gaze was like a touch, and she felt it trailing like a finger up her inner thigh.

Suddenly he lay down in the shallow water and rolled onto his back. He yanked her on top of him. Water splashed onto her thighs, her belly, her breasts, and her soaking hair slapped on her back. He spread her knees so they braced on the pebbles on either side of his hips. Splayed across his loins, she felt him—the hardness—straining against the fibers of his braies.

She gasped at the feel of it, so hot and hard against her. She flattened her hands on his abdomen to brace herself. Water seeped into his shirt, outlining the ripples of his ribs. Droplets gleamed on his face, and his eyes blazed a blue to match the sky.

He filled his hands with her breasts and her nipples tightened into knots in his palms. He massaged her in ways she'd never been touched. The nuns had always told her that God gave women breasts for one reason alone. But no motherly thoughts of feeding babes had ever sent hot sparks through her, or made her breasts feel so heavy or made her nipples ache, or made her want to arch like a cat, begging with her body for a rougher touch.

She imagined how he must see her right now, sprawled half-naked across his loins, her hair a tumble of snags, nothing shading her nudity from the eyes of the world but the wet linen plastered to her skin, and a thin lacing of tree boughs. She was happy he found her worth touching, kissing, loving.

"I won't have you blaming me for your ruin," he said, as he dragged his hands to her hips. "If you really want this, Maura, you'll have to take it."

She leaned over and pressed her lips against his. Her tight nipples grazed his chest. She welcomed his tongue and slid her own against his the way he'd shown her that one night by the inlet shore. On his tongue she tasted the sweetness of honey she'd used in the oatcakes that morning and the lingering trace of hazel-mead he'd purchased in Clare.

He kissed her back in new and wondrous ways. He kissed with the bite of his teeth on her lower lip. He kissed by wandering all over her mouth while his fingers played upon her spine. Aye, it was no surprise that he could play upon her body like a master harpist upon strings, knowing where to strum, and how hard to do it, and how long. No matter how he touched her, every single brush of flesh was as potent as the hippocras the sisters doled out at Christmastime.

Her mind spun. She grasped moments of sensation—the rasp of his unshaven cheek against her neck, the yank and pull of his fingers on the hem of her under-tunic as he tugged it free between them, the roughness of his linen undergarments on the tender flesh between her legs. He throbbed and her body answered. She loved how he felt lodged against her, she soaked it in as swiftly as her under-tunic soaked in the cool river water. But as his kisses continued, she grew impatient with the masterful play of his hands.

"Is this to be all teasing kisses and love play, then?" She sounded breathless and husky as she pulled away from him. "Or will you finally make a woman out of me?"

"As you wish, my lady."

He thrust his hand between them and his knuckles brushed her cleft. Her whole body tensed at the intensity of the sensation. He loosed the cloth of his braies to set free his cock. She only glimpsed it— long and thick and throbbing—before he lifted her body so she balanced atop it. The tip was hot against her, *inside her.* She found herself slipping around the tip of it, gyrating her hips, searching for where it fit, feeling pressure, a sweet, burning, welcome pressure as she settled down a mite.

She groaned aloud at the feel of him so close to the ache. She heard him make a sound, too. He was grimacing, looking between them, and she looked down, too, and saw their flesh merging.

Pebbles rolled under her knee as she eased down, a little more, feeling a resistance, a stretch that bordered on pain, as her body gripped him tight.

"Easy," he said, as his fingers dug into her hips. "Easy, Maura."

She wasn't having easy, not anymore. She rolled her hips again and pressed harder. She gasped at the pinch as the resistance gave. Then the long, hard, hot length of him slid within her, all the way in, until she felt the bones of his hips against her inner thighs. She held still, breathless, as both of their bodies throbbed and his cock pulsed inside her.

She threw her head back. *So snug.* The warm summer sun caressed her face as his cock touched her deep, deep inside. She felt a fullness she'd never ever experienced and it excited her that they were here, coupling upon the banks of some river, she with her legs spread to welcome him, merging their flesh in a way too wonderful to not be forbidden.

"Are you hurt, lass?" His voice was strained.

"No," she whispered. "No."

Then he moved. She gasped at the swelling against her inner muscles. He moved again, kissing her deep inside with his cock as he had kissed her lips with his mouth. He gripped her hips and showed her how to slide up his rod and then plunge down again. She did it herself, feeling the full length of him stroking the skin inside her. She felt the insides of her thighs grow slippery and slick, like her body was licking him each time she rose up and sank down anew. He was breathing hard now, like she was breathing, for each plunge was a higher, tighter sensation—over and over and over—and he gripped her hips and made a grunting sound as he moved faster—still faster—until suddenly beyond the film of her eyelids the light intensified, and a cry gathered in her throat. She threw her head back and it was as if the sun shone so bright and so hot that the light burst over her and rained showers of sparks over her heaving body.

For moments uncounted she quivered with waves of sensation even as Colin continued moving, his cock swelling tight so that it filled her up. He thrust so hard that he lifted her knees off the riverbed. He made a strangled, grunting sound and she felt liquid warmth. And she understood yet another thing about the world that had never occurred to her—that this coupling between a man and a woman could be beautiful, could be joyous, could be as close to Heaven as anyone could come while still living on earth.

It took some time before she noticed the flow of the cool water across her knees. Spread as her legs were, her thighs began to ache. She lowered her head and looked down upon the man who'd just made her a woman.

Were she looking into a silvered mirror, she'd expect to see the same sort of expression upon her own face as she saw on his—the same half-lidded eyes, the same faint smile, the same slowing breathing. She didn't think she could speak even if she wanted to. He took her hand in his, raised it to his face, and brushed a kiss in the hollow of her palm. She rasped her hand across his unshaven cheek and bent over him, so her damp hair hung as a curtain around their faces. He thrust his hand through her hair and combed it with his fingers, as his gaze roamed over her, full and hungry with promise.

She knew with a certainty that went straight to her bones that whatever happened in the days to come, she would never regret this moment by the riverbed.

"You'll be sore, lass, if you don't climb off me."

She bit her lower lip and swung her leg over him, feeling his cock slip out. He took her in his arms and rolled her out of the water—rolling, rolling, laughing as they tumbled onto the dry grass of the riverbank.

They lay for some time. She pressed her ear against his chest to hear his racing heart. A chill breeze twisted around the wet black boughs, sending a confusion of leaves dancing upon the wind.

A strange peace flooded through her. She closed her eyes and basked in it for uncounted moments.

"I like it here." She made no effort to rise from their bed of grass as she traced little circles upon his chest. "I like lazing about on a riverbank in the middle of the day."

One eye winced open. His lips twitched.

"So is it true what they say," she said, as he made no attempt to touch her, to kiss her, to take her in his arms again, "that once a man beds a woman, he doesn't want her anymore?"

"You know that's not true, lass."

"Well, look at you. You're like a butcher's dog, lying quiet and bored beside the beef."

She expected him to roll her over in the grass and make a mockery of her words. Instead, he trailed his fingers down her spine, his gaze still on the sky above.

She lifted herself up on her elbow and frowned at him. "It's a fine pretty sight, to see you counting the boughs like a merchant counting his day's takings."

"I'm thinking."

"Aye, I can smell the wood burning."

"At Emain Macha," he said, "the master *filidh* would each day give us a theme. Then he would send us into the dark to lie on our backs to contemplate the theme, and compose a poem."

She held her tongue, surprised at his words. There was so much she didn't know about this man.

So much of his past hidden from her, so many days ahead for discovery.

If he willed it.

"It was always as cold as Hades when he sent us to task." His lips curled in a rueful smile. "The school worked only from Michaelmas to March, and the man who ran it had no will to waste good peat on a bunch of boy poets."

"It would seem easier to sleep than to think, laying in the cold like that." Odd mood he was in. "What strange things are churning in your mind?"

"Just thinking, Maura. Just thinking." Then he looked at her and his face changed. He rolled her on her back in the grass. "Help me make it stop."

She opened her arms to wrap them around his body, and then parted her thighs for his touch.

Suddenly, a voice came from the trees, calling Colin's name.

"Go away, Maguire," Colin mumbled, as he tugged the linen off her breast with his teeth.

Maguire stumbled out of the trees and skidded to a stop. She knew she should be embarrassed caught like this, Colin's mouth on her, her thighs bare to the world. She waited for a rush of shame, of regret, of guilt, but all she felt was irritation that Maguire would come bother them just when Colin was slipping his tongue across the tight peak of her right nipple.

"About time," Maguire cackled. "I was thinking I'd have to stop calling you a beard-splitter, Colin, if you didn't tumble the lass soon."

Colin raised his head. He replaced his tongue with his skillful fingers. "Go away, Maguire."

"I'll be off and on my way, then." Maguire's cackle echoed through the woods. "It's sure you've got a task before you making up for all those nights she left you with ballocks as heavy as lead—"

"Wait." A ripple of lines appeared on Colin's brow. He raised his head and went very still.

"Please." She pressed her hand over his, for Colin had stopped rolling her nipple between his fingers.

"Shhhh."

Then she heard it, too. A faint ringing through the trees, the sound of unfamiliar voices, all coming from the direction of the road.

She whispered, "Don't stop, Colin."

He said, "I hear horses."

"Oh," Maguire said, his voice bright as he backed away, "they belong to a deacon making his way to the next parish—"

"You're lying." Colin abandoned her breast altogether. "That's the jangle of a rich man's harness." He stood up and tied his braies. "Who is it, Maguire?"

"I told you, just a deacon. I thought the Abbess might want to confess—"

"For a poacher, you're the worst liar of all."

Then Colin was gone, striding back to the road.

Maura made a huff of frustration. "What were you thinking," she snapped, scrambling for her clothes, "following him out here when you knew the plan was for me to hold him fast?"

"I was thinking of saving the man's life."

"And a right bad job you did of it," she said, sweeping up her tunic, "lying like a child who ate a pie set to cooling."

"How was I to know you'd finally hike those skirts of yours? You, who've been keeping them as tight as an innkeeper's fist?"

"Never mind about my skirts." She scrambled into her overtunic. "What have you sent him off to?"

The Mudman didn't answer. He didn't have to, she saw the answer upon his grim face. She swept up her slippers and tossed her stockings over her shoulder as she followed Colin's path. She found him hidden at the woods' edge, his back pressed against a tree, gripping the bark with a hand gone white.

Beyond, upon the road, stood a horse and rider. The shiny bosses of the horse's harness gleamed in the sunshine. She must have made a noise, for the man upon the horse gave her a sharp glance as she stumbled half-dressed through the trees.

For modesty's sake, she bowed her head and slipped behind the same tree that Colin was hiding.

"But the songstress," Arnaud was saying, shrugging his massive shoulders, "she's not feeling so well, an affliction of the throat I think."

"An affliction of the throat, is it?" the man said.

"Yes, yes."

"Maybe," the man said, "she shouldn't be bathing in the cold river in the middle of the day."

Behind the tree, Maura felt her cheeks heat. She glanced at Colin but his face was as blank as stone.

"Come, come," the man continued, "I've never heard traveling players to strike such a hard bargain. Let this be the balm for your songstress's throat."

Maura heard the clink of coins.

"Tomorrow," the man said, "is the St. Vitus's Day feast. You'll be expected at the castle."

"But—"

"Don't disappoint me, minstrel." The horse's hooves scraped on the road. "More importantly, don't disappoint my master, Lord William Caddell."

CHAPTER THIRTEEN

Maura drummed her fingers against her crossed arms. She paced in front of a wattle screen, kicking up bits of chaff and hay. Here, in this musty upper room of the castle of William Caddell, she'd spent the last hours suffering Matilda's poking and painting and Arnaud's bellowed warnings, while all of the minstrels acted as if this was just another evening performance. Now the furious jig of Padraig's pipe siphoned up from the stairwell, punctuated by shouts and laughter, the clapping of hands, and the shuffle of dancing feet. Just another St. Vitus's Day feast. As if they all weren't deep in the heart of the home of a man Colin intended to kill.

Soon Arnaud would be coming for her to sing before Lord William. She closed her eyes and pressed her fists against them. She would sing, aye, she would sing. If she had her way, she would sing Colin—wherever he was—right out of a hangman's noose.

"Hello, Maura."

She dropped her hands and there he was,

outlined in the glow of the open stairway. She flushed with fresh anger that this afternoon, without a word of good-bye, he'd disappeared into the woods less than a mile from the gates of Shrule.

"Where have you *been?*" Her bells jangled as she trembled with agitation. "The twins and Matilda were chewing their fingers off with worry—"

"That worry will be done, soon enough."

He sounded deadly calm. He stood wide-legged in the portal. With the glow pouring in around his figure she could imagine the gleam of armor plates upon his elbows, the glitter of chain mail upon his legs. Though his gaze was fixed upon her, she sensed one part of him was already looking through her.

"Colin." She swallowed what tasted suspiciously like a sob, "just lay a curse upon the man, as you did O'Kelly back in Tuam."

"A hundred thousand curses have already been rained upon him and they slide off his back as if the devil forged his armor."

"Can't you just—"

"No."

He crossed the room in two long strides and dragged her up into his arms. He seized her hair, arched her head back, and muffled her cry with his mouth. She wanted to curl his tunic in her fists and shake him, shake him, shake him. She wanted to scream until her voice wore raw. She wanted all these things, even as she pounded on his chest only to fling her arms around his neck.

He wore a leather strap across his chest fitted with a buckle that bit into her breast. He pushed her behind the screen until they slammed against the castle wall. He dragged his hands down her body. She gasped, broke the kiss, and arched against him.

He yanked the borrowed silks above her knees. She dug furrows into his shoulders as his tongue slipped around the lobe of her ear and then the hollow behind. She should be pleading now—while he wanted her, while he was vulnerable—but she couldn't speak with the rush of feeling.

This was no soft roadside loving. Her blood coursed through her, wanting him all the more now that she knew what it felt like to be with him. He yanked down the neckline and palmed out her breast. Lowering his head, he sucked her nipple between his lips. She squeezed his hair as he suckled her puckered nipple, over and over and over, over and over, over and over, and she knew that if he asked her to be his traveling whore for days uncounted, she would beg him to take her with no second thoughts.

Then he lifted his head, leaving her breast wet and cooling. His eyes were in shadow, but his breathing rasped. Holding her gaze, he thrust his hand between her legs. She peeled open her thighs to give him leave, and he seized one of her knees to open her legs more. As he braced that knee high upon his hip, she lurched to one side, unbalanced, but he pressed his body against her—pinning her to the wall.

She made a noise she didn't know she could make. His cock pressed against her cleft. He shifted his weight until the hot tip of him nudged through to the eager heart of her body. She stretched her hiked leg to the limits of the sinew, wanting him to fill her up. Once positioned, he grasped her buttocks and lifted her whole body against the wall. With his cock he stroked her from front to back, rubbing, rubbing, only to pull himself back and stroke between the folds again. Her throat filled with a moan, for she was sore and tender but she felt everything, the pounding of the veins in his shaft and the shared dampness he spread over her inner thighs.

Take me, Colin. Take me. Take me. She didn't realize she was speaking aloud until he tightened and braced himself, squeezing her hips in his hands as he thrust through the clench of her muscles. She heard the echo of her own cry at the feel of him stretching her open. He stood there for a moment, his face in her throat, his breath hot against her collarbone. Then he jerked back, leaving her gasping, clasping for handfuls of his tunic until he thrust again, a short thrust. Then again. Another. Then another. She stretched for him, arching her back to increase the contact, trying to hike her leg higher to make room for him. At each stroke she thought she would burst from the sensation, but he jerked back again, leaving her aching. She sensed by the tightness of his shoulder muscles and the cramp of his abdomen that he was controlling this, that he was winding her to the very razor's edge of pleasure.

Please…

His face was tight, his eyes intense, and a muscle moved in his jaw. His hands dug into her hips almost to the point of pain. Just as he pulled out from the clench of her muscles again, she bucked against him, wanting more. He made a throaty sound and shoved his cock so hard into her that she threw her head back. He started to grunt and she saw a sheen of sweat on his forehead. She sensed a desperation behind this loving, the same knuckle-gripping, bloody-toothed desperation he'd shown in the fights he'd had in so many village squares, all but putting his jaw in the way of one meaty fist after another.

Again and again, he stroked, filling her, filling her, filling her, her buttocks slamming against the wall with each thrust. He grit his teeth, and she saw veins bulging in his throat, and then sensation swamped her—a rush of blood to her head, a snapping of bonds, as if something set loose within her, something wild, raging. She groaned as she felt him swell inside her. She closed her eyes as her senses lifted, and she felt hurled off to a bright place, knowing nothing but the hurried stroke of Colin's hardness inside her, the vibration of his groan, the hot sensation of being washed with his seed.

She floated and floated and floated and floated, reveling in the feeling, her heart pounding, her body held up by his clenched hands. Slowly, she drifted downwards, sidling into the musty room with its drafts. She became conscious of the bulk of Colin's shoulders holding her against the wall, his face buried against her cheek, her fingernails snagged in the wool of his tunic, his cock still throbbing inside her.

Then the sound of someone clearing his throat filtered through the fog.

Damn it. She blinked her eyes open to see Arnaud's ponderous shadow cast upon the screen.

"I waited as long as I could." Arnaud's voice was pitched low. "Lord William is calling for the songstress."

No. Panic drove away the last of the languor. *No.*

Colin pulled away. Her hair tangled in the buckle of his leather strap—he stopped to set it free. Her feet jarred against the floor and her silken tunic tumbled free of its folds. He gripped her by the shoulders until she found the strength to stand.

She searched his face, but there was no mistaking the tightness of his jaw.

"Colin—"

He placed a finger upon her lips. Then he trailed his hand over her cheek, down her jaw, her throat, then up again, into the tangled sweep of her hair. Maura stared at the familiar fall of that lock of his black hair, the crook of his nose, the mouth that now lacked a smile, and she thought, *I can't save him.*

She unlocked her fingers from his neck. Something soft brushed her knuckles. That's when she realized he wore a quiver of feather-tipped arrows across his back.

"Have done with it, will you?" Arnaud paced in a circle beyond the screen. "The whole hall awaits."

Colin backed away and fumbled with something in the bag slung around his waist. Seizing her hand, he pressed into it a circular brooch, winking with bits of colored gems. Across the diameter of the metal curled a visage of a long-necked swan.

"The MacEgan brooch," he said.

She shook her head, not understanding.

"If a child is born from this night, I would see that he has a name."

Then he was gone, his cloak snapping as he whirled around the screen, his footsteps silent upon the stairs—moving so fast that he had already disappeared from sight by the time she ran around the screen to follow.

Arnaud seized her before she reached the door. "Colin will do what he must. And now, you must do what you must."

No.

She shook her head even as she knew she had no

choice. Her body still throbbed from their lovemaking, but her mind had gone numb, and Arnaud didn't release her until she stopped shaking. She stumbled down the stairs, squeezing the brooch in her hand, hoping to glimpse Colin. Instead she found herself in the main hall.

She swept the room with her gaze. On one side stood a single trestle table, covered in white damask. A half dozen well-dressed nobles sat behind it, sharing a chalice of gold set with jewels, the crumbs of honey wafers littering their clothes. Retainers milled around, red-cheeked from dancing to Padraig's pipe. A grand tapestry swayed behind the trestle table, moved by the drafts that sang through the castle—a depiction of the slaying of a stag, the arrows jutting bloody out of the beast's hide.

Colin was nowhere in sight.

A piercing sensation brought her attention to the brooch. She'd held it so tight the pin had burrowed into her skin. She swiftly covered it up with her fingers and slipped it into one of the many secret pockets in her tunic. Then she walked into the hall.

Men paused with cups to lips, eyeing her from the tip of her head to the toes of her boots as conversation fell to a murmur and then a hush. Arnaud had made his way around her and now he gestured as he told a romanticized tale about her being found on the convent steps—an abandoned babe with the voice of an angel. Fingar, planted on a stool by one of the roof-trees, strummed his harp. She must sing now. Colin was somewhere in the shadows, and she must sing like an angel, to stop a good man from becoming a murderer.

Arnaud fell silent. All eyes were upon her. She

waited for the blind harpist to begin the plucking. Then she closed her eyes and let the song shimmer through her.

"The Minstrel to the war is gone…"

Colin, she thought, listen to me.

"His father's sword he has girded on, and his wild harp slung behind him…"

It was an old song that Padraig had taught her, though she'd changed the words. As she sang it she became aware of a rustling in the room, a shuffling of feet. Though her heart trembled, she opened her eyes. She startled, because a nobleman stumbled to a stop before her.

She knew, by the richness of his clothes, that he could be none other than Lord William Caddell.

The song trailed off in her throat. Fingar halted mid-strum and an expectant silence engulfed the room. Maura stared at this older man, his salt-and-pepper hair cropped above the shoulder, waiting for him to say something. His lips hung open to show a wine-stained tongue, and as he took a step closer she was overwhelmed with the sickly scent of cloves.

This is the man Colin would kill. She waited with her heart pounding for an arrowhead to burst from beneath his tunic, for blood to bathe the fine silk.

"My senses must be leaving me." The Englishman spoke in a whisper, then he raised his voice. "Richard, come here."

A man, sporting a long mustache in the Irish way, emerged from the shadows. "Father?"

"Does she remind you of anyone?"

The young man gave her a cursory look. "No."

"She is the very image of Eleanor," the nobleman said. "It is as if your mother has risen from the dead."

A spurt of panic gripped her as gasps rippled through the crowd. The man must be crazed, deep in a forgetful dotage. How could Colin think of killing this shadow of a man, no matter what he might have done? As his son took him by the arm, Maura lowered her gaze and backed away, but he called for her to wait.

She ventured, "Milord?"

"That tale the Gascon told," he said, "about you being a foundling. Is it true? Or did he tell it for amusement's sake?"

"I am a foundling, milord."

"What convent took you in?"

She hesitated. She had told no one the name, lest the tale find its way back to the Abbess or the sisters. They would be devastated to know she worked as a common player with a traveling troupe. They would wear their knees out in prayer for her redemption—a redemption she wasn't sure she wanted anymore.

But this bleary-eyed baron waited for an answer, and the whole hall listened, and it came to her that Colin might be holding back from shooting an arrow only because she stood so close to his enemy.

That was something, at least. "I was found at the Convent of Killoughy. Outside of Killeigh."

Lord William's brows twitched. "How old are you, child?"

"I was found in the harvest time in the Year of Our Lord 1285."

"The same year you were born, Richard," Lord William said, glancing at his son. Disappointment rippled across his features. "This cannot be then."

Sympathy speared through her. *He's just an old*

man. A man like any other.

"Forgive me, my dear girl." Lord William reached for her hand as if to kiss it. "These past years I'm full of imaginings—" His words ended on a swallow. He yanked at her hand. "By God! By God!"

Then the whole room was full of shouts and exclamations, and the son stepped in to grasp her hand, the two of them tugging on her finger to better see her ring. Her heart dropped and her throat closed up and it was as if the smoke of the rush lights choked her along with the stench of cloves.

"This," Lord William stuttered, "is Eleanor's ring."

"It's stolen," the son Richard said, eyeballing her. "It's a trick, Father, it's a minstrel's trick."

"It's *not* stolen," she said, surprised at her own audacity. "It was in my swaddling clothing."

Then out of the shadows barreled an older woman. Her veil flew off her graying hair as she looked at Maura and then flung herself at Lord William's feet.

"Forgive an old woman, my lord."

"Have you gone mad?" Lord William bellowed, glaring at her in annoyance. "Up, woman, and off with you—"

"Hear me," the woman cried, rising to her knees as guards surrounded her. "By the blood of the Virgin Mary, I will swear to this. This foundling, this songstress—she is your daughter, and Lord Richard's twin."

CHAPTER FOURTEEN

Colin had once witnessed the spectacle of the taking of Jerusalem by the First Crusade, played in a Gascon noble's home by a group of Italian mummers. Complete with a pool of water, roaring lions, flowers springing from meadows, grapevines growing long to mark the passage of time, and showers of scented water and sweetmeats. A spectacle so rich in machinations that he'd spent hours with the men as they dismantled the pieces, trying to figure out the magic of it all.

Yet no troupe of Italian mummers could match the drama taking place in the hall below. No guild actors could play these parts better: the stunned, long-lost daughter; the teary, amazed father; the weeping maidservant, prostrate, blurting out an impossible tale of a babe hurried away in the midst of night, of a dying mother so fervid in her religious beliefs that she'd chosen to secretly send away the second-born of her newborn twins rather than be thought of as a woman who had lain with two men.

And he himself, the thwarted avenger, standing just off the stage with his bow half-strung, flexing his fists as he watched his enemy claim his lover as flesh and blood—as he watched the chance for his vengeance snatched away.

Colin curled his fingers tight over the bow. It was not too late. Caddell stood there—as straight-backed and proud as the day he led his Englishmen into MacEgan lands. Caddell stood there, just in range of his arrow, and so stood the end of ten long years of delay.

He slid the arrow back, pulled the sinew tight. One single arrow. Through the heart. The vow would be fulfilled. His father would be avenged. He would be worthy of the name MacEgan. It all would be over, finally.

And Maura would lose the father she'd just met, and then curse his name for the rest of her days.

No. *No.* This was all a scripted farce, it had to be. Yet his fingers paused on the sinew. He crouched in the shadow of the stairwell, above the heads of the crowd. The haze of the smoke settled like a transparent blue cloud. She stood as still as stone, listening to the maidservant's babbling, her hands still caught in Caddell's grip. Her hair shimmered like dark gold in the rush light, and he found himself remembering the feel of it against his cheek.

A bubble of laughter threatened in his chest. He choked it down, for he knew it for what it was. If he barked it aloud, he'd tumble off the tight rope he'd been walking on for too many years and there was no telling where madness would bring him.

What difference did it make? He yanked the sinew back again and squinted down the length of the slender arrow. Maura could curse him to Hell, because she would believe this impossible story that she was Caddell's daughter. But he wouldn't hear her curses, for he'd be hanging on a gibbet before tomorrow at sundown. He pulled the bow taut. He fixed his sight upon the lower tip of the embroidered neck-slit of William the Black's surcoat, the cloth that covered his black beating heart.

He willed the old memory back to him. The acrid stench of blood. The cries of wounded men and horses. The sight of his father laid low in the mud. Fergus's blazing blue eyes defying the coming of death, his father's fist curled in Colin's boiled leather tunic, willing him with his last bit of strength to vow a death upon William the Black Caddell, the man who had stolen everything from the MacEgans, who had blinded one brother and killed all the rest and stolen what should be theirs.

The man whose life hung at the tip of Colin's iron arrow. The man who stood there in the hall claiming he'd spawned one such as Maura.

Shoot him.

The sinew cut into his fingers.

One single arrow.

Through the heart. A kinder death than the Englishman deserved.

Shoot him.

And all would know that Colin MacEgan had returned from ten years of exile to avenge the death of Fergus MacEgan, to avenge the injustices rained upon all the MacEgans, to make a man of himself.

His fingertips tingled.

Do it.

His work would be done, and so would his life.

And so would Maura's.

With a muffled curse, he raised the arrow off the bow. The sinew snapped against his bare wrist. In four quick strides he descended the stairs, then pushed the door of the castle open to the night, ignoring the guards he startled into wakefulness, not bothering to hide his face with the minstrel's mask he'd used to slip into the castle without being recognized.

He marched blindly, conscious only of the balm of the air rushing in and out of his lungs, the mocking gleam of the stars above, the burn in his chest. He stomped over the inner moat, through the portcullis, over another trough, through a break in another wall, into the dark maze of the streets with its night people beckoning from the alleys, into the blackness of his thoughts.

He'd lost his one opportunity to fulfill an old vow.

So what was he now? A man without pride, without honor.

Not a man at all.

Maura let herself be led up into the darkness at the top of the stairs while below, in the hall, the guests of William Caddell murmured in excited whispers as they found their way to their rooms, their pallets, their horses. The servant girl who Maura followed raised her candle as they passed the shadow of several doors. Maura expected Colin to jump out at any moment, to confront her, to take her away. Where was Colin with his iron-tipped arrow and his silent resolve? What was he thinking about this turn of events? She needed someone to pinch her out of this strange dream.

At the end of the hall, the servant pushed open a heavy door. Maura stepped into the room and gazed at a canopied bed with rich damask hangings, the kind of bed the laywoman Sabine would have loved.

The servant closed the door and placed the candle on the mantel. "My lord asked me to fetch for you some of Lady Elizabeth's—your sister's—nightshifts." She gestured to some gossamer fabric lying across the bed. "I'll help you undress."

Maura stared at the servant. Everything about this girl was neat, from the pressed sweep of her wimple, to the scrubbed pinkness of her cheeks, and the slight questioned raise of a single brow. Though the servant's face remained impassive, Maura sensed an element of scorn, as though the servant knew that she had been forced to wait upon a guest well beneath the stature of those she was accustomed to serving.

Maura turned away from her. She didn't want to change clothes—she wanted to sneak away and seek out Colin and try to make sense of all this—but she found herself raising her arms as she was bid, turning at the servant's urging, letting herself be stripped of Matilda's borrowed silks until she was bare and shivering with something more than the kiss of a cool draft. When the servant tossed the silks on the bed, the MacEgan brooch fell out of a pocket and winked at her from the bedclothes.

Suddenly she felt like two women in one body. One wanted to race screaming out of this room. The other was determined to stay and meet the sisters and brother she hadn't known existed until this very night.

Colin had insisted that things like this didn't

happen. He said that noble infants weren't whisked away by maidservants and left on the convent steps. Yet in front of a room full of guests, Lord William Caddell had claimed her as his own, and it all rained upon her head again, the whole impossibility of it: Lord William's over-bright eyes, the teary confession of the nursemaid, the excited din of the crowd, the eye-smarting smoke of rush lights, the chill of a golden chalice in her hands, the vinegary taste of Gascon wine, the swelling urge to shake her head, to back away, to say *no, no, this can't be.*

She'd been searching for an Irish *mother.*

A soft knock on the door made her start. The servant pulled a shift over her head, then wrapped her in a robe that was stiff and warmly quilted. As the heavy door swung open, she felt her heart stumble with hope to see Colin, but it was Lord William Caddell who stood in the frame, looking her over with those rheumy eyes.

She couldn't help herself. She searched his face, taking in the stubborn shape of his chin, the wrinkled span of his brow, the pale color of his cheek, the dull color of his remaining hair under the nightcap he wore, seeking some common feature that she could set upon and say, yes, yes, and then feel a deep tug of familiarity, a sense of homecoming.

"Wait outside," Lord William ordered the servant. "I want a moment alone with my daughter."

She winced at the word and then hid her shaking hands in the sleeves of the robe, telling herself she must be calm, she must be wise, she mustn't let this man who claimed to be her father know that only hours ago she'd made love with an Irishman who wanted him dead.

The door closed quietly behind him. He took a few steps deeper into the room, his gaze steady, assessing, very unlike the bewildered look he'd given her when he first laid eyes upon her in the hall.

"I understand," he said, folding his fingers together, "that you may be as shocked by tonight's revelation as I am."

Speechless, she twisted her ring around her finger.

"In the days to come, there will be many people questioning the truth of the story. You understand that, yes?"

"I will be first among them," she confessed. "I can scarcely believe it myself."

"Oh, but I need you to believe, Maura."

His lips lifted in a half-smile, and one bushy eyebrow arched above his eye, and Maura wondered how he could be so at ease when her whole world had upended.

"We'll begin with a little honesty. I expect you will tell me everything I need to know. Your position here depends upon it."

"My position?"

"Your position in this house, as my long-lost daughter, a young woman worthy to carry the name Caddell and all the benefits that go along with that."

"Benefits."

"Come, you are not so innocent, I think." He splayed his fingers to indicate the warm, well-appointed room. "Many might take advantage of such a situation. I am a rich man, as you can plainly see."

Lord William Caddell. Protector of Kilcolgan, Lord of Athenry, the Baron of Shrule. The man her lover had sworn to kill.

"Come," he urged into the silence. "You must understand what I'm saying. I know you haven't lived in such fine lodgings while traveling the roads with a minstrel troupe."

"I've only been among them a few weeks, my lord."

"Is that so?"

"I grew up in a convent, and before these last weeks, I hadn't been beyond my village, not ever."

He raised an amused brow. "Make sure to speak of that in the coming days. It'll serve you well."

She blinked, not understanding.

"To silence the naysayers," he explained. "There will be many. That's why my advisers will insist that I seek verification for the story that you are the foundling of which that nursemaid spoke. I'll be writing to the Abbess at Killoughy tomorrow morning. Will she confirm everything you've told me?"

Maura couldn't imagine how the Abbess would react upon receiving a parchment with an English baron's seal, one that asked about *her*, no less. "The lady Abbess will confirm it. I'm sure they're all still worrying about me, I left the convent without warning."

"Are you absolutely sure?"

She wondered why he was questioning *her* when it was *he* who'd claimed her as his daughter. "My lord—"

"Father," he corrected sharply. "Best you start calling me that."

She bit her lip and wondered why he didn't speak with more warmth than authority, like he had in the hall below. Maybe this whole evening was a cruel farce. Maybe he suffered from bouts of madness. Maybe his son would be the next person through the door, asking her to gather her things and leave with the minstrels in the morning, when Lord William was sure to forget the drama of the night.

Her heart leapt at the thought of leaving with Colin, even as she silently scolded herself for not paying more mind to what was being offered to her.

"Father," she began, the word sticking in her throat, "it seems you may have some doubts about my provenance yourself."

"I have no doubts." He didn't seem in the least bit dull-witted, standing here staring at her with such intensity, combing his fingers through the pointed tuft of his beard. "You are my daughter, I have proclaimed it so."

She twisted the ring again, anxious for him to leave so she could seek out Colin or even the minstrels in the stables.

"So to start," he said, "you must start living like a daughter of a baron. Dressed," he continued, "in the finest clothes, fed at my own table, and tended by many servants. You will find your stay exceedingly comfortable."

She spread her arms to indicate the warm robe. "I thank you for your kindness."

"In return for that kindness," he continued, "you must begin to behave like the daughter of a baron."

Maura blinked. There had been no daughters of barons at the convent, but there had been many daughters of the lesser aristocracy. She had been closest to Sabine, a laywoman who adored pretty things, like birds and squirrels and jewels and ivory combs and making pets of little girls.

"You must be modest," he continued, his voice gravelly. "No more of those obscene silks, no more rouging your cheeks. No minstrel stories, or bawdy puns or language not fitting for church."

She thought of Maguire Mudman and his riddles, Matilda and her painted lips, the twins and their easy laughter, and felt a strange tug in her heart.

"My dear," he exclaimed, nodding his head. "You play the innocent well, I'm quite impressed."

"Innocent?"

"Indeed. Remember, though, I have eyes in all places—in the castle, the stables, in churches, on the bridges, and everywhere on the road." He made a grunting noise that he stifled by clearing his throat. "I'm not the failing old man my son wishes me to be."

"I…I don't understand."

"I suspect you do, despite your protestations." He turned and headed toward the door. "It may take a while for you to adjust to your new position, but I think you'll find that the benefits outweigh the drawbacks."

"Drawbacks?"

He paused, clearly irritated. "You're carrying my name, and my protection, and I expect a certain amount of decorum."

"Decorum."

"Must I be blunt?" He curled his fingers over the edge of the door. "As of today, Maura of Killeigh, there will be no more swiving in the fields with minstrels."

He closed the door behind him, bolting it from the outside.

CHAPTER FIFTEEN

Colin urged his mount up yet another slope in the foothills of the Partry Mountains. Rain splattered from the trees, soaking his six-colored cloak, now glued to his horse's flanks. He backhanded a rivulet off his chin and urged his mount around the crackle of gorse that choked the old trail.

Something hissed by his cheek and then *thunked* into an oak nearby. To his right, the shaft of an arrow quivered.

A voice sifted from the sky. "Who comes into MacEgan lands?"

He recognized the lilt of the Connemara dialect as easily as he'd once recognized musical scales by the ringing of pitched chimes.

"I am Colin." He sensed more than one pair of eyes upon him, more than one bow drawn against him. "Son of Fergus MacEgan."

Colin's tongue rolled around the surname as it would roll around a bone found within the meat of a fish. It had been ten years since he'd called himself by it, and longer than that since he'd considered himself worthy of it.

A man dropped out of a tree and landed flat-footed upon the trail. Beneath a tunic of deerskin, knotted sinew held the warrior's hose to his legs. The warrior strode closer, assessing him with narrowed eyes. Colin didn't recognize Aedh the blacksmith, not at first. All that remained of the once burly vassal was a tunic that caved in around his belly and cheeks that had sunk deep into his skull. But the drooping mustache was the same, as russet as autumn leaves.

"Unless Fergus himself has risen from the grave," Aedh said, lowering his bow, "then it's Colin for sure."

Men dropped from the trees like ripe apples in September, men in ragged dress with wood-handled knives strapped to their waists. He saw among them familiar, older faces—scarred, the skin tight to the bone, all with eyes full of a strange brightness.

Aedh said, "Your brother Murtough returned yesterday and told us he'd found you alive in Kilcolgan."

"I sent him ahead."

"Brendan, your cousin, holds the rod of the clan now."

Colin tried to hide his surprise. He'd been led to believe, by the Connacht exile he'd stumbled across in London, that Brendan was all but dead.

That was months ago.

"Aye, Brendan lives still." The blacksmith curled his fist into the bridle of Colin's horse. "I'll lead you to him."

Colin tugged on the reins. "I know the way."

"Not anymore you don't. We've more than one

trap set for the likes of the English along this path, should they show their faces here. We move from mountain to mountain with the change in seasons, and watch the paths well."

Like rabbits beneath the sight of a fox.

Colin allowed Aedh to lead him down a path wide enough for only one horse at a time. They hugged the edge of the woods, keeping quick in the shadows, though nothing disturbed this rain-drenched world but the leap of a roe deer. They sifted their way through the narrow pass that led up to the old MacEgan stronghold, but rather than head toward it, they took a sharp turn to the east, up a rocky ledge, through a pasture speckled with bow-backed cattle, to a clearing beneath a blue haze of smoke.

The makeshift homestead consisted of a shallow trench surrounding a cluster of wattle buildings. As they came closer, Colin noticed men clattering dice against a stump. Women bickered over an open fire and half-naked children chased a stray dog around a tree. Colin heard the ripple of his name across the land, a strange murmuring—*cullin, cullin, cullin, cullin.*

He was used to drawing attention whenever entering a settlement. But during his time as a minstrel, it was laughter and joy and applause that had greeted him. Not the sight of women clasping their hands against their chests, or children reaching out to brush their fingertips across the hem of his cloak. Not the sight of warriors rising from their duties, their faces blanching as if he were a ghost.

In their gaze he saw the look they had given to his father Fergus, all those years ago, when Fergus bright in his new-forged chain mail, Fergus with the bloodlust of righteousness in his eye, had set out to take back for the MacEgans what had been seized from them.

He wanted to shout for them to stop.

Men stood sentinel at the door of the mead hall. The door swung open as Colin approached. Brendan MacEgan stumbled out on the arm of another warrior, his king's cloak of many colors wrapped around chain mail. At the sight of his cousin, Colin hissed a breath through his teeth. Brendan was Fergus's brother's oldest son, older than Colin by less than fifteen years. Colin remembered him as a man quick of thought, strong of opinion, and unstoppable in battle. Now his cousin stood in the doorway little more than hardened flesh upon bones. Only his black eyes showed life, fierce beneath half-drooping lids.

"Colin." Brendan spoke the name in a gravelly voice. "We thought you dead."

"Aye." Seizing the horse's mane, Colin swung himself off the beast's back and stood before his cousin. "But you sent me off so that I might live."

A silence settled over the clearing. Colin knew the source of it. More than one cousin or brother or uncle had killed his own kin for the sake of power. Looking at this proud but wasted warrior, Colin understood why Aedh had spoken of Brendan's recovery with weariness. These men anticipated a change of leadership—hoped for it—for as Colin stood in their midst, they didn't grip their sword to protect the man they now called The MacEgan.

Brendan shuffled a foot. Grasping the shoulder of his guardsman, he started to bend a knee. Colin stepped forward and seized him before his cousin could sully his hose upon the wet ground.

"No."

Brendan raised his hooded gaze. Beyond the etching of weariness, Colin could see the wheels of his cousin's sharp mind turning. It was Brendan who had stayed behind with the clan when Colin had been hustled onto the boat out of Galway Bay. It was Brendan who hid in these hills what was left of the MacEgans, their cattle, and their women. It was Brendan who had kept these clansmen alive while Colin danced under the sun and drank in alehouses and made love to the women of Gascony.

Brendan had earned the title. Colin had not.

"The MacEgan," Colin said loudly, "does not bow to his heir."

And with a rush Colin remembered when he had come charging back from Emain Macha with a harp of horsehair and thongs, his head roiling with wild swaggering poems. He'd played a song of war to the elders. He'd been like a torch to dry tinder, starting a conflagration that would swallow everything— everything but this ragged band of clansmen clinging to life in the barren slopes of a place not even the English bothered to conquer.

Now he felt a hot rush of emotion as he turned to meet the eyes of those watching him, seeing how dirty his people were, how worn, how thin, how wide their eyes rested upon him. The years under the eye of William Caddell had taken their toll: His people had forgotten who they were. They'd lost their pride.

That much, a bard could change.

"There will be time enough to choose a new king," Colin said, "when William Caddell is dead."

Colin swung Fingar's harp off his back. With the old poem singing in his ears, he set his fingers to the strings.

CHAPTER SIXTEEN

The Caddell household ran on a schedule as rigid as the bells of the convent of Killoughy. Precisely at Sext, Maura pattered across the rushes of the main hall in the donjon to take her place next to Lord Richard—her twin brother. In the weeks that she'd been here, she'd discovered that to be late for the midday meal was a sin almost as egregious as that of helping harvest carrots on a warm afternoon with the kitchen servants in the castle garden.

She heard the whispering as she crossed the hall. Wherever she walked, whatever she did, that buzzing always followed her, cruel words spoken just loud enough for her to hear. *Look at her, dressed up in Lady Elizabeth's tunics, fit to split them at the seams. Look at her walking around as though she's queen of the place, as proud as a cock—and she has had enough of them, I wager.*

Her cheeks burned by the time she sidled into her place. Fortunately, Lord William strode in through the front door and put an end to the muttering. A knight of advanced years walked by his side. She recognized Sir Maurice, one of Lord William's vassals, who was introduced to her in the early days. Lord William gestured Sir Maurice to the place beside him, then seated himself in the chair at the head of the table. He nodded to his son, his daughters, and his vassals as they sat down too.

Lord William's gaze rested upon her a moment longer, as it always did, as he eyed every detail of her hair and dress. She could tell by the slight incline of his head that he approved of the blue tunic she'd labored over these past days, though she thought she caught a hint of a frown when his gaze settled upon the embroidery stitched around the neckline. In the solitude of her room, with Nutmeg dozing on her shoulder, she had found herself stitching with fine golden thread the swirls and whirls of ancient Celtic patterns, the rounds of Celtic crosses, as if by needling the designs into her clothing she could somehow convince herself she was still Irish-born.

Rebellion spurted through her. She'd spent a lifetime as a kitchen maid in a convent more Irish than English. She couldn't instantly turn into one of his other daughters, with their lisping talk and wasteful ways, who flirted with the castle vassals with a skill that would put Matilda and the twins to shame. She'd approached those half-sisters several times, yearning to get to know them better, but they'd glared at her, mute, as if she were still wearing minstrel bells and painting her cheeks red.

For the hundredth time, she wondered what had happened to the troupe. The very morning after the revelation, she'd slipped off to the stables to seek Colin, Arnaud, Matilda—anyone—but found the place deserted but for Nutmeg's basket, hanging on a post, and her quivering pet hiding in the rafters. Maura couldn't have been in the stables more than a few minutes before a flustered servant girl barreled in, breathless. Maura asked the girl what had happened to the minstrels, and the girl told her they'd left in the night. When Maura asked her *where, how, why,* the servant shut her mouth so tight that a blacksmith with pliers couldn't pull the truth from her.

Not for the first time, she wondered with a pang if the twins were dancing down some road again while Padraig piped their way to yet another fair.

Her reverie was interrupted when a fleet of servants arrived with the first course. On the table they set a flock of roasted partridges and quails seasoned with rosemary and a school of carp swimming in a sauce tart with a spice she'd never tasted before. She picked at the sauce-drenched meat upon the trencher bread she shared with Richard. The thickness of the sauce clung to her teeth, her tongue, her throat. It was all too rich, but she didn't dare say anything. The last time she mentioned that the cook of this house had a heavy hand with the spices—an expensive habit, she knew, having once been in charge of the same—she'd received nothing but a frown of disapproval from Lord William, along with the high-pitched giggling of her younger half-siblings.

Now she contented herself dreaming of wild rabbit roasted over a fire under the bright blue sky.

"You're not eating enough, dear sister."

She glanced up at Richard. He hadn't spoken a word to her since that night she'd been discovered. Her so-called twin spent every meal sitting ramrod-straight by her side, grinding his jaw.

She said, "I'm not used to such rich fare."

"That doesn't surprise me." Richard nudged a piece of partridge breast to her side of the trencher bread. "Still, you should eat while you can. Riches like this may disappear as quickly as they came."

Maura took the meat but not the bait. He held no faith in Lord William's story of her birth. The more she looked at the young man who was her twin, the more she doubted as well. In coloring, she supposed there was a resemblance. They were both fair-skinned and had light brown hair. But Richard's eyes were a muddy brown, like a churned-up springtime river, and his face far more angular than her own.

"Eat, Maura." He did something strange with her name, rolling over the 'r' in a way that hinted of insolence. "I beseech you."

She glanced at the trencher bread and saw that he poked with the end of his knife a dead beetle. His lips curled in a cat's smile as he lifted their shared wineglass to his lips and drank it to the dregs.

"Richard, you surprise me," she said, keeping her voice neutral so as not to attract attention. "A man grown, and yet you're still playing with beetles. What shall I find next? A frog in my stockings? Mice set loose upon my bed?"

"I wager your bed is crowded enough."

"And yours as empty as last year's wine barrel," she countered. "Why is that, Richard? Are you too busy playing with your stick-boats upon the moat?"

Richard's fair face flushed. "My bed is full enough, and with better women than you."

"Kitchen maids and laundresses, I hear."

"Better kitchen maids and laundresses," he said, with a hiss in his voice, "than a common whore plucked from the road."

"Shall I tell our father what you just called me?" She ignored the fury tightening her throat. "Here, with so many ears listening?"

"You can tell *my* father," he said, "whatever you'd like. Tonight, when he fucks you again."

She went very still at the words. Suddenly, it all pieced together. Her stepmother Lady Isabelle refused to even look at Maura when she passed her in the hall. And Maura remembered the whispers in the garden about Lord William's mistress, a mistress that everyone in this room apparently believed was *her*.

She spoke without thinking. "Do you want to know what the kitchen girls say about you, dear Richard? They say, *quick, quick, Richard is quick, lean right over and you hardly feel the prick—*"

"Quiet your filthy tongue!"

Richard shot up out of his seat. She leaned away and summoned false tears so quickly that she found herself ruing her decision not to join Maguire and Matilda in the minstrel plays.

"Richard?" Lord William said into the tense silence. "Is something amiss?"

Maura watched the shift of Richard's jaw as he debated whether to say anything. Whatever Richard *did* say, she was sure Lord William would include it among his litany when her father took her aside later to list her failings. For now, seeing Richard squirm in indecision was worth her act of petty vengeance.

The Mudman would have been so proud.

"Forgive me, Father." Richard flexed white-knuckled hands as he settled back on the bench. "Nothing of import, just a…sibling argument."

"As my eldest son," Lord William said, "I would think your attention would be on this side of the table, where there *is* a discussion of import."

"Yes, Father."

"We'll be sending some men into Lord Maurice's lands. He is having trouble again with the MacEgans."

She tightened her grip on the silver knife so it wouldn't clatter upon the table.

"There's an Irishman recently arrived in the area." Sir Maurice hiked an elbow upon the table. "He claims he's the son of Fergus MacEgan."

The world receded but for the echo of that name.

"He's the youngest son." Lord William chewed and swallowed a hunk of quail. "We assumed he'd gone into hiding because we haven't seen him in a decade. He spent most of his youth training to be one of those Irish bards."

"You mean an Irish spy." Sir Maurice raised hairy brows so upswept Maura was sure he'd combed them that way. "Well, this son looks for all the devil like his father, I've been told. All the scattered MacEgans have rallied under his banner."

"Ah, my dear friend." Lord William thudded his knife down and grasped his wine cup. "When I received your message, I feared that there was more to this visit than a renewal of an old friendship."

"I meant not to salt your meat with such bad spice, nor spoil good company with the ghost of troubles past." Maurice glanced down the table, his gaze settling only for a moment upon her. "Let us talk of other things."

"You tell us of the death of kings then wish to talk about horse-breeding." Lord William's face crinkled in grim humor. "It's good to see that years away from war have not changed you."

Vaguely, Maura was aware of the shuffle of servants around the table, the removal of the platters for the next course. Some part of her mind registered the gamey scent of venison and the sharpness of new cheese, but her attention was elsewhere.

"Frankly, Lord William," Maurice said, as he sliced himself a sliver of cheese, "if I thought this man—Colin—was no more than another MacEgan determined to lift my cattle, then I'd have seen to the MacEgans as I always have. But this man is different, as I've seen to my detriment in the latest skirmish."

Skirmish?

Richard glanced at her and she realized she had spoken aloud. She dropped her gaze to the hunk of cheese. She must be wary. Her interest in such affairs would take too much explaining, and her thoughts whirled too wildly for lies.

Maurice continued. "He has rallied more MacEgans than I knew existed in those dreary mountains. And now he's sunk his teeth into the castle at Fahy."

Fahy.

Maura remembered the name, remembered Colin talking about it upon the hill outside of Kilcolgan. He was heading in that direction, so he said. There, in Fahy, was the old castle-keep of the MacEgans. She remembered the cow-path that led off the road a mile or so before Shrule, the path in the woods into which Colin disappeared before the minstrel troupe trudged onward to Lord William's castle.

"That castle at Fahy," Lord William said, settling back in his chair, "was well defended?"

"It was not as well-defended as it has been in the past, and that blame is on my part," Lord Maurice said. "But this man took it by sending his warriors out of the darkness like animals, screaming war cries, and pouring over the walls."

She had a vision of Colin fighting the blacksmith in the square at Tuam, charging across the cobblestones while blood dripped into his eyes.

"Will it ever end?" Lord William clanked his wine chalice back upon the table. "I don't have the vigor of those terrible old years, when I inherited the barony from my cousin. Nor the same blind foolishness."

"Father," Richard said, leaning across the table. "Let me lead the men to defeat these Irishmen."

Lord William's gaze drifted over his son's visage. "See what all this talk of war does? It gets a young man's blood pumping for adventure, and he not even knowing the wherewithal of it."

"Father, I am knight enough—"

"Who will become the baron if you fall?" Lord William tilted his head toward his daughters. "This war started because my uncle died with only female heirs. Back then, the MacEgans nearly succeeded in capturing this castle, until I returned from abroad and brought the war against them."

Maurice added grimly, "If this son of Fergus is anything like Brendan he will fight until the last drop of MacEgan blood has sunk into the earth."

Lord William cut the meat and lifted a small bite to his lips. "They are still to the north, yes?"

"Yes. A small contingent holds the castle, while the rest are spread across the Partry Mountains."

"Then we shall ride tomorrow."

Sneaking out of Lord William's castle was easier

than Maura had expected.

She strode across the open courtyard. The summer sun blazed upon her linen coif. She eyed the open gate, and its swarm of guardsmen and traders, tripping an excuse easily upon her tongue. *I'm just setting off for a walk in the countryside to gather some nuts for Nutmeg.* Her gathered belongings banged her thighs where she'd tied the pack beneath her tunic. Nutmeg's basket thumped against her back. She could only hope that any curious guardsmen didn't dare question the daughter of the lord of the place.

She passed through the gate, but she was not yet free. Clusters of tradesmen lived amid the narrow streets, and many might stop her to ask why Caddell's daughter traveled unguarded. She held her head high, looking neither left nor right, passing through as if she had a place to be and a time to be there. She made her way until the town gave way to a stretch of cleared pasture, dotted with cattle.

Nutmeg whirled within his basket, popping up to whisker the air in excitement, daring to skitter onto her shoulder as they left the confines of the city. Still she kept walking until she found the cow-path where she'd last seen Colin. Plunging into the woods, she noted by the moss growing on the oaks the direction in which she set her foot. She knew that Lough Corrib gleamed a two hours' brisk walk to the west of here. If she followed the shore northwards, she would come to the hills between it and Lough Mask, to the entrance of the Partry Mountains. From there, she suspected there had to be some kind of clear way to the castle in the mountains around Fahy.

With each step deeper into the woods came an excitement, and anticipation, a lightening of body and mind, a surety that what she was doing was right. She started to run, racing through the spindly saplings, racing away from the hateful whispers of the Caddells, from those prison walls of stone, away from the English—even if they were her family. She hadn't been welcomed like one of them, and as day after day passed in shame under strangers' disapproval, she'd come to the inescapable conclusion that even twenty more years of living among the Caddells wouldn't make their hearts any warmer.

She didn't want to be Maura Caddell any more than she'd wanted to take the veil, or be the butcher's wife. She wanted something that she was afraid to confess, even to herself, even as she raced like a kestrel set free of the mews, soaring across the earth with only one destination in mind.

Hours later, as she shared bilberries with Nutmeg while working her way around the banks of Lough Corrib, a man dropped down from the trees with a whoosh and a thud.

Nutmeg screeched and dove into his basket. The skirt of her tunic slipped out of her hands. Bilberries scattered across the forest floor.

"Look what I found, lads." His lips tightened into a grin beneath his mustache. "A nice bit o' hind wandering alone in the woods."

Coarse laughter echoed from the trees. Maura noticed the toe of a boot dangling from a branch.

"You're far from home and hearth, lass."

Maura looked at him hard. He didn't have the look of a common vagabond. This man had painted his face with woad, and the leather stretched across his chest looked tough and hard-boiled. His quiver bristled with arrows.

"You came from an English hearth, by the look of you." He spoke a thick and unwieldy English. "Have you no tongue? Or will you be having me look for it and use it the way it was meant to be used?"

"You do me harm," she snapped in Irish, "and The MacEgan himself will see you punished."

"Will he now?" She could see his crooked teeth now. "And what do you know of The MacEgan?"

"He is close, I know he is."

"And why do you think Brendan MacEgan would give a damn about a lost English wench?"

"I don't know Brendan. It's Colin I speak of. The minstrel turned warrior."

The man's eyes narrowed behind the caking of the woad, and the tenor of his attention shifted.

"I've come to see him. I am Maura—" She hesitated, wondering what these men would do if they thought her a Caddell. "I am Maura of Killeigh."

"Colin," the man said, "knows many women."

"Be that as it may," she said, "he won't take kindly to see me maltreated."

"You speak an easy Irish for an English wench."

"I'm not English."

A lifetime of thinking Irish didn't make it easy for a lass to swallow the idea of being born English. A lass could choose, couldn't she?

Then she thought of something else. Sweeping open her cloak, she fumbled with the sack tied about her waist.

A sliver of steel chilled her throat.

"Move slowly, lass." His breath brushed her cheek. "I've no liking to be nicked by the slice of a lass's knife, and even if you were to draw blood, there's a dozen healthy lads in the trees above who would see you'd regret the act."

"It's clear enough," she said, her breath short in her throat, "that I'd not get through that thick hide of yours with the sharpest of daggers. If you'd let me be, I'll give you proof that I know The MacEgan."

The man backed off, but not so far that she didn't smell the fumes of him rising up to choke her. She fumbled in her pack until she found what she looked for—a small package wrapped in linen. She unwrapped it to show the circular brooch winking with bits of colored gems.

The man lowered his knife. Someone called from above, and, another man dropped from the trees to stare at the brooch winking in her hand.

"Malachy—you keep watch in the pass." The leader adjusted his bow across his chest. "The MacEgan has a visitor."

He headed into the brush without another word. Maura shoved the brooch into her sack and hurtled through the woods to keep up with the leader's swift stride. He wandered around rock and hill, through the thickest of gorse, taking no mind of any marker she could see. She cursed her lack of forethought for not wearing her own sturdy boots instead of slippers used to nothing rougher than dried reeds spread across castle floors. But when she set her mind on Colin, the man couldn't walk fast enough for her.

As the shadows stretched long across the hillside, they came to a copse of wood. Shouts rang from the trees and a stir began in the midst of it. Men emerged from behind every rock and bush. The jangle and clank of sword and dirk against metal boss rang in the air as the crowd swelled.

Maura's heart skittered. There were so many

warriors camped in this site in the mountains. The height had a good view of the valley below where a slate gray elbow of Lough Corrib gleamed. She felt the men's eyes upon her as she approached the stone rampart on a rise, her legs wobbly, and not from the climb. Colin was near, somewhere amid the bustle of these warriors, somewhere within those walls. Soon, she'd lay eyes upon his face, feel his arms around her, and maybe even the pleasure of his kiss.

She shivered with anticipation.

Her guide strode through the wooden gates and across a bustling courtyard. She heard the ding-ding of a blacksmith and smelled stewing meat. Her escort pushed open the wooden door to a squat building in the middle of the courtyard. She blinked in the sudden darkness until she noticed several men seated around a trestle table. At the call of her guide, all the men glanced up. One man rose to his feet, dragging a coif of chain mail off his head so the links collapsed in a jangle upon his shoulders. One man, taller than all the others, his eyes as blue as the summer sky.

She stuttered to a stop. The air buzzed around her ears. A sword hung from his belt, banging against his mail-covered shins as he approached, weighted easily on him as if he'd worn it all his life. A snatch of memory came to her, of the story of Cú Chulainn, the famous Ulster warrior who during the heat of battle was seized by a bloodlust so fierce and so blinding that he paid no mind to the path of his sword, to whether he killed kith or kin.

This man wearing chain mail, this man with the bristled cheek and stony gaze…he was Colin.

But she did not know this man at all.

CHAPTER SEVENTEEN

"Where did you find her?"

He barked the question at Aedh while staring at *her*, the blue silk tunic, the flush of her cheeks, the two plaits bound back in the English way, thinking of the last time they'd touched, making love against a wall in the shadows of Caddell's castle.

"We found her wandering up the pass—"

"Alone?"

"Aye, alone." Aedh frowned. "She claims she knows you. She has your father's brooch to prove it."

He wanted to shake her for wandering around these war-torn woods alone with a fortune in her hand. When he'd given that brooch to her, he had not expected to live another day. He had hoped that she would conceive a son. Now he hoped she hadn't, for all he had to leave that son was a hard life in the hills and a desperate, bloody, endless conflict.

"Send ten more men to the pass." His mind raced. Caddell was crafty, unpredictable, and the news of the capture of this castle had no doubt reached him by now. "Double the watch on the ramparts," he ordered. "Eoin, fetch your sharp-eyed boy to climb to the ledge and report on what he sees to the north."

Men ran to his orders. He planted his hands on his hips and tried to make sense of seeing Maura standing there, blinking up with him with that dangerous innocence in her eyes. He couldn't take his eyes off her face. How pale she looked. It was a delicate, aristocratic pallor—the May-milk skin he remembered from before their weeks on the road, when the summer sun had burnished it gold. He wanted to capture that moist, pink lower lip. He pressed his knuckles against his chain mail to crush the itch he had to drag her into his arms.

It would be just like Caddell to send her as a secret weapon to distract him from vigilance while the bastard amassed fighters to attack.

He barked, "Did Caddell send you?"

"Of course not." She sounded startled. "I escaped the castle on my own."

His heart stopped, a painful thump. He ran his gaze over her body, looking for bruises, scratches, injuries. He wouldn't put it past Caddell to torture her for information. Nor would he put it past Caddell to use her as a pawn—willingly or not.

He said, "You're a spy then."

She flinched, and the motion sent a dart of guilt through him that he crushed instantly. He knew she expected jokes and gentleness, but in the heat of war, acting cautious meant eager boys might die.

"You've come here," he pressed, "thinking I would let you go and then you could report back on my whereabouts."

"If I'm a spy at all, then I'm a spy for *you*."

Colin watched the tendons in her neck flex. She wasn't lying. Maura had never mastered that minstrel's trick.

"Speak your mind then." He wondered when his voice had become like this. Hoarse from barking orders. Hoarse from screaming warnings. Hoarse and harsh and unrelenting. "Lest you haven't noticed, we have a war to wage."

He pretended not to see the ripple of hurt that passed across her face.

"Today," she stuttered, "Sir Maurice arrived at the castle. He told Lord William of your raids, of your capture of this stronghold."

More truth. The capture of the Fahy castle was a fresh victory. It was his first success—more kindling on the fires of the illusion that Fergus had come back from the dead. In truth, it was the ever-weakening Brendan who deserved the credit, for though Colin had led the attack it was his cousin's strategies that had guided his hand.

"Lord William is planning to gather a sizable army, if he must," she said. "He is being pressed to win back this castle—"

"This is not news." He seized a bladder of ale upon the table. "Caddell has been trying to crush the MacEgans since he came into the barony."

"He doesn't want war."

"Doesn't he?"

"He says he's tired of it." She glanced around the room at the men. "He claims it is the MacEgans who will not surrender—that your clan will fight to the bitter end, like your father before you."

"So Caddell *did* send you here, to negotiate."

"No." She found interest in the rushes by her

feet. "He knows nothing of who you are, of what we…"

A flush crept up her throat. He ignored it, for the eyes of the clan were heavy upon them.

He said, "Go on."

"Caddell doesn't give a fig about me," she said, "or about what I do with my days. He certainly wouldn't send me to do something as important as negotiate. I came here to tell you what I know, in the hopes that I can stop this madness and…"

She swallowed the rest of her words, but he heard them in his heart nonetheless. "You're still trying to save me from a hanging."

She looked up at him with those confused hazel eyes and he felt his determination weaken.

He barked to the room, "Leave us."

Then the men hiked weapons upon their shoulders, grasped wooden cups of ale, and strode across the rushes to the door thrown open to the sunshine. While it remained open, the light poured in around her. He saw how thin she'd become, how bright the loose strands of her plaits.

When the door finally closed, she crossed her arms in the silence. "Look at you," she said. "Dressed up like a shiny new pot."

"It's my father's chain mail." As was everything else he lived and breathed these days, his father's men, his father's clothing, his father's cause.

"I can't help but look at you and think you're prepared for a play. What happened to Arnaud and Matilda and the others?"

"They're here."

"Here?"

"Camped up on the hill," he said, debating how

much to tell her about his fears for their safety after Caddell caught her in his web. "Matilda's time draws nigh, they needed to stop for a time. I offered safety."

"There'll be no more plays then, not for a while." She cast her gaze over it again. "The armor fits you well."

She did not speak those words as a compliment. When he'd first tried on the armor the closeness of the fit had struck him as strange, for in his mind his father had always loomed large. The armor might be the only thing that fit him well in this new life. For everything else he'd taken his cues from Brendan, who loved this clan better than any wife, better than any god, better than his own fading life.

He shook himself out of brooding. "Did he hurt you?"

"Your blue-faced warrior? No, though if I hadn't shown him your brooch, he might have—"

"Not Aedh," he interrupted. "Caddell."

"Why would my father hurt me?"

Colin's jaw tightened. He turned away from her and walked to the other side of the trestle table to compose himself. Her innocence had saved her again.

He said, "Caddell never mentioned me to you?"

"He told me I couldn't go about swiving minstrels anymore, if that's what you mean. He didn't specify which one."

He glanced over his shoulder and the look that passed between them shimmered with remembrance. He tore his gaze away. He couldn't think about the afternoon by the river, or the evening before they parted, when he took her against the wall like it was his last night on the face of the earth.

"It's good to see you, anyway," she said, swinging

Nutmeg's basket off her shoulder to place it on the trestle table, "even if you are as garrulous as Padraig used to be when he was woken up too early in the morning."

In his memory he heard the ringing of the pipes—not the discordant clash of the pipes of war but the free-reeling music of moonlight and passion—riffling up memories of a lightness of heart, a lightness of being. He tightened his jaw to shut it out of his head.

"So I'm to believe," he said, mustering up some control, "that you've come here to betray your father."

"He's been a father less than a season, and less than kind."

"But you embrace him as your father nonetheless." He had enough worries upon his mind, without thinking of Maura lost in the castle at Shrule, a lonely outcast among the English. "You set off from a convent just to find him."

"I set off searching for something," she said. "Clearly I hadn't the faintest idea what I'd find."

Just then, her squirrel nosed the hinged lid of the basket. She leaned in and spoke soft words to him. The pet scrambled out of the basket, freezing when he caught sight of Colin, and then the beast darted for a piece of bread abandoned upon the table.

Colin stared at her braided hair and her silks, clinging so close to her curves, and then forced himself to look into that hurt-filled face as he asked the question he couldn't hold back anymore.

"Is there a babe?"

She startled and stared down at her own belly. She gripped it, thinking, and then she shook her head no.

"That's for the best." The words came out like stones. "A little loving on a summer's afternoon, a taste of paradise upon the road, and no consequences at all."

She grabbed a cup, took a deep gulp of ale, and then wiped a drop off her chin. "You were a much better liar when you were playing the minstrel."

He felt like a harp's string that had been twisted, played, and twisted again, still not striking the right tone, and so twisted, twisted some more, stretched too tight between the posts.

"Colin, hear me." She placed the ale back down and rounded the table. "You once told me that having a family can be a terrible burden. You are right. I don't want to be a Caddell."

She approached too close and a buzzing rose in his ears like the humming of a hundred thousand bees. Beyond the walls rose the murmurings of his men, the jangle of harness, the neighing of horses, the twang of a bowstring, the creak of boiled leather hauberks. All he had to do was lean forward, take those ripe wet lips she offered up to him. He could make her his again—she wanted it, too. His blood rushed as it did before battle, his loins hardened as it did after the battle was done, when he wanted to beat his chest and scream victory to the skies, and slake all that fiery energy with a woman.

Suddenly her hands were gripped in his, and he looked down at them, seeing her ring wink in the pale glow of the fire.

"I'll throw it out," she said. "I swear it. I can play many parts in minstrel's plays, but I can't play the part of an English lady."

"You don't have to, Maura."

Something in her eyes flickered. He looked into that innocent face and realized that he couldn't keep the truth from her any longer.

"You are not William Caddell's daughter."

Her mind felt like an egg broken and set upon by a whisk. Somehow Colin maneuvered her to the bench before her knees gave out. On that hard wooden bench she landed, jarring herself to the teeth, trying to absorb another piece of impossible information like a cake soaked with spirits still swimming in more.

She smelled something bitter and looked down to find he'd thrust another cup of ale under her nose.

"Drink."

It was a command, not a request. She sucked down the ale in a gulp and a half and felt the warmth of it sweep through her veins. She stared at her slippers and wiggled her toes idiotically, as if she wasn't sure they were still a part of her. Nutmeg, sensing the drama, clambered onto her shoulder.

I've always known.

Hadn't she sensed it all along, from the moment Lord William had approached her in that great hall, and that midwife had rushed, wimple flying, out of the shadows? She remembered feeling as if she'd stepped into some other minstrel troupe's play. She'd struggled to play along. She'd taken up her part because that's what was expected of her, that's what she was supposed to do.

But in her heart, always in her heart, whispered the thought *this cannot be.*

This cannot be.

She reached up to give Nutmeg a scratch. "I am a fool."

"No." He dropped to one knee before her, startling Nutmeg into dashing away again. "He played it masterfully. You had no reason to think he'd concoct such an elaborate lie."

Colin was being kind. She had every reason to disbelieve Lord William Caddell. The story was more preposterous than any that Maguire Mudman could come up with. But she'd been blinded by the one part of her that *wanted* it to be true—the part of her that ached for a loving mother, a kind father, siblings to share a life with, escape from the veil or marriage to the butcher's son.

She couldn't look at him. "How can you be sure he's lying?"

"There are many attendants in a highborn lady's birthing chamber. Among them are the unnoticed, like young Irish servants." He gave her a half-smile. "Some were MacEgans."

"Oh."

"And that so-called midwife," he said, shrugging. "Sometimes it takes one traveling player to recognize another."

"I should have seen through him when he first spoke to me—"

"Your innocence saved you. Once Caddell got you away from that crowd, he must have seen that you weren't play-acting. I don't know why else he'd keep up the pretense all this time."

"I thought he was protecting my honor." She remembered the sound of the bolt sliding on her bedroom door. "But really, I was his prisoner."

"I spent every night of these past weeks wanting to storm that castle and get you out." Colin's grip tightened. "Tell me he didn't touch you."

"Caddell came to my room every evening," she explained, "but only to give me lectures on behavior."

Perplexity wrinkled his brow. "No more?"

"No more." She rubbed her head as she tried to make sense of why this was happening. "If he took me prisoner…it must be because he knew about us, he knew he could use me against you."

"The messenger on the road," he said, slipping onto the bench beside her. "He must have caught a glimpse of us and then sent spies to observe."

Her heart tripped. "Then he knew you were in the hall that same night."

"Yes."

"He must have known," she continued, "that stepping close to me would protect him, that you wouldn't kill him if he stood so near."

"Yes."

"Why the ruse?" She shook her head. "Why didn't he just send men to seize you?"

"He's up to something." Colin stood up and began pacing in the rushes, his mind turning. "Did he truly introduce you to Sir Maurice?"

"On the second or third day of my stay. He's introduced me to many other of his vassals as well."

"He's holding to the ruse that you're his daughter."

"He's always irritated," she said. "He looks at me as if I'm a squirrel that won't dance to his tune."

"His men melted into the woods when my men attacked. They hardly put up a fight when I took this castle." Colin rubbed his jaw, trying to figure out the mystery. "For years my father looked upon this occupied castle and wanted it more than anything else. This was the heart of MacEgan lands, the jewel in the crown. It burned in his gut that it had been lost." Colin turned an eye on her. "Letting you come to me must be part of his plan."

"He made sure I was listening when he mentioned you at the dinner table." She felt very small, very stupid. "He must have hoped, or guessed, that I would leave. That I would seek you out."

"He's crafty, Will Caddell. My cousin says that the Englishman has some grand plan to herd us into a slaughter. But if there's a grand plan that includes giving up this castle, I can't make any sense of it."

Colin kept pacing, drawing circles in the rushes with his boot. Maura felt no smarter for her travels than the day she stepped out of the convent.

"Lady Sabine was right," she said softly. "The world *is* dangerous, and full of trickery."

"There's a reason at the bottom of every trick." Colin stopped in the middle of the hall. "But you can't always know it unless you play along."

"Play along?"

He approached, and the look in his eye made her knees soften like butter in the summer sun.

"A captured daughter," he said softly, "will fetch a fine, high ransom."

Ransom.

She tried to focus on his familiar blue eyes, the ones that so often had crinkled in laughter, and ignore the gleam of the chain mail on his shoulders, and the fear that she didn't know this man anymore.

"You won't send me back," she said, her voice quivering. "You won't make me his prisoner again."

CHAPTER EIGHTEEN

The answer was in his kiss.

He thrust his hand through her hair. Warmth seeped through her body at the feel of his cheek brushing hers. When he turned his head she offered her lips to him without hesitation. She clasped his shoulders so tightly that she felt the bite of the chain mail in the skin of her palms. His kiss was deep and hungry.

He loved her, she was sure of it. She felt it in the gentleness of his fingers against her head, in the way he drew her body against his, in how he couldn't stop kissing her. *This* is what she wanted, maybe from the very moment she'd stepped out of the convent in Killeigh. She hadn't known it then—she hadn't known *anything* then—she hadn't understood that such a love existed.

No, she thought.

Colin wouldn't send her back.

Then she pushed away all her doubts and tilted her head at his urging, loving the wet merging of mouth and teeth and tongue. He dragged his hand down to the hollow of her lower back, pressing her up against the root of him swelling through the cut-out of his hauberk. Memories of that day by the riverbank flooded through her mind, and other, hotter ones of the upper gallery of Caddell's castle, sweet promises of the pleasure soon to come.

He broke away long enough to shout something over his shoulder. She glimpsed a spear of sunlight as someone came through the outer door, but only for a moment, for Colin was walking her backwards. She followed his urging as if they were dancing under the eaves of the alehouse with the sea roaring in her ears. She felt the boards of a door give behind her, heard it slam shut behind Colin, and then they were swept into a twilight darkness, the only light coming from some arrow-slit on high.

She stumbled back against a post. She opened her eyes long enough to realize they were in a bedchamber. The hardness lodged in the middle of her back was a post belonging to the canopy. She buried her hands in his hair as he kissed his way down her neck. She closed her eyes, thinking of what it was going to be like to spend an entire night lying in his arms, uninterrupted.

He kissed the pulse throbbing in her throat, then the hollow of her cheek, then her temple, while she breathed in his hair, smelling the fresh summer breeze in the softness of it, breathing it in as if it were her last breath. She curled her fingers into the mail on his shoulders and wished she had the strength to pluck it off him.

He pulled away from her and cupped her face in his hands. "I'm not doing this standing up again."

She managed a shaky laugh. "You did a fine enough job of it before."

"I blame that on you, for being so tempting as to make a man mad."

"It's good that I'm not the only one half mad."

He kneed her thighs open to make more room for him, and he spoke in a hoarse voice. "I've waited a lifetime to stretch you out on a bed, Maura."

"There's a fine noble bed behind me." She plucked at the links of his chain mail. "But unless you shed this, you'll crush me beneath you."

His sideways grin caused a delicate rippling sensation between her legs. He stepped back to unbuckle his sword belt and toss it upon the floor. He reached behind his head and hauled his surcoat off his back. He tossed the cloth into the dimness. Scraping it out of the way with his foot, he worked on the buckles of his hauberk with one hand, hasty, fumbling, his gaze fixed on her, until she couldn't bear it anymore and she moved to help him, flipping the leather straps out of the metal tongues, one after another until he shrugged off the mail. The links slipped like cool water across her palms to settle into a pool of dull silver on the floor.

Then the padding, so many ties. His chest rose and fell beneath her hands as she worked this strange clothing free. She wanted to see him in simple linen—she wanted to see the poet beneath the warrior again. She felt a hurried tug on her side and realized he was unlacing her surcoat at the same time. The world went dark for a moment as he lifted it over her head, and when she blinked anew he was shrugging out of his padding so he stood before her only in his linens.

He reached down to pull off a boot, hopped on

one foot to pull off the other, but his eyes never left hers.

"Take everything off," she heard herself whisper. "I want to see you."

She blushed at her audacity, but she didn't take the words back. He was beautiful, standing so tall before her like this. He gave her that sideways smile. Her body thrummed with excitement. He hefted his shirt over his shoulders and made short work of his braies so that the linen fell in a heap upon the chain mail.

There he was, long and tall and lean and full of muscles that swelled in his shoulders and arms and tapered down his abdomen to the root of him. Her hands itched to run over his skin, to feel the swell of those muscles beneath her palms. Her eye was drawn to the narrow protrusions that edged his hips on either side and led to the darkness between his legs, and the powerful cock that thrust away from it.

Her body went liquid, her knees weak, and she felt a yearning to feel his hips sliding between her legs, to feel him filling her up, stretching her until she couldn't take any more of him in.

Then, suddenly, she was holding it. She curled her fingers around its thickness. She sensed the shock that shot through him and felt a rush of power for having caused it. His cock hardened even more, pulsing in the grip of her hand.

Oh, there weren't enough Hail Marys in the world to save her from this sin, if it were a sin at all.

Then with a groan he uncurled her hand from his root and tugged her neckline down. She shrugged her shoulders close so he could pull the linen off them. She wriggled, helping him slide it down her arms along with her chemise, rolling her shoulders as he tugged, until her tightening nipples sprung free of the constriction. He paused in his tugging to suck a nipple deep into his mouth.

His hot mouth was a shock. The scrape of the edge of his teeth made her squeeze her eyes shut. She pressed her head back against the bedpost at the swirl of his rough tongue. She couldn't touch him—her arms were pinned to her sides by the constriction of the bunched-up linen. He released one nipple to suck the other one into his hot mouth, and the sensation of one nipple cooling, tightening, while the other felt the rough lave of his tongue made the blood rush out of her head until black spots threatened before her eyes.

She heard the sound of something tearing, felt the linen loosen around her arms. She shucked it off and grasped his hair in her hands, torn between the need to press her nipple deeper into his mouth and the urge to drag his head up so she could feel the pressure of his kiss.

Then the whole world tilted and his hands were wrapped around her backside. The softness of the bedclothes sank under her, and she felt the warmth and weight of Colin's naked body atop her.

"Maura." Light fell from the arrow-slit to make a halo around his head. "Maura."

She opened her mouth for his kiss, a kiss unlike any other they'd shared, though she couldn't explain why. All she knew was that during this kiss she felt a breeze sift through the arrow-slit, a breeze that smelled like summer grass, a breeze that whorled around them and caught in the folds of the draperies, a breeze she felt herself caught up in, that seemed to bring, from afar, the piping of Padraig's pipe, rising and falling and seeping into her blood until she found herself so breathless she had to pull away.

"Colin."

He ran his fingers across her lips and then slid down her body, palming her breasts in his hands, stopping to lay another kiss on the tips. His hands roved lower then, rubbing down her ribs and then the curve of her hip. She watched as he kissed his way down to her navel, as his tongue flickered out to wash circles in the indentation. All sensation poured through her to focus on a pinpoint place throbbing in the folds between her legs.

"Colin," she whispered, breathless, as he slid lower, his hair tickling her side. "What…what are you doing?"

He looked up at her with those blue eyes as he grasped the underside of one thigh and raised it above his shoulder. "The French," he said, sliding lower, "have a different way of loving."

A new flush tingled over her. "I like the Irish way, you know."

"We'll get around to that, too," he said, as his chin trailed over the slight rise at the junction between her legs. "Eventually."

Then, watching her face, he slipped his hot tongue into her cleft.

She arched up, her fists full of bedding. She arched up as her whole world centered on the trail of his tongue. She let her knees drop wide. She cried out as his hands slid up her sides to grasp her breasts. She gasped for breath, aching for the suck and tug of his mouth between her legs. She lifted her hips to meet this new kiss, moving against him and making noises she didn't know she could make. She glanced down past his hands kneading her aching breasts and saw him tonguing her. She watched breathlessly as he licked her cleft from back to front, watched as she dared to reach down and run her hand over his dark head lodged between her legs.

In the most sinful of her fleshy dreams, she'd never imagined opening herself so widely to the touch and kiss of a man. With each probe of his hungry tongue, her body tightened and tightened and tightened until, finally—blissfully—spasms shuddered through her as she shattered into a thousand pieces under his touch.

With the taste of her sweet in his mouth, Colin slid up beside her to watch her face. Her lips were swollen, and on them was a streak of angry pink from where she'd bitten the lower one. A flush lay upon her cheeks, as did her long lashes, closed over her eyes as if she were dreaming. He wanted to touch those lashes, trace her cheek, but he did not want to rouse her from the pleasure that still throbbed through her body. It made his cock pulse, to remember how fiercely she'd responded.

He wanted to bury himself in her tightness, lose himself as he'd lost himself in so many women over so many lost years. How easy it would be to seize that moment of exquisite forgetfulness and the freedom from anxiety that always followed, at least for a night. But he couldn't do that to Maura, not to this sweet woman who deserved better. He would take himself in hand, if that's what he had to do.

"Colin."

Hazel eyes upon him, wide and dewy. He traced a strand of hair off her brow and took pleasure basking in the glow of her smile.

He murmured, "You like the French way."

She slipped her lower lip between her teeth. At the sight, his scrotum tightened.

She must have sensed the twitch of his cock, for she glanced down between them and then back up. "But you…"

"I wanted to watch you."

Her color deepened.

He said, "You're beautiful. All of you."

"You've seen more of me than anyone else."

"Yes."

He spoke the word like a possession, felt a rush of pride that he—and only he—had brought her this kind of pleasure. She turned onto her side to face him. She traced her finger over his collarbone as she pressed closer. Then she leaned up for a kiss, but he cupped her cheek in his hand, stopping her.

"What's wrong?"

"We can't risk it, Maura."

"Risk what?"

He rubbed a thumb across her cheekbone. "A child."

Her lashes fluttered and that little line deepened between her brows. "But…before, when we were—"

"We were fortunate." He pressed his lips against her brow. "I was unwise."

He would not risk siring a MacEgan son. He would not burden a child of his with bloodied histories and a destiny no man should inherit. And certainly, he would not burden the woman he loved with a child from a man who'd likely die a violent death, like all the MacEgans before him.

She stilled for a while, her face against his, long enough for him to know that she understood what he was saying. He was making her no promises of any real future. He wished the world were different. He wished he didn't have to lie here and feel what little honor he'd gathered around him weaken.

She pressed her lips against his, a kiss full of hope and fear and passion. He tried very hard not to open his mouth, not to welcome more, even as he felt his cock throb against her thigh.

She pulled away and licked her lips. He suppressed a groan at the sight of that little pink tongue.

She said, "You taste like me."

"I like the way you taste."

"I want to taste you."

He tried to breathe. It suddenly became very difficult. She pressed a hand on his chest to push him onto his back. Then her soft hair trailed against his chest as she slid down the bed, until he felt her breath against his abdomen.

"The French way will work for you, too," she murmured. "Won't it?"

CHAPTER NINETEEN

The Partry Mountains split the shores of Lough Mask from those of Lough Corrib with a ridge of hills that petered out beyond the lakes to grassy plains. In the late summer, the sun didn't climb over the hills until midday. Here, in this elbow of mist and mud, Colin waited. His horse pawed the grass, while his guards perched in the slopes all around, watching for the coming of the English.

A shout pierced the mid-morning gloom. It echoed beyond, to the stone walls of the castle. *His* castle, now, though the English had rebuilt it in stone long after the MacEgans had been cleared of these lands. Waiting in the pass, Colin had a fuller sense of the strategic importance of the fortress than he'd had when he'd heard his father talk of it in his youth. By taking it, the MacEgans claimed all of the hills west of the lakes—and guarded those lands by guarding no more than this single mountain pass.

The shout came again. His horse flicked his ears. Colin tightened his grip on the reins. All around the clearing, the men rustled, settling into rock and crag and tree trunk. At the far end of the pass, something red flashed between the trees.

The first Englishmen emerged into the pass. He wore a jeweled swath of crimson, bright against the muddy gray forest. Colin had expected one of Caddell's trusted knights, armed and braced for treachery, not a man dressed in silks as bright as a minstrel's. Then Colin heard Maura suck in a breath.

There he was, William the Black himself, calmly riding straight for him.

Colin's horse skittered. He forced himself to loosen his choke hold on the reins. His blood rushed hot, swelled in his head, and started a painful throbbing behind his eyes. Ten years he'd waited for vengeance, and here it was, appearing before him unprotected but for a few retainers. To kill Caddell now would be a breach of honor, of all accepted conventions of warfare, an act of incivility that would foment all the neighboring English lords into vengeance. But killing Caddell would be so very easy.

"It's true what they say." Lord William pulled his horse to a stop a few feet in front of him. "You look very much like your father."

Colin didn't respond. The war Colin's father had raged had been one of quick raids, surprise skirmishes, and one desperate attempt to seize Caddell's castle. Colin had never seen the Englishman as closely as now. Even lurking in the rafters of Caddell's castle, Colin had noticed only a gray-haired lord, well-dressed, loud-voiced. Now, up close, he saw a man with a face carved in lines, his hair oiled but thin, his belly bulging against the crimson tunic.

But the Englishman's eyes…his eyes held an intensity as they shifted focus to Maura, perched on a Connemara pony just behind Colin.

"You look well, my daughter," Caddell said. "I trust you have been treated with respect?"

"I've been treated," she said, "as family."

Colin wondered if the Englishman heard the hardness beneath the words.

"Fear not," Caddell said. "Soon enough, you'll be back in my castle safe with your siblings."

Colin frowned. *So Caddell will keep to the falsehood.* The Englishman had something up his sleeve, though Colin couldn't fathom what it might be.

"We have business, you and I." Colin swept his leg over the saddle. "Let's be done with it."

"Ah, the fiery impatience of the young." The fine leather of Caddell's saddle creaked as the Englishman loosed himself from the mount. "I suppose I should expect no less from the son of Fergus MacEgan."

Colin didn't answer as he headed with his guard toward a small fire in the lee of the hill, where he and his enemy could speak in some semblance of privacy. He took his place and stood by the flames, ignoring the smoke stinging his eyes. The perfumed stench of the man reached Colin long before the Englishman's riding boots squished in the mud.

Aedh stepped forward and handed Lord William a bladder of ale. The Englishman took a sip, then held it out to Colin. Colin's first urge was to slap it away, but Aedh took the ale from the Englishman and handed it to Colin with a look in his eye that urged patience, that spoke of the virtue of courtesy, that reminded him of the danger of the situation, even as they stood in a valley ringed with MacEgans and their Flaherty allies.

So Colin took the silent advice, seized the bladder, and choked down the ale.

"It speaks well of you," Lord Caddell said, gesturing back toward Maura, "that my daughter has suffered no harm from this adventure—"

"No thanks to you."

With a flick of an eyebrow, Lord William said, "I believe it is you who made her a hostage."

"The girl was found by Lough Corrib by my own men. Had she been found by others, who knows what may have befallen her." Colin eyeballed him. "You should hold closer that which you hold dear."

"Do you have children, Colin MacEgan?"

He thought with a pang of last night's conversation with Maura. He pushed the thought away and shook his head.

"Are you married, then?"

"When The MacEgan marries, you'll hear of it."

"I have six daughters, much like my uncle, the baron before me." Shuffling closer to the fire, Lord William gathered his tunic and settled himself on a boulder set there just for that purpose. "Each of those daughters is more obstinate than the next. Haughty rebelliousness seems to run on the distaff side of the Caddell family."

The Englishman ran his hand over his head, dislodging the careful comb-tracks in his hair, looking, for a moment, exceedingly human.

Colin pushed that aside. "There is the matter of ransom."

"Yes. Ransom." Caddell tipped his head. "Indulge my curiosity for a moment. That was you behind the bear mask, that first night with the minstrel troupe?"

So it was true, his presence had not gone unnoticed. "Your sight hasn't faded with age."

"Your clansmen all have jaws as hard as the Connemara hills. Why didn't you kill me then?"

Colin tried to read the Englishman's gaze as he would read a blacksmith sizing him up for a fight, but Colin was becoming increasingly aware that this wasn't the same kind of battle. He wished Brendan was here. His cousin would know what to say, how much ransom to ask, how to handle the golden moment when William the Black stood before them, unprotected.

But Brendan had finally died last night, leaving this world with an exhalation that had sounded very much like relief.

Colin said, "If you knew I was behind the bear mask, why didn't you seize me and have me hanged?"

"For the same reason you didn't kill me that night as your father surely bade you, many years ago."

"You talk in riddles." Colin didn't like this strange, indulgent communality. He reached for the ale and brought the conversation back to the topic at hand. "There's the matter of ransom."

"Mmm. How much is a daughter worth these days?" Lord William rubbed his hands together as if feeling the morning's chill. "It has been years since I've had to think of such things. Fifty head of cattle? Sixty? With a couple of bulls as well?"

Colin stiffened. Maura was worth all the cattle in Ireland, but apparently not to this Englishman.

"And after this ransom we settle, what shall you do next?" Lord William squinted across the clearing. "Shall you steal more of my vassals' cattle? Burn the harvest? Attack another castle? Win the Caddell lands back to the MacEgans, hill by hill, field by field?"

"I'll win it back the way you took it—with the

blood of Irishmen, with the blood of Englishmen."

"How very difficult." The Englishman stretched his hands over the fire. "And so very wasteful, too."

"You've never had any compunction over spilling blood."

"Grant me some small amount of consideration, MacEgan. Your father, friends and brothers died in the heat of a battle that I did not start."

The words held a glimmer of truth but Colin deflected it. "And Murtough?" Colin trailed a finger across his left eye. "Was that cruelty just the heat of battle, as well?"

"I blinded your brother to stop the fighting. I reasoned that, without a head, the clan MacEgan would be subdued—and peaceful—and that is what I wanted more than anything."

"My brother feels no peace toward you—"

"I could have blinded him in two eyes. I could have killed him outright—it would have been fair. You know this. For ten years, there has been a sort of peace in these lands. An Irish peace, of course, full of cattle reeving and thievery, but an all-but-bloodless peace nonetheless." Caddell gestured to Colin. "Now here you are, riling the clan up again. Fergis had too damn many sons, and all the people of these parts pay the price—English and Irish."

Colin remembered the bloodstained banks of that pond east of here. "Killing didn't hurt your conscience ten years ago."

"Ten years ago I was ten years younger," the Englishman said. "Even then, I'd lost the stomach for the kind of war your father took grim pleasure in."

Colin clamped his hand over the hilt of his sword. "You speak ill of the dead."

"It's a difficult to avoid since most of the men I've known, both loved and hated, are long since in the grave *because* of this war. Please," he said, throwing a hand up in surrender. "The very sight of you, standing there with fury in your eyes, as I'd seen your father so many times, is enough to weary me."

And what kind of target was a weary old Englishman? Colin dropped his hand from the hilt of his sword. "I didn't summon you here to chatter about the past. Talk of ransom, and be done with it."

"Sir Maurice will be the one providing the ransom. He, too, is weary of the demands of our situation." The Englishman squinted toward the hazy outline of the castle atop the hill. "You may have noticed that the Fahy castle was not well guarded. Sir Maurice has grown lax in his twilight years."

Colin's gaze drifted to the English knights in the clearing beyond, to the bushy-browed one among them, his oiled beard gleaming.

"Maurice has buried his children, and his wife," the Englishman continued. "He has no direct heirs, only distant cousins who can easily be put off. I have offered him a place in my household, and he has agreed to surrender his lands to me now—something he'd have to do at the time of his death nonetheless."

"You think me stupid." Colin tilted his head toward the castle. "You offer me for ransom something that I already possess."

"You possess it by force, and thus it can be taken by force. But I'm offering it to you as an end to our war. What remains to be seen is if you can stomach being my vassal for the price of a few coppers a year."

"You'd have me bend my knee?"

"Your father was vassal to my uncle, once. Life

was peaceful then. Think of that if you can't bear the thought of bending your neck."

"My father would have fallen on his own sword before bowing to you—"

"Your father paid homage to many a man when it suited him. Before I came to defend my birthright, he'd bent his knee to The O'Conor."

Colin clenched his fists. William knew too much of Fergus, more, Colin sensed, than he did himself. In his mind's eye, Colin sensed the rage of Fergus's ghost. But Fergus was dead. And so were many of his aspirations—lofty, impossible ones that they were. Across this fire sat the man who could bring peace to a world that had not known it for too many years. And he himself, the man who had been the spark for the whole conflagration, was the only one who could now throw sand upon the flames.

How easy it would be, to agree. Take one third of what the MacEgans once had, and be satisfied. Such land would be more than enough to divide among his men. Rich land, too. It meant an end to sleepless nights, to raiding. It meant giving his people land to till, instead of Englishmen to kill. It meant laying down the sword he'd spent a month sleeping with.

It wasn't enough.

"Again," Colin said, "you offer me that which I already possess and then expect me to pay homage."

"You'll have more. You'll have enough land to satisfy all the MacEgans, that I promise on one condition."

"Condition?"

"Just one." William the Black lifted his head. "You must agree to marry my daughter."

CHAPTER TWENTY

Colin took one lunging step toward Caddell and the English guards stepped forward and grasped the hilt of their swords.

"Hold." Caddell shot to his feet. "Hold, all of you. There'll be no bloodshed this day."

Colin felt his own breath go hot. He looked around at the circle of guards, tense and waiting. "All of you," he said, "*leave us.*"

His own men eyed the English. With a nod from Caddell, the English guards drew back out of the circle of the fire. Colin's men followed. Colin waited until they were well out of earshot while a hot coal of fury banked inside him. What a puppet master, this Englishman was, playing with Maura's fate so cavalierly. It infuriated him that he still didn't understand the Englishman's intentions.

"Which daughter," Colin asked darkly, "would you consign to an Irishman?"

The Englishman fluttered his white hand toward Maura. "Your fiery hostage, of course."

Colin had suspected so, but Caddell had many daughters, and before Colin spoke his mind he wanted the offer to be clear.

"I should cut you down for offering me insult. I know Maura is not your daughter."

Something flickered in those eyes—surprise perhaps, but this man was hard to read. "It's true," he conceded. "She is not my daughter by blood."

"I am not the only man who knows this."

"Perhaps." Caddell shrugged. "But in public I have declared her my own child, multiple times, to many highborn people. I have installed her in my household, dressed her, fed her, and introduced her to noble guests. And I have come here, publicly, to pay a hefty ransom for her freedom."

"Your own family thinks she's your whore."

"People will think what they will." Caddell's face shuddered. "But I am William Caddell, the Baron of Shrule. I have declared her my daughter. Tell me, MacEgan: Who would dare naysay me?"

"And the dower you will give her? Is it to be nothing more than the castle I already own?"

"More lands than that."

"So you will take land from your own vassals and give it to me? Take land from your true daughters, and your only son?"

"My son will inherit all these lands, along with the conflict." Caddell sank a thumb into his belt. "So yes, Colin MacEgan. Yes, I will trade land for peace in my time, in order to preserve it in his. It's a price I'm willing to pay to stop the bloodshed."

Colin's heart pounded in his ears, a pounding of thwarted fury, a pounding of disbelief. He and Lord William stared at each other across the blue snapping haze of the fire and, for a moment, Colin began to think the man was speaking the truth.

Colin said, "I don't trust you."

"You have reason."

"This is another of your ruses."

"I won't deny that I have been planning this for quite some time."

"You will have me married to Maura, and once the vows are made, you'll deny her, and you'll deny me all your promises."

"If I do that, I'll find myself in a war again, except this time you'll be ensconced in that castle," he said, pointing toward the stone keep on the hill, "almost impossible to dislodge, if you keep it better guarded than my faithful, though negligent, servant."

He planned that, too—he let me seize this castle. The insight bounced off his mind, impossible to believe.

"Why now?" Colin asked. "You could have made peace with Brendan at any time, married him to any one of your six daughters."

"Now you go too far."

The Englishman's voice went dark, and Colin felt a flicker of understanding. The Caddells could trace their history back to the sister of William the Conqueror. William's father was a third cousin once removed to King Edward I. Caddell was too proud to give up a daughter to a mere Irishman. Which explained the ruse with Maura.

"It would have been useless to make this offer to Brendan, in any case," the Englishman continued. "Brendan is a bitter-ender, like your father before him. He would accept no half-measures. He would die on his sword first."

True, Colin thought, and it bothered him that the

Englishman knew his enemy so very, very well.

"In fact, I expected to see your cousin here." Caddell glanced over his shoulder to scan the Irishmen watching from afar. "I expected to see him propped up, the power behind your throne. Has the old goat finally gone the way of us all?"

"I am The MacEgan now." For the first time since he'd arrived at the MacEgan settlement, the words came to him without hesitation, without shame, and without any doubt.

"That will make this negotiation easier." The Englishman combed his fingers through the point of his beard. "I suspect you are very different from your cousin. You want peace."

"You don't know what I want."

"I can think of no other reason why you left Ireland ten years ago and played the part of a traveling minstrel for so long."

The way the Englishman phrased those words raised a niggling suspicion in his mind, a suspicion that took on a life of its own. Colin thought about the night Caddell discovered his so-called daughter. He thought about the swift capture of the MacEgan castle. He thought about the offer that Caddell was spreading before him.

He began to wonder at the extent of the ruse and the wily old fox who'd engineered it.

"Oh, yes, Colin MacEgan." Caddell's eyes glittered with triumph. "I have been expecting you for a very long time."

Maura watched her false father and the man she loved lock forearms in a warrior's handshake. She wondered how many cows a false daughter was worth. She wondered how many bulls were considered a good exchange. She wondered whether they took into account how good a cook she was, the sturdiness of her hips or the health of her teeth. They did not seem to have bickered for long.

Then she closed her eyes and told herself not to be bitter. This situation was of her own making. She'd always known that Colin was a leader among men. From the very first day she'd seen him in Killeigh, fighting in the dirt, she'd assumed he was the head of the minstrel troupe. Yet she had come here yesterday foolishly expecting the Colin she'd known upon the roads—the irresponsible, irrepressible minstrel who had teased and seduced her into loving him. What she'd arrived to find was a more complicated man bowed under the burden of responsibility—a man who'd finally revealed his true self. A man who loved her, but had other demands upon him, far more important than one wayward orphaned girl.

And she'd changed, too. Her younger self would have been scandalized by the heedless woman she had become in Colin's bed last night. She felt as though the person she had always been had now finally emerged.

At the sound of footsteps, she looked up and saw Colin striding straight toward her. She swallowed the lump that rose to her throat at the sight of him, long-legged, that loop of black hair falling over his brow, the nose that had been broken one too many times. She wouldn't fool herself that they could go on as they had last night and not invite the risk of a child that he didn't want born. She figured that he would set her aside somewhere, out of war and trouble, and likely out of his life. As he neared, she summoned every last ounce of strength she had so she wouldn't shame herself by crying as he determined her fate.

Colin grasped her hand. "Come with me."

He didn't slack his stride, so she followed him up the slope that led to the walls of the castle. She grasped saplings to pull herself up and cursed the thin shoes that slipped upon the matting of leaves and old grass. She eyed the flex of Colin's legs, envying his surefootedness, forcing herself not to remember all the other days she had followed him upon the roads, watching the wind sweep through the wildness of that black hair. She took comfort in the warmth of his hand as she followed him to the clearing before the castle where a cool wind rose up from Lough Corrib.

He released her and leaned back upon a rock, crossing his arms. A frown stitched his brow. If the whirling of thoughts could spin a spit, she thought, she could cook a goose with the thinking Colin was doing right now.

"So," she said into the silence, her annoyance the only defense against tears. "What did he offer you for a false daughter? Sixty good milk cows and two bulls along with it? A half league of land by the edge of the sea? Another castle and a handful of coppers?"

"He offered me exactly what I wanted." He stared up at the walls of Fahy, much in need of repair by the look of the crenellations. "He offers peace."

"Peace."

"I don't know whether to think him senile, or to credit him for his genius."

Maura pulled the edges of her mantle close. Hadn't she been the one to tell him that Lord William wanted peace? "Is this a man's strange way of admitting that a woman was right?"

He grinned at her. She looked away from that grin, as potent an arrow as any iron-tipped one. It didn't matter that she'd been right, because it didn't change anything. But Colin's odd behavior, the eerie whistling of the wind rising from the Lough, the distant chatter of birds in the greenery, made her feel as jittery as a drop of water dancing upon grease.

"Maura."

She knew the sound of that velvet voice, skittering across her nerve endings. She met his gaze and for a moment she couldn't think at all. Her body fluxed with a rush of emotions too confusing, too complicated to sort from one another.

Then she blurted her worst fear. "You're sending me back to him."

"Yes."

Her heart stopped. A ringing started in her ears. She went numb from her scalp to her toes.

"But," he added, "only for a short while."

She must have swayed, for the sky moved above her head and the ground slipped beneath her feet and then, all of a sudden, Colin was there, seizing her hands and holding her still and staring down at her with those blue, blue eyes.

"Maura, listen," he said, speaking in a rush. "I was not born to be The MacEgan."

"I know."

"It is not my choice."

"Family," she stuttered, "imposes obligations."

I thought you'd never send me back.

"If I asked you, right now," he said, "to leave these lands, to go back on the road with me and live the life we choose—"

"You cannot." She pressed her head against his chest. "You have responsibilities here. The fate of a clan depends on you. I understand that."

"But if the world were different," he persisted, so close that she could feel his breath upon her hair, "and I asked you to leave with me—"

"But—"

"Right now, right this moment." He tightened his grip on her hands. "Would you run away with me, Maura?"

A sharp, sweet ache speared through her. This is what she'd been hoping for when she'd come seeking him yesterday, leaving her so-called family's house with her head full of silly dreams. She had come with a trill in her heart and joy in her mind, with no thought of anything but being with Colin, free to live the life of her dreams and love the man of her choice.

So why did she hesitate to speak her heart, even if he spoke folly? This was the face she would dream about in the months and years to come. Even if she found herself forced to wed the butcher's boy—or take the veil—she would fall asleep each night envisaging a lanky minstrel with a crooked nose and eyes full of mirth. What harm was there in playing along, building impossible reveries?

She spoke around the lump rising in her throat. "Are you finally offering me marriage, Colin MacEgan?"

He didn't laugh as she expected him to. He released her hands and then cupped her face, lifting her chin so he could look in her eyes.

He asked, "If I did, would you say yes?"

His face went blurry beyond her tears. How ironic that he would offer her a future, when the future between them was lost for sure. "It would be a poor wedding," she whispered. "Done on a roadside by some traveling friar."

"Fingar would play the harp." He rubbed his thumbs across her cheeks. "And Matilda would supply the silks for your wedding dress."

"Wouldn't that be a sight."

"The roadside would be filled with flowers."

"Aye, that's true."

"But we could find a church that would take us," he said, "if that's your wish."

"Padraig couldn't pass the threshold without raising up hellish smoke. And someone has to steal the ring."

"We could use this."

Colin tapped the ring on her finger, the ring that had been tucked in her swaddling clothes.

His blue gaze settled on her with growing intensity, waiting for an answer to an impossible question, an answer that must be glowing on her face. He pulled her into his arms. She pressed against his chest. A buckle under his surcoat bit into her cheek. He held her so tightly that she found herself gasping until finally he loosed her and laid a kiss upon her lips that stole the very last of her breath.

He said against her mouth, "I have another question for you."

"Questions, questions. Doesn't a man have better things to do with his tongue?"

"I won't be able to walk this slope if you keep talking like that. Caddell is waiting for my answer."

At the sound of the name, she remembered herself. "Caddell is waiting?"

"As am I."

She searched his eyes and realized that this whole strange conversation had something to do with William Caddell and the ransom he'd come to pay.

"Colin," she said, her voice breaking, "I've no stomach for japes."

"It's no jape. You will have to go back to Shrule with him, for appearance's sake. But only until the marriage."

"Marriage."

His smile was slow. "I've been offered your hand in marriage, Maura. But I'll only take it if you'll agree to have me."

She blinked at him, disbelieving. Her lips, fingertips, nose, went numb. She blurted, "It's a trick."

"No." He shook his head. "I think he speaks the truth. I marry you, and there will be peace."

Hope leapt in her breast, a treacherous thing. Could it be possible? Could it be possible that Colin would be The MacEgan openly, without fear, the war and skirmishes over? And she—the foundling from Killeigh, a mere kitchen servant—become the Lady MacEgan, the mistress of the castle looming over them from above?

It was too odd, too impossible, too fantastic to imagine, a player's midnight tale come to life.

He wiped a strand of hair off her brow to draw her attention. "You already told me you'd marry the minstrel. Would you marry the warrior as well?"

She traced the scruff of his jaw, the indentation of his chin, and then the sweep of his lower lip, whispering, "Aren't the two men one and the same?"

CHAPTER TWENTY-ONE

Maura shifted the stool so that the light streaming from the arrow-slit fell upon the swirling design of scarlet and gold threads along the collar of her bridal surcoat. Her silver needle flashed as she pierced the rose-colored silk. By her bed, two maidservants bickered as they struggled to re-hang the newly washed drapes of her bed. Before drying the cloth in the late August sun, they had steeped it in a heather rinse. As they shook out the first drape, the scent billowed over her.

She found herself thinking of warm hillsides. She found herself yearning for Colin's lovemaking. Most of all, she found herself wondering what niggling concern kept dampening what should be delirious joy at the prospect of marrying the man she loved.

She winced as silver pierced her flesh. A drop of blood pearled out of her thumb. She sucked its coppery tang into her mouth before it could stain the fabric. Maybe her discontent arose from nothing more than being back in this castle with this false family. She hated being steeped in the lie that she was Lord Caddell's daughter, but Colin had convinced her that all the pomp and fuss was necessary. Many wars ended in a wedding, but only if the wedding had a multitude of witnesses.

She felt the patter of little feet and looked down to see Nutmeg on his haunches in her lap, twitching his nose.

"Aye, you feel it, too," she said, putting her embroidery aside to scratch his belly. "I suppose we'll both feel better once this wedding is done and we're out of this place."

Feeling the servants' eyes upon her, she set her attention back on her embroidery. Nutmeg skittered off her lap to sniff in an unoccupied corner. Lord William's announcement of the upcoming wedding had overturned the rigid, well-worn protocol of the castle. The last of the banns had been read yesterday at Mass. Though the wedding was ten days away, the guests had already begun arriving. The first pavilions rose up in the fields outside the walls—haphazard rows of dun-colored tarps, with brightly colored pennants flapping at their peaks like cock's combs of competing roosters. Servants bustled as if possessed, tradesmen roamed the halls, selling spices and cloth and ribbons and baubles to all who needed a new robe for the wedding day, *brehons* had arrived to draw up the wedding agreement, bickering with the English clerks, priests came to speak of marriage and take confession. She couldn't even escape to the kitchen for peace, for those rooms buzzed—a hive of kneading and baking and smoking and plucking.

To Maura's great relief, Lady Isabelle had taken the handling of most of the arrangements out of

Maura's clumsy hands. Instead, Maura concentrated on her bridal gown, on making the tiny tight stitches Sister Agnes had taught her to make. She set her mind to dreaming of how her life would be, once Colin and she were married. She wondered if they would ever have a moment of privacy again.

The door to her chamber flew open and servants flooded in. One came directly to her and bobbed a curtsy.

"Beggin' yer pardon, milady." The elderly woman's gaze darted around the room. Maura found herself thinking of those tiny, dun-colored birds that always flitted in and out of the stables, feasting on fleas and the occasional bit of grain. "I beg for a moment of your time."

"No need to beg." Maura would never get used to all the bobbing and curtsying. "Speak your mind."

"It's about the matter of your servants."

The woman had switched to Irish, so Maura did the same. "My servants?"

"Aye, milady. After your wedding, blessed be—" the woman made the sign of the cross, "you'll be off to your own household. And it's no secret that you'll need some women of your own to see to you."

Maura blinked. She supposed once the wedding was over it would be her responsibility to hire servants to keep Colin's castle running properly.

"I was wondering when you'd be picking them," the woman continued, fussing with her bird-boned hands, "and if you'll be taking many from the castle."

"I'll have to speak to The MacEgan."

"Of course," the woman said. "It's a wise thing, to consult with your husband before making a decision. But as to the matter of servants, the mistress picks her own."

Maura dropped her hands into her sewing. "Has someone sent you?" *To remind me of my duties?*

The elderly woman shook her head. "I come to speak for myself, milady."

Maura nodded in acknowledgement. Another consequence of becoming a chieftain's wife was that she must listen to the complaints of the village women in the expectation of speaking quiet counsel to her husband upon the bed pillow.

"Do you not remember me?" The elderly woman glanced over her shoulder at the other servants and then leaned in. "'Twas I who risked my old bones and what life I have left, God save me, to come forward on the St. Vitus's Day feast and tell the…tale."

Maura looked at the elderly woman with more attention. She remembered little of that night except an elderly nursemaid sprawled upon the rushes of the mead hall blathering on about twin babies and the vow she'd made to a baroness long dead.

"Lord William has treated me well," the servant continued, tugging her gray mantle close as if she were cold, "but once you're gone, I fear he won't want me around as my mind grows feeble, in case I go about speaking out of turn."

The older woman plucked at the edge of the mantle with nervous fingers. Her gaze kept darting about, to the servants and back.

Maura asked, "Has Lord William threatened to send you away?"

"No," she said. "Not yet. But I beg you to think on me, my lady. I may be old, but I can be of service. By the look of your future husband, it's likely you'll have a new babe in your arms every year."

Her cheeks grew warm. Yes, there would be many children in the years to come. A welcome responsibility. But another responsibility nonetheless.

"And since I know that kind of work," the old woman continued, "being a nursemaid and all, I was thinking you'd take me in."

Maura glanced at the woman's arms and thought they looked like they'd break under the weight of a pail of water. Then she thought of the cold gray eyes of William Caddell and imagined this Irishwoman begging outside a church, or silenced in a far worse way. She thought of the other servants she would have to hire, the children she would raise, the household she'd be responsible for on the height of that mountain. Her neck tightened up. She felt, all of a sudden, like she had to cook for thirty honored guests with nothing but a single ham, one pot, and two dull-witted servants.

Her stomach turned over like she'd swallowed a flock of birds.

"You are welcome in my household," she murmured, distractedly. "I thank you—all the MacEgans thank you—for your service."

After the servant bowed and left, Maura put her sewing aside. She paced to the window, and then back to the chair, and then back to the narrow window again, Nutmeg following, his little claws skittering on the floor slates. Then, without thinking any longer, she swept up her pet and headed for the door.

The next thing she knew, she was striding through the pavilion field. Catching sight of the pennant flapping with the serpentine swan, Maura stumbled past a startled Irish guard straight into Colin's tent—and a gathering of laughing, roughly-dressed Irishmen.

Colin rose from his crouch. He wore a fine tunic of crimson today, edged with silver embroidery. Gone was the chain mail. Gone, too, was the bristle that had darkened his lip and jaw. Clean-shaven, he had the look of a young English nobleman at leisure.

With one look at her, he waved his men out of the tent.

Colin held out a skin. She slipped Nutmeg to the ground and then took a sip of the ale. She couldn't catch her breath. She couldn't stop the racing of her heart. So she sank her face into his silk tunic. She curled her fists into the cloth, holding him close. He held her tight against his chest. His chin rested upon her head, his heart beat steady under her ear.

The cries of a ribbon-peddler sounded in the path between the pavilions. From outside came the barks of men's laughter, the murmur of women gossiping as they plied their needles in the waning sunshine. The smell of roasting meat wafted in through the flaps.

He said, softly, "What happened, my love?"

She murmured, "The world is changing."

"Aye, lass, it is. Very fast."

"I don't like being here with this false family."

"Neither do I."

"And I still have my ring," she said, "and no answers."

She pulled away from him and splayed her hand. When she'd first been given this shiny gold ring, she'd felt great gratitude for the gift. But this gift had birthed a thousand unanswered questions, impossible to answer in a life full of responsibilities. The mix had made her so restless that she'd abandoned those responsibilities just to seek the truth.

Now that gold ring still lay heavy upon her finger, a weight of a mystery unsolved—a mystery that might never be solved, if she didn't set out to resolve it before taking up the new responsibilities of the Lady MacEgan.

"You once made me a promise, Colin."

She blinked up at her lover. His smile was slow and warm.

"I did, didn't I?"

"A pilgrimage! But the wedding is in *ten days.*"

Maura tried not to flinch at Lord William's roar. Her false father stood behind a desk littered with books in tooled leather bindings, bristling with white quills and inkstands. The air of the room smelled of sweet beeswax, of great men in silk tunics discussing matters beyond the knowledge of a common girl.

Then Lord William glanced at Colin, who'd slipped his hip upon the desk. A strange smile flickered on his face.

The Englishman said, "Am I to assume you have agreed to this nonsense, MacEgan?"

Colin shrugged. "It's only St. Patrick's Purgatory. Less than a week's travel in good weather."

"You'd risk missing your own wedding day."

"Only by a few days. I know how to be quick upon the roads."

"And what sins," the Englishman said, tapping a seal upon its dish, "does a girl of that age have that hang so heavy upon her shoulders that she feels the need to go to a shrine and delay a wedding for which all of Connacht awaits?"

"Sins aplenty, Lord William," she said, forcing him to face her, "as you very well know."

Lord William waved a ringed hand. "Rather than take a pilgrimage, why don't you find a matron to give you a talking-to. Whatever sins you wish to confess don't need to be confessed on pilgrimage—"

"You mistake me." She cocked a brow at him. "I have little need of counsel in the matters of swiving."

Lord William's expression stilled. He glanced at MacEgan, who offered nothing but upturned palms.

"It's best I leave today," she said. "You can send guards if you wish to have us chaperoned. Though I'd prefer to travel with the minstrels."

Dancing and singing and piping their way down the roads.

"The minstrels indeed." The Englishman pointed to the window. "And what are we to do with the guests gathering in my fields outside? In the midst of harvest time, no less?"

"You could always make up a play yourself," she said. "You're very good at that."

Lord William sighed. "MacEgan, put an end to this foolishness. Take her on pilgrimage when the marriage is done."

"After the marriage," she said, once again drawing his attention, "I will have many responsibilities and little time for travel."

"Why St. Patrick's Purgatory?" he asked sharply.

She hesitated, her spine stiffening. She had woven such pretty fantasies about the purgatory. She had imagined herself arriving and falling at the bedside of some elderly clergyman whose body ailed, though his mind remained sharp, some priest who would clutch her hands, recognize her instantly, and finally gasp out the twenty-two-year-old secret of a mother's terrible confession, before slipping off to Paradise while she sobbed by his bedside.

Well, she wasn't that foolish little dreamer anymore, but that didn't mean she didn't need to put the fantasy to rest.

"Certain pilgrims passed by my convent around the time of my birth," she said, lifting her hand so that her ring winked by the light sifting through the narrow window. "I was told they were going to St. Patrick's Purgatory." She glanced at the guard by the door, carefully weighing her words, as she'd done every day since she'd returned to this castle. "I vowed I would go someday, too, in respect for those good people. That vow has remained unfulfilled."

Lord Caddell's face darkened. He glared at Colin. "Why are you encouraging this?"

"I made a promise."

"You also made a bargain with me." The Englishman fluttered a white hand toward the window. "Two hundred and seven people are coming to witness it. Yet you wish your future wife to set out on a quest whose motive—" he lowered his voice "—risks all these well-laid plans."

She said, "It's just a pilgrimage, my lord."

"You'll find nothing at St. Patrick's Purgatory," the Englishman insisted. "Nothing but barefoot, fasting pilgrims preparing themselves to enter the cave. Nothing but strips of linen fluttering from the tip of every branch of every bush, flags marking the visits. And no priest old enough to remember one set of pilgrims from the thousands and thousands and thousands that have passed through, in the twenty-three years since *my wife's* nursemaid left you on the convent stairs."

Ever sticking to the play, this false father of hers. "Do you ever visit your late wife's grave, my lord?"

"Every year," he snapped. "On her name day. What of it?"

"You're fortunate to have someplace to pay your respects to the one you loved. For me," she added, raising her ringed finger, "this is all I'll ever have."

Maura watched as his expression shifted, as a measure of understanding flickered in those eyes. For so long she felt as if she lived somewhere in-between—knowing that she had parents who cared enough about her to swaddle her and leave her a treasure, but not knowing who those parents were. It had been a purgatory, of sorts. But she understood now that she would never know who her parents were. Before she started her new life, she needed to say good-bye to the old.

The Englishman placed his hands on his desk, resting his weight so his fingertips turned white.

"There's no use in going to St. Patrick's Purgatory. But I can tell you something about that damn ring."

The words shocked her like a blow to the ears. She was sure she hadn't heard them right, and so it took her a moment to understand. When she did, her body went very still, very numb. A throbbing began in her head, a relentless dull pressure. She wondered if, when she emerged from this fog, she would be able to forgive men who took a strange, morbid pleasure in spinning webs of intrigues.

"I'm surprised, with all your travels," Caddell said, raising a brow at Colin, "that you didn't recognize it, too, MacEgan."

Colin glared at Caddell with a face full of questions.

"That insignia," William Caddell began, "is much faded, but I've seen that design before, when I was a young man traveling on the continent. A hundred thousand peddlers sold trinkets like that, tokens that a pilgrim could take home as proof that a certain journey had been made. Thousands of pilgrims wear that insignia, my dear. It's from the church of St. James of Compostela."

Suddenly Colin was beside her, taking her hand in is, uncurling the fingers she'd tightened into a fist, as if he was untying the strings of a bound guinea fowl.

Colin traced the lines that projected to the edge of the ring face. "We once worked among the Pyrenean passes—part of the road to St. James. The symbol of that church is a cockleshell." Colin flattened his hand over the smudged, faded lower half of the ring, so that only the rays were visible. "I should have recognized this," he said. "It's a seashell insignia. But the ring is so worn."

"Sabine wore it all her life." The men looked at her in question, that's how she realized she'd spoken aloud. "Sabine was a laywoman in the convent."

Colin said, "Why was she wearing your ring?"

"I'm not sure." The Abbess had been vague about that, waving away Maura's questions with the comment, *you know how Sabine was about pretty things.* "Sabine had always been partial to baubles. Since I was too young to have it, I just supposed the Abbess let her wear it." Maura frowned as the memories flooded through her. "Nutmeg was hers, before she gave him to me, too."

Colin tightened his grip on her hand. "And Sabine—or the Abbess—never told you this was a token from St. James?"

Maura shook her head. His words gave her pause. Even *she* had heard about that church on the shores of Spain. Some of the wealthier novices talked about having made the pilgrimage with their families. It ranked third in the great pilgrimages—behind Jerusalem and Rome.

"This Sabine," William Caddell said, with a darkness in his voice, "is she still living?"

"No."

Relief spread across Lord William's face. That sight, more than anything else, caused the back of her neck to tingle. She couldn't believe—no, it couldn't be true—not Sabine, silly Sabine, growing ever fatter in her bed overflowing with pillows, the laywoman who'd loved to comb Maura's hair when she was a child but lost interest as she grew into a woman…no, it couldn't be. She could not have lived in that convent all her life and heard no whisper of such a secret. Not even by the Abbess after Sabine's death.

The Abbess, who'd come to Ireland from Avignon, who must have been familiar with the insignia of St. James of Compostela.

"Lord William," Colin said. "We shall forgo the trip to St. Patrick's Purgatory."

"I knew you were a man of good sense—"

"The wedding will be delayed a little longer." Colin threaded his warm fingers through hers. "Tomorrow we're off to Killeigh."

CHAPTER TWENTY-TWO

The minstrels danced into Killeigh. Padraig Smallpipe led the way, his tunic twirling, his bare feet slapping upon the mud, rat-tatting his tabor while the Mudman piped a wheeling jig. The twins tumbled on either side of a donkey, flashing bare thighs for all the world to see. Arnaud followed behind, trailing a donkey that carried Matilda nursing her newborn son. The two guards that Caddell had insisted chaperone them swept off their horses the minute they came within sight of an alehouse. They waved them off with barely a good-bye.

Maura clutched the pommel of her saddle and drank in the sight of her home village. Everything looked the same, and yet everything looked different, the muddy little houses and the crooked little lanes, the sheep that scattered away at their approach, the barefoot children who watched from doorways with their fingers in their mouths. It looked like a toy village, a miniature that Sabine would have played with, not the sprawling dangerous streets she'd been constantly warned about.

The Mudman paused by her horse, stopping his piping long enough to give her a sooty grin. "We'll be off to the square," he said, making a deep bow. "Best of luck, your highnesses."

Then with a wink he was gone, following the twins down another street. She had an irrepressible urge to follow him and leave this quest behind.

"Strange, isn't it?" Colin said. "To come back home?"

She cast her handsome soon-to-be husband a wavering smile. "I can hardly believe I've spent my whole life here."

"Coming home gives you double vision," he said. "You see the place how you remember it…but you also see it how it actually is."

She knew he was thinking about the MacEgans, and the long war, and how his expectations had been upended by an Englishman who'd had enough of fighting and a clan weary of bitter-enders.

"Maura." He held his hand out to her. "Whatever you discover, I'll still be here, as will our new life."

She brushed her fingertips against his until the horses bumped apart. She felt the buzzing sensation that warmed between them, remembering last night's tussle in the grass. She held the memory close until her nervousness ebbed.

Then the convent of Killoughy came into view. She and Colin nudged their horses through the archway into the courtyard. Everything looked smaller than she remembered here, as well, probably because she'd never observed it from the high seat of a fine, caparisoned palfrey.

A nun raced out of the convent proper. Maura

suppressed a shout of surprised recognition. Here was Sister Agnes, as round as ever, running toward them as if she was late for Mass.

The nun said, "My lord and my lady MacEgan?"

"I am MacEgan," Colin said, shifting off his horse and handing the reins to a stable boy. "This is my betrothed, the lady Maura Caddell."

Sister Agnes glanced at her, then startled in mid-curtsy. Maura gave her an apologetic shrug. It was no surprise Sister Agnes hadn't recognized her. Maura had never visited the convent in a dove white tunic and a rose-colored surcoat edged in rich silver thread.

"Maura! *Our* Maura!" Sister Agnes patted her chest and flushed right to the edge of her starched veil. "We thought you were lost forever!"

"I was always in good hands, Agnes."

"Did you say *betrothed?*" She grew flustered as Colin walked around to help Maura down. "We'll be praying blessings for the happy day, then." The nun all but tripped back toward the door, trying to find her balance. "We've prepared for your arrival—the Abbess is waiting for you—I must run ahead and tell her the good news!"

Agnes ran off as Colin's hands encircled her waist. Maura slipped off the saddle into his arms. He held her longer than was necessary, and she welcomed his embrace. It had taken more than a week to arrive here in Killeigh, but she couldn't call it hard travel. The nights had been full of the music of Padraig's pipe, the bellow of Arnaud complaining of the pace, the mewling sounds of Matilda's new child wanting to nurse. In the evenings she'd stared up at the bright sparks of the sky, the only blanket she needed for her bed, thankful that Lord William's guards were hardly vigilant—especially with the twins on their laps—so she and Colin could sneak off and sleep in each other's arms.

"Milord," she said, flattening her hands against his chest. "We're in a convent now, if you please."

With a wink he curled her hand under his elbow and led her into the convent. Maura breathed in the scent of frankincense, of laundry, of old crinkling rushes with a rush of nostalgia. They passed through the hall where she had seen served so many meals— the chairs lined up just the way they'd always been, the tapestries just as bright. They passed the cells where the nuns slept, and the bright, cold rooms where the novices took their lessons.

She paused for a moment when they passed the cell where Sabine had lived. Once, this small cell had rung with the chirping of birds, the cracking of nuts, and the scent of perfume far more exotic than any incense. This cell had been a magical place of wonder. Now she wondered with a mix of hope and resentment if this room had also been her nursery.

When they reached the Abbess's rooms, the great oak doors opened to a blaze of light. A draft ruffled a single piece of vellum and twisted a quill around the edge of an inkwell. Upon a tilted rostrum nearby lay a leather-tooled Bible, a page lovingly marked with a scarlet silk ribbon.

The Abbess leapt up from behind a battered oak table. "By the blessed milk of the Holy Mother Mary." The Abbess pressed a hand in the hollow below her bosom. "Sister Agnes said it was you, Maura, but I could hardly believe it. My dear Maura!"

"Lady Abbess." Maura bobbed like the maid she once had been. "It's me, whole and healthy."

The Abbess strode toward her and gripped her hands. The Abbess had lively, unusual eyes, bright and expressive against the white of her wimple, and now that gaze darted across her face, up and down her dress, while the muscles in the Abbess's face quivered in odd ways.

"We thought you were lost," the Abbess said. "Or stolen away. We've been saying prayers for your soul every day, worrying what had become of you."

Maura felt a pang of guilt to go along with a pang of pain for the tightness of the Abbess's grip.

"Did you doubt it, Maura? Didn't we all raise you since you were barely out of swaddling?" The Abbess gave her a twitchy smile. "And our daily fare has not been the same since you disappeared so abruptly. I fear half the sisters prayed not just for your safety, but also for your venison baked in jelly. Or your salmon in butter sauce. And of course, the butcher's son, he all but abed with worry for you—"

The Abbess bit down on her own chatter. She raised her chin as if she was trying to get herself in hand.

Maura's heart softened to see her so affected.

"But look at you now." The Abbess gestured to Maura's silver embroidery, the fine rose-colored surcoat, the well-tooled leather shoes peeping out beneath the hem. "Such a lady. And betrothed to an Irish chieftain. There's a tale in this, I see."

The nun sidled a glance at Colin, and in her eyes swam suspicion and uncertainty and a growing coolness of manner. The Abbess cleared her throat and stepped back into her straight-backed authority. "Will you stay awhile, tell me what has happened?" She strode to the hearth and rang a pulley hanging by its side. "Surely," the Abbess continued, "it's the stuff of the French romances our dear Sabine used to smuggle in from fairs and hide under her pallet."

"I shall tell it to you," Maura said, hesitating. She wasn't sure she'd be able to explain everything that had happened without lying, and just the thought of lying to the Abbess brought back too many youthful memories of the threat of the paddle. "But first," she said, "I need your help."

"My help?"

"Did you receive a letter from the Baron of Shrule?"

"The Baron of—my goodness, Maura, what are you talking about?"

So William Caddell hadn't sent a letter as he'd threatened. He probably didn't believe her story at all. Maura shook off the thought and splayed her hand, letting the gold ring wink in the sunlight.

"Do you remember this ring?"

"Of course I remember that ring." A knot tightened in the Abbess's forehead. "You could speak of nothing, but that ring, that ring, that ring in those weeks before you disappeared." She sank into the chair behind her desk. "I thought maybe you'd been taken captive by thieves who'd seen the ring. All these weeks, I wish I'd never given it to you."

"It was this ring that sent me out of the convent." Maura rubbed the face of the gold. "I left to find my parents."

The Abbess looked from her to Colin in confusion. "I don't understand. How did you think that the ring could ever help you?"

Because I was foolish, and young, and curious, and ignorant of the world. "You told me about the pilgrims who passed by here around the time I was abandoned on the steps," she stuttered. "The ones from St. Patrick's Purgatory."

"Yes, yes I did." The Abbess took a deep breath, lines deepening below the hem of her wimple. "You were so full of questions, I had to tell you something to make them stop. But that ring," she said, "is from St. James of Compostela."

Maura was thankful she was already sitting, for at those words she would surely have fallen in a heap. "You never told me that."

The Abbess's shrug was stiff. "I didn't think it of importance."

"Why did Lady Sabine wear it, then, all her life?"

"The Lady Sabine tended to excess in all things. You know this." The Abbess's expression darkened. "I wasn't aware that she'd borrowed the ring from me until I found it among her things after her death."

"She *stole* the ring?"

"I will not speak ill of the dead." The Abbess's jaw tightened. "I can only speculate how she found it. I was keeping the ring for you, you see. For your wedding day, if you chose to marry the butcher's son. For a donation to the church, if you chose to take the veil. I'd put it in a safe place and didn't give it another thought. There was no reason for me to imagine it was missing until I found it amid Sabine's things."

The door squealed open. A novice poked in her head. The Abbess glanced blankly at the intruder, as if she forgot that she'd summoned her moments ago with a tug of the bell-pull.

The novice looked past the edge of the door to grant Maura an excited smile. Therese, Maura remembered. A bright spark of a novice, far too lively for the veil.

"Bring wine," the Abbess said. "The knight and his lady need refreshment after their long journey."

The girl bobbed her head and closed the door. The Abbess gathered herself, then leaned back in her straight-backed chair, grasping the arms. "You announced yourself as Lady Maura Caddell. So in your travels—and adventuresome they must have been—you have found your father?"

"Lord William Caddell," Maura began, "has claimed me as his firstborn daughter, aye."

The tendons in the Abbess's throat tightened. "A highborn father. So unusual, to have found your relations."

"More unusual than you know, Abbess."

"You must tell me, my dear, how you found this family, for I fear I find it very hard to believe."

Maura glanced at her lap. Along the road, she and Colin had talked long and hard about how much to tell the Abbess about their situation. There were risks involved in exposing herself as the false daughter of William Caddell. Colin had been surprisingly calm about it. He said that any woman who'd gone to such lengths to hide a secret baby would not want it exposed now, lest it put the convent in a bad light.

Now he gave her a nod, his strength flooding over her like a warm wind.

Maura dug her fingers into her tunic. "Lord William Caddell, my father—" the word still stumbled over her tongue "—has agreed to my marriage to The MacEgan to forge a long-awaited peace. It's an important marriage, a marriage that will bring peace to a place that has not seen it in a decade."

"A marriage to forge a peace."

"Yes."

"Maura, my dear, this story is like—"

"Bear with me, Lady Abbess," she interrupted, surprised at her own temerity. "What I really need to know, what I came back to discover, is whether my natural mother lived here, in this very convent. If my mother were perhaps…Sabine."

The Abbess made a choking sound, then leaned forward and grasped the edge of the desk. Maura was halfway out of her chair, frightened by the thought that the Lady Abbess was choking on something, when a knock came from the oak door.

The Abbess leapt up, undeterred. She strode through the rushes and swung open the door. Hiding behind it, she muttered something to someone just outside and then backed into the room holding a tray of wine and cups.

The Abbess crossed the room and clattered the tray on the table between her and Colin. "I suppose," she said, her voice oddly hoarse, "that Sabine's special treatment of you gave you the impression that she might be your mother?"

"Her affection wasn't always steady," Maura confessed, tightening her grip on the arms of the chair. "And she liked me less as I grew older. But she did hold my ring, and hold it a long time—"

"Maura, Sabine was *not* your mother."

Maura felt as if one of the legs had been pulled off the chair beneath her. Colin's hand on her arm was a steady weight, keeping her still.

"But," the nun continued, "I can see how you may have concluded such a ridiculous thing, considering Sabine's affection for you."

Maura remembered the dolls, the birds, the little

songs Sabine would sing as she combed Maura's hair.

"Sabine lost a child," the Abbess said, splattering wine into two cups. "A stillborn baby girl."

Maura struggled to breathe.

"Illegitimate," the Abbess explained. "That's why she was sent to this convent by her father in the first place." The Abbess handed her a cup of wine. "You must have known that she wasn't the most excellent example of piety among the laywomen."

Maura stared into the ruby depths of the wine, watching the shimmer of her own reflection.

"That's why, I suspect, she liked you so much when you were young." The Abbess backed up to the edge of her desk without taking a glass of her own. "You were willing to have your hair pulled with her endless brushing. And I just broke a solemn vow to a powerful nobleman by telling you that."

Maura caught the worry in the Abbess's eyes, a glimpse of guilt she'd never seen before.

"I take my vows very seriously," the Abbess said. "I always have, from the moment I left my home in Avignon and came here. I do not lightly break vows, or tell secrets that others have entrusted me with."

Months ago, Maura would have heard this tone of voice from the Abbess and she'd have never dared to ask another question. But Maura had been out in the world now. Now she realized that the tremor in the nun's voice wasn't fury. There was something else behind her words, something the older woman hesitated to say. Maura didn't come all this way to leave without finding out.

"I must trust your discretion, Abbess, and you must trust mine. I have a future that lies bright before me." She closed her hand over the one Colin had placed on her arm. "Before I walk that path, I need to know why I have a ring from St. James of Compostela, why it was buried so deep in my swaddling clothes, and, most of all, who put it there."

"Oh, Maura, the story is common," the Abbess said, a weariness in her words, "and as old as time."

The Abbess headed around her desk. She stumbled against the corner and then paused, her fingers on the surface turning white.

Maura could almost hear her will cracking.

"Once upon a time," the Abbess began, in a voice so low that Maura had to lean forward to hear her, "a young woman went on a pilgrimage to St. James of Compostela. She was headstrong, ill-guarded among the children of a large family, beloved but given more freedom than she deserved."

Maura's heart stopped for a moment—another, yet another—and then throbbed hard in her chest.

"That woman," the Abbess continued, "took interest in a tall, dark-haired stranger on the same roads. He had an accent so charming, and his eyes were warm, and his touch was the closest she'd ever gotten to Heaven."

The Abbess turned her face toward her, flaming with color now, and Maura's throat swelled with understanding.

"I took two things back from that pilgrimage to Compostela," the Abbess said. "The first was the ring. The second was you, growing in my womb."

For the second time in his life, Colin sat as still as stone outside the center of events, listening to a woman tell a wild tale about how Maura came to be a foundling left on the convent steps.

But this was no elaborate spectacle. This was no well-orchestrated set of players. The Abbess's bright gaze lay desperate upon Maura's face as she told the story of returning home to her village in France only to discover that she was with child. The Abbess's voice trembled as she spoke of her fear of her father, who she knew would take the child away forever. She'd loved the man she'd met on the pilgrimage no matter how brief their acquaintance. She wanted his child so she kept the pregnancy a secret. She told her father she wanted to join a neighbor who'd taken vows in an Irish nunnery the year before. With six daughters to marry off, her piety was a relief to him, and would cost no more than a small chest of gold. Within a few months she was on a ship to Ireland, her only companion a trusted nursemaid who would see the child born in an Irish field outside of Wexford, see the novice that would become an Abbess escorted to the nunnery, and see the child left behind on the convent steps.

Colin stood up and poured wine for all of them as the tale unfolded, soft in the darkening room. A tree branch tapped a rhythm upon the leaded panes. Maura herself had sunk into the hard-backed chair, clutching a chalice with white fingers. Colin laid his hand upon Maura's shoulder and felt, through the fragile silk, the slow loosening of her muscles as the final mystery was made known.

"None of the sisters knew the truth," the Abbess continued, "though in later years some wondered why I insisted that you run the kitchens, and not one of the novices or the nuns. You were a fine cook, Maura, but to those watching the books, you were an extravagance." With a pass of her hand, the Abbess gestured to the ink and papers upon the table. "Sabine's family's yearly contribution to the convent was a bounty that helped support your position here, but it didn't continue after Sabine's death."

"That's why," Maura said, breathless, "you wanted me to marry the butcher's son."

"I was about your age when I fell into… sinfulness. I thought the butcher's boy was a fine, honest young man. I didn't want you to waste away as a simple kitchen servant. I wanted you to be happy." The Abbess's gaze flickered to Colin's face. "But it seems blood will seek its own."

The Abbess talked more and more. She spoke of the years of Maura's childhood, sharing how she'd slipped, in small ways, and revealed her special affection. Allowing her in for lessons in Latin and French. Special tasks rewarded with time in Sabine's room, the only place where there were toys of a sort—birds and shiny pennies and dolls. The Abbess spoke until her throat went rough, until she could not speak any more.

"Forgive me, Maura," the Abbess said, wiping her cheeks. "I could have given you over to a family to be raised. That would have been the wiser thing to do. But I wanted to watch you grow, even if I could never claim you as my own."

And Colin found himself thinking how family means obligations, and what desperate sacrifices a good woman would make for the love of her child.

They didn't notice as Colin headed toward the door. As he closed it behind him, he glimpsed his future wife rushing around the desk into the Abbess's open arms.

CHAPTER TWENTY-THREE

Maura shifted her weight upon the bench. Under the cover of the damask tablecloth, she pinched her thigh to wake her leg out of tingling sleep. Around her, women rustled in their fine silk tunics, talking of the labors of childbirth, of the faraway English court, and the strange cut of a French guest's tunic. She stifled a yawn, bored of the stately harp music and the watered Gascon wine.

High Masses had more vigor than this wedding. Surely this was the dullest event she had ever attended. Or perhaps it just seemed that way, after spending so much time on the road with minstrels.

And her mother.

Her heart swelled. She and her mother—the word still felt a little odd on her lips—had spent a long time talking, for the Abbess had shared the road with the minstrels all the way to Shrule. It took Maura by surprise how well the Abbess tolerated the folks she once so disparaged, and Maura had told her so. The Abbess had given Maura a wink and confessed she had a weakness for fallen women.

Unfortunately, the Abbess had long abandoned the mead hall, so Maura was no longer entertained by her sharp observations of the English gentry, spoken in whispers. Before she'd retired, the Abbess had pressed a warm kiss upon her brow, wished her happiness in her new life, and laid a very public blessing upon her. That fact that her mother was an Abbess was almost too perfect a guise for the secret they held fast between them. Even William Caddell remained ignorant, his mind put to ease with the harmless, whispered story that the late laywoman Sabine had been her true mother.

I will make her godmother of my first child, Maura thought. Then the Abbess would have an excuse to visit often.

Now she searched the room until her gaze lit upon Colin. Their gazes locked. He raised his brows toward Maguire Mudman, who darted among the crowd playing the wild man, desperately trying to inject some mischief into this wedding. *Aye, Colin, I know where your heart is.* He, too, wished he was listening to Padraig pipe a lively jig, or hearing Maguire tell an earthy story full of human weakness. He probably wished, as she did, that they were both reeling in a merry dance alone under the moonlight instead of watching the stately dances of these English nobility and smiling stiff smiles and talking of inconsequential things.

She sighed and splayed her hands upon the tablecloth. Her wedding ring winked in the amber light. Upon the church steps this morning, Colin had slipped the ring upon her third finger and promised to love and honor her for as long as she should live—

and thus bound them both to a strange new life.

She couldn't wait for this dull wedding to end and the true marriage to begin.

Then a rustling rose in the hall, like a gaggle of geese rising from a pond. She knew the sound by now, for she had sat before this table and been served what seemed like a hundred courses over the afternoon. This time, it was the waferer who presented himself. A fleet of servants followed in his wake. Gleaming silver platters heaped with figs and apples and round glistening orbs of an orange fruit said to come from the heathen country were presented at intervals all the way down the table.

The guests settled back at their places. She felt Colin's breath upon her shoulder as he came up behind her. "When is the bedding, dammit?"

A tingling skipped down her spine. He clambered over the bench and eyed her as she reached for an orange.

"I trust," she said, rolling the orange between her palms, "that the bedding will be more lively than the wedding."

"A burial would be livelier than this."

"Why did Lord William bother hiring the minstrels if he isn't going to use them properly?"

"He's using Fingar."

"Aye, to pluck at that harp like he's a boy learning his scales."

"Maybe Lord William has heard too many stories from your guards upon the roads." Colin lay his hand over his chalice to prevent a servant from refilling it. "Maybe he thinks if Padraig pipes or if Fingar sets loose his talent, or the twins start tumbling, then you'll tear off your veil and let your hair fly free and dance barefoot."

She leaned into him, brushing her cheek against the soft wool of his tunic, not caring if they were being watched. "If you think you can get me out of the witnessing of the bedding, Colin, I just might dance for you tonight. And it'll be more than my feet that will be bare."

Under the table, he tugged her tunic to make way for his hand. "I'm holding you to that promise, lass."

Lord William suddenly rose from his seat and swung his chalice high. Silence fell upon the crowd. The Englishman's pronouncements of good health and happiness and peace to Connacht seemed to come at more and more frequent intervals. But she wasn't really listening. Colin's fingers had traced their way up the inside of her leg, even as her husband turned to politely look up at his father-in-law.

"Ladies, knights, worthy men and maidens," Lord William began, spreading his arms so the embroidery of his silken surcoat glimmered in the firelight. "You all know the wonders that God has bestowed upon me and my family these past months. First, by sending my eldest daughter, my long-lost daughter, back into the fold of our family. And now, by gifting me with a wise son-in-law."

Lord William pinned Colin by the shoulder. Colin covered the Englishman's hand with his own, even as Colin tightened his grip on her thigh.

"But," Lord William continued, "all those months ago, I had sent for this very same troupe of worthy minstrels, not in the thought of finding a daughter, but in the hopes of hearing a certain lady of renown—to hear the voice of a songstress. A foundling who could sing with the voice of angels."

Maura's mouth parched, but not from his words, for Colin had begun tracing circles on her inner thigh.

"Maura."

She startled and looked up at the Englishman.

"Maura," her false father repeated, "grant me this one last favor, as my still maiden daughter."

"F-favor?"

"Sing to your grieving father," he said, "and let me hear the voice so long denied to me."

The Englishman had summoned a tear to gleam upon his cheek. Around the room came shouts of encouragement. She didn't want to sing. Not now. And not for Lord William, of all men. But she realized that if she tried to demur, it would seem as if she was demurring out of modesty—and that was a hypocrisy she couldn't bear.

She glanced at Colin, who gave her a shrug as he slipped his hand off her thigh. He slid away to give her room to climb off the bench.

"Yes, father," she said. "I'll sing for you."

Amid polite applause, she worked her way around the long table and took her place in the middle of the hall. Fingar shifted the harp upon his knee. His yellow grin gleamed in the rush light.

"What will it be, Highness?" Fingar brushed his fingertips across the strings. "'*Angelus ad virginem*'? Or will ye be wantin' one o' those soggy love songs the women sobber over?"

She supposed the Angel's address to the Virgin was what everyone expected from her. This banquet had the taste of the church to it. She should give them a good hymn about Christ's wounds, or some such thing, to put them all in the praying mood. She could sing about love, too, she understood that well enough.

Then she thought of another kind of love she craved…a way of loving that Colin had so thoroughly taught her.

It was her wedding, after all.

Maura breathed in the torch smoke and felt the thrum of the Gascon wine in her blood. She looked across at the man who'd traveled with her upon the roads, who'd taught her how wonderful life—and love—could truly be. Then she tilted her head back, opened her mouth, and let the song unfurl.

As the words fell from her lips, she was very glad that her mother the Abbess was no longer in the room.

Colin shoved the door open so hard that it cracked against the wall. Through the haze of her laughter, Maura sensed the heat and blaze of beeswax candles and the billowing fragrance of lavender and roses. She lifted her face off of Colin's shoulder just in time to realize he was tossing her upon the bed.

She squealed as she hit the wool and furs, a toss forceful enough to send her bouncing back up to her elbows. Servants skittered from all corners of the room and clogged the door like so many mice battling to be the first to escape.

"Did you enjoy playing the lusty minstrel, woman?" He turned and bolted the door. "On the wedding day of The MacEgan, no less."

"Did you see them?" She gasped for breath. "Did you see them all standing as if they'd been turned to wood?"

"The women behind you," he said, wrestling himself out of his tunic, "were opening and closing their mouths like so many fish.''

"Arnaud, in the corner, was choking in laughter.''

"Can you imagine what Lord William is saying now to all those guests?''

"I should have sang 'The Ball of Ballymore.'" She rose up on an elbow. "Or 'The Young Man and His Maid.'''

"A fine, lusty wife you'll make.''

He seized her ankles and dragged himself over her. His face was lit with the flickering amber glow of candles. His surcoat was gone, his hose untied, his braies in a linen heap on the floor. He pressed his naked body upon hers, his bare skin hot. She crushed the petals of late-blooming roses beneath her back, filling the room with their scent. He ran an eager hand down her side to her hip to tug up her tunic. His hair fell over his brow, slipping out of the civilized bit of something he'd used to tie it back. The *culans* slid over his shoulder and tickled her cheek. He gripped her face and his eyes filled with an emotion she recognized now, for she knew her own eyes were filled with the same.

He kissed her. A deep, long, slow kiss, filled with shared laughter, filled with something else, too, something warm and comfortable and sweet. She couldn't place it right away, not while he muddled her thoughts with his touch. He was her husband, aye, her lover, oh, aye, but somewhere upon the road he'd also become something unexpected—he'd become her friend, a closer friend than ever she had.

Suddenly, from outside the door, came the high roiling reel of Padraig's unmistakable pipe.

"It seems," she said, tugging on Colin's Irish braid, "you stopped the witnessing of the bedding.''

"That I did."

"Didn't I make you a promise," she whispered, pulling up her tunic, "about dancing naked for your eyes alone?"

THE END

**Turn the page for a sneak-peek of
HEAVEN IN HIS ARMS, another
romantic road-trip adventure by Lisa Ann
Verge**

"An absorbing, exciting romantic adventure!"
                                    —RT Book Reviews

*"Lisa Ann Verge breathes fresh life into the romance genre
with a novel that should gather her award nominations."*
                                    —Affaire de Coeur

Paris, 1670

Struggling to survive on the streets of Paris, Genevieve agrees to a dangerous masquerade: She switches places with a King's Girl, a young noblewoman about to be shipped to the colonies. It's a risky venture with a high price—once overseas, Genny must marry a stranger.

PROLOGUE

Paris, July 1670

This was her only chance.

Genevieve pressed against the stone wall. The dampness seeped through her woolen dress and chilled her skin, already clammy with fear. She dug her fingers into the bundle clutched to her chest. She had come this far. All that was left was to pass the guard at the end of the hallway, and she would be free.

The distraction had already begun. A slip of a girl emerged from one of the doorways. That girl raced toward the dozing female guard and startled the woman from her nap. The guard blinked at the wild-haired creature while the young girl—a deaf-mute—gestured frantically toward the gaping door of her cell. Sighing, the stocky guard hefted out of her seat, grasped a sputtering candle, and followed her.

As soon as the guard disappeared into the

chamber, Genevieve leapt out of the shadows. She raced on bare feet toward the oak doors. She would only have a few moments before the guard realized that the young woman's unspoken fears were imaginary—then the laywoman would shrug it off and return to her station.

But by then, by ruse, Genevieve Lalande would have already escaped.

The brass handle chilled her hand. She eased the door open to prevent the hinges from squeaking. When it was cracked enough, she slipped through and closed it behind her. She leaned against the door for a moment, sucking in the night air as she waited for her blood to stop pounding. But she was already late. If she didn't hurry, her second accomplice would lose courage and destroy all their plans.

She scanned the enormous courtyard of the Salpêtrière, her prison for the last three years. The night was clear but moonless. Bits of gravel scattered the starlight, making the courtyard glitter as if it were covered with frost. There was no sign of her accomplice, but she'd hoped that the girl would have more sense than to stand like a lost child in the middle of the open courtyard. She glanced at the debris scattered at the opposite end, where the church of Saint Louis was being built. There was no better place to hide than among the hewn stones, the piled earth, and the skeletal wooden scaffolding.

She clung to the walls as she worked her way over. Chips of gravel bit into her feet. A breeze swept through the open courtyard, heavy with the stench of the Seine River. The rows of windows in the opposite building winked at her like a thousand eyes and she was so distracted that she stubbed her toe against a pick abandoned by some day worker. She squeezed her eyes shut until the pain passed. Then she limped on until she reached the shadows of the scaffolding.

Marie should have been here by now. The last note Genevieve had sent her was specific: Tonight was the night they were to meet in this courtyard to complete the plans they had so painstakingly formed over the last three weeks. She and Marie had been passing notes back and forth through the same system without fail for too long for there to be a sudden mix-up.

Come, Marie. Come.

Somewhere in Paris church bells rang. Above her, birds startled with an anxious fluttering of wings. A stream of silt filtered down from the higher scaffolding, dusting her shoulder. As the church bells faded, she saw a figure separate from one of the buildings.

Genevieve sucked in a breath and pressed back against the masonry. If one of the guards saw her, she'd be right back where she started, and who knew when she'd get a chance like this again. But as she watched the figure enter the courtyard, she realized this was no guard. It was a woman, a young woman by the quick pace of her walk, an anxious woman by the way her head pivoted back and forth.

Genevieve intercepted her near a pile of bricks. "Marie?"

The young woman stopped short and pulled back the edge of her scarf, revealing a pale, drawn face. "Genevieve?"

"*Oui.* Come into the shadows."

She had never seen Marie before today. With relief, she noticed that they were of about the same height. Height would have been the most difficult to disguise.

As she approached, Marie loosened her head rail and pulled the scarf off her hair. "Thank God you are here. I feared you would leave. The housekeeper on my floor would not fall asleep. I had to check three doors before I found one unlocked."

Refined speech. Well, Genevieve could mimic that well enough. "You had nothing to fear," she said. "I would have stayed until dawn."

The young woman squinted at her. "I have never seen you before."

"Nor I you." She didn't bother to explain that she was housed in a separate building, isolated from women like Marie. Marie was a *bijou,* a jewel of the Salpêtrière, an orphaned daughter of the petty nobility, pampered and educated and protected.

"You write with such a fine hand," Marie murmured, glancing at Genevieve's common russet skirts. "I thought you might be one of the noblewomen housed in another building."

Genevieve felt the muscles of her neck tighten. In another time, in a better world, she might have been worthy of being called a *bijou.* But that was long ago and best left forgotten. She gestured to Marie's skirts. "Is that what you planned to wear tomorrow?"

"Yes." Marie parted her cloak to show a dark blue traveling dress. "I've packed a small case and left it by my bed. In it, you'll find several other dresses and a few gold pieces. This is all I can give you for what you are doing for me."

Such foolish, innocent generosity. "You should have kept the money. You'll need it more than I—"

"No, that isn't true." Marie twisted her scarf in

her hands. "You do know what you're doing, don't you? I couldn't live with myself—no matter how happy I'd be to escape this place—if I misled you."

"I'm the one who suggested this plan."

"But I'm going to be sent away—*you're* going to be sent away," Marie corrected. "King Louis XIV himself has dowered me. He has paid my passage to some horrible place called Quebec and he intends to marry me off to some coarse, half-savage settler—"

"I know you're a king's girl." Every year since she'd arrived in the Salpêtrière, dozens of girls had been given a dowry by the king and sent off to the Caribbean islands or to the northern settlements of New France, to marry and settle in the colonies. "I chose you because you're being sent away from here."

"Do you know anything about Quebec?"

Genevieve took the mangled scarf out of the other girl's hands to stop her from crumpling it. "I know enough."

"The forests are filled with red-skinned savages. The winters are long and frigid, and there's so much snow that it tops the rooftops." Bereft of the scarf, Marie's smooth white hands knotted and twisted and pulled at each other. "And the voyage—over the sea—halfway across the world, in storms and sickness. Why are you doing this? Why would you take my place and go to that dreadful colony and leave all this behind?"

Genevieve glared at the long buildings of the Salpêtrière and thought, *I'd rather sell my soul to Lucifer than spend another hour here.*

But Marie wouldn't understand that. She and Marie both lived in this "charity house," but they lived in entirely different worlds. Marie lived in the

Salpêtrière of King Louis XIV, the charity house that succored aging servants with no pensions, old married couples of good birth, and the younger daughters of impoverished petty nobility, a charity house staffed with religious women and headed by a benign Mother Superior. Genevieve lived in a place ruled by brutal guards, a place peopled by orphans and waifs and beggars taken forcefully off the streets of Paris. Since the day she herself had been captured, three years ago, she'd found no charity in this place.

"I'm surprised Mother Superior didn't recommend you to the king himself," Marie continued into the silence. "I've been told she's having a difficult time finding enough girls of modest birth to fill the king's ship."

"I'll make a better match in marriage disguised as a Duplessis." Genevieve folded the silky scarf and laid it upon her own bundle. "Because of your birth, you'll be set aside for the wealthiest men in the colony."

Marie cast her gaze down. "I didn't think of that."

Of course she wouldn't. This woman had never tasted a stolen apple. She had never raced through the streets of Paris after cutting a nobleman's purse, fearing hunger more than the threat of capture and punishment by whipping.

"But of course, it makes perfect sense." Marie's hands fluttered white in the starlight. "When I found your first note among my laundered shifts, I was sure someone was playing a trick on me. The girls are terrified of being shipped off to this dreadful place. They're sobbing for me and Cecile as if tomorrow the two of us will be executed in the square."

"But you won't be going now. Have you heard

from him?"

"Yes. Yes." Her face lit with joy. "I received a note this morning. François is waiting for me, just inside the gates of Paris."

So that was the name of the French Musketeer Marie loved enough to risk everything to marry. Genevieve dearly hoped this François wasn't like the other strutting, shifty-eyed Musketeers she had known in her younger days. In their blue coats and shimmering braid, they had terrorized the city, taking whatever women pleased them and pulling their swords at the slightest provocation.

"We mustn't delay any longer." Genevieve nodded to Marie's cloak. "Take off your clothes."

The young woman started. "Here?"

"Quickly."

"But what am I to wear?" Marie glanced up at the skeletal scaffolding of the church and crossed herself. "I can't escape in your clothing."

Genevieve footed her bundle toward the girl. "You'll wear the clothing of a governess—a black wool skirt, a white coif, and a black mantle. Then you can walk out the front gates without being stopped."

"Where did you get it?"

"Never mind that. Hurry."

Genevieve unlaced her bodice, tugged it off, and then slipped out of her russet wool skirt. The night was balmy, and the breeze toyed with her tattered shift as she stuffed her old clothes beneath a pile of bricks. As Marie fumbled with her own laces, Genevieve scrutinized the girl more closely. Marie's tresses were long and chestnut-colored. Genevieve's own hair was a mass of copper, a gift, her mother had once told her, from the father she had never known.

Marie's skin was smooth, while Genevieve had a sprinkling of freckles across her nose. Problems, she thought, but nothing that couldn't be overcome by brushing the roots of her hair with an ashy comb, covering her head tight with a scarf, and patting her face thick with powder.

Genevieve snatched Marie's bodice and thrust her arms through the sleeves. "Tell me about your family. I'll need to know their names, ages, and everything about them that's important."

As Marie struggled out of her skirt and petticoat and reached for the bundle of clothing, she told Genevieve that her mother had died in childbirth when Marie was only a few years old. Later, impoverished by the civil wars flaring through France, she and her father had lived on the charity of distant relatives until her father died, leaving Marie to the mercy of an unscrupulous second cousin. He refused to dower her or pay to put her in a convent, so she was sent to the Salpêtrière. Genevieve noted all the names and dates as she slipped on Marie's petticoat and skirt. She would need to know as much as she could remember for when she got to Quebec.

But her mind wandered from Marie's monologue as Genevieve slipped on the blue travelling dress. The feel of the soft cloth against her skin brought a rush of memories. She blocked them out. The past was the past—it was the future that mattered now.

"Cecile awaits you tonight," Marie said as she knotted the last lace of her bodice. "She'll open the door and guide you to my bed."

"Good." In her new clothes, she twirled before Marie. "Well?"

"You have the carriage of a noblewoman." Marie

plucked at her plain black robes, hesitating. "Perhaps this shall all work out as you planned."

I swear that it will.

"But," Marie began, her voice catching, "if you are caught—"

"I won't be."

"—the punishment for what we are doing is severe." Her breath came fast. "We're switching places under the very nose of Mother Superior. It's like tricking the King himself—"

"The king and Mother Superior want girls to fill their ships, no more. They won't look too closely after counting."

"If we're caught, they could force us into a convent," Marie stuttered. "They could shut us away from the world forever."

They'd shut you into a convent, Genevieve thought, but they would find a far more painful punishment for her.

Marie ventured, "You are sure?"

"Yes." Any risk was worth the possibility of freedom.

"Very well." Marie took a deep breath. "You'll be leaving at dawn tomorrow for Le Havre. Cecile will shield you from Mother Superior as you board the carriage, but it'll be tricky."

"Mother Superior is half blind," Genevieve said. "She'll never even notice me. And I'll be crying like an onion seller into my—your—handkerchief. Will we be traveling in a public carriage?"

"Oh, no!" She rested a hand on her throat. "The carriage will be sent by the king, of course."

"Who else will be in it?"

"Some guards will ride outside to see that we are

protected until we reach the ship. But there will be other girls from here, I'm told."

"Do those girls know you?"

"No. I don't know anyone coming but Cecile. But what if one of them recognizes you?"

She forced her feet into Marie's boots—a bit too small. "None of the women who live in my section were chosen, so I don't have to worry about being recognized. Go, Marie." She waved toward the gates. "Your Musketeer awaits."

Marie lurched forward and seized Genevieve's hand. "I will never forget you for the sacrifice you've made for me—oh!"

Genevieve pulled away but it was too late, for Marie had already dropped Genevieve's chapped hand like a hot poker.

Marie staggered back, her mouth falling open.

"Obviously," Genevieve said, raising her chin, "I'll need gloves. Even in Quebec, no one will believe that a fine young lady has the hands of a washerwoman."

Marie made a choked sound and then raced away. Genevieve stared sightlessly at the place where the woman had been. She'd been right, it seemed, to hide her true identity as she slipped notes amid Marie's clean laundry. Marie would never have agreed to this desperate scheme if she had known the truth.

The only women who washed linens in the Salpêtrière were the whores.

~Excerpt, *Heaven In His Arms,* copyright 2014 ~

ABOUT THE AUTHOR

Lisa Ann Verge is the critically acclaimed RITA-nominated author of eighteen novels that have been published worldwide and translated into as many languages. She started her career writing emotionally intense romance about hot men and dangerous women, and now as **Lisa Verge Higgins** she also writes life-affirming women's fiction. A finalist for RT Book Review awards five times over, Lisa has won the Golden Leaf and the Bean Pot, and twice she has cracked Barnes & Noble's General Fiction Forum's top twenty books of the year. She currently lives in New Jersey with her husband and their three daughters, who never fail to make life interesting.

9 781940 963129